SECRETS IN FEATHERWOOD FALLS

FEATHERWOOD FALLS SERIES

HEATHER REYBURN

Cover design: Frank Honsa

ISBN 978-0-6451234-8-7 Print Edition

Heather Reyburn

www.heatherreyburn.com

For my Family and Friends
Thank you all for your love and support

1

Constable Rhys Morton brushed the sweat from his forehead and swallowed, silently cursing the struggling air conditioner's pathetic attempt to cope with the thirty-eight-degree heat of Queensland's mid-summer. Folding his long legs under the chair, he stared at the heavy, wood-panelled door.

Why had he been called in to the inspector's office? He'd submitted a written report on his investigation into the run of car thefts the previous week. Was this summons to do with his conduct during that investigation? Had he done something wrong? Overstepped his authority, perhaps? Or had someone made a complaint about him? Some of the other officers could be like that—their enthusiasm often mixed with a desperation to be noticed ... and promoted. Rhys himself was the opposite—introverted, diligent and, to his own detriment at times, brutally honest.

The door burst open and he jumped to his feet, meeting the faded, grey eyes hooded by bushy eyebrows of Inspector Jones.

'Good morning'. The older man's chin wobbled as he spoke, a smile deepening the creases on his face. 'Come in, Rhys. Take a seat.'

After striding into the office and lowering his lanky frame onto the chair, Rhys leaned forward slightly, fingers knotted together under the smooth, laminated desk.

The inspector cleared his throat and met the young constable's curious gaze. 'You're probably wondering why I've called you in to see me.'

Rhys remained impassive, giving the barest hint of a nod.

'I won't keep you in suspense. You've been at the Warwick Station for four years now and I've noted your performance has been quite exceptional.'

Rhys blinked at the unexpected compliment as the inspector rattled on.

'You've qualified for the rank of Senior Constable ... and we have a situation at the moment which has required some considerable thought.' Jones paused to consider him. 'Do you know Stan Brennan at Feather-wood Falls Police Station?'

The older man's formal manner and speech drifted over Rhys's head while he searched the recesses of his memory. 'Yes,' he finally replied. 'Brennan was sworn in at the same time as my father. I don't think they were friends, but they knew each other.'

The inspector nodded. 'Right. Well, he's had a heart attack and is in hospital.'

'Sorry to hear that,' Rhys said gravely.

'Hmm. Don't think he'll be returning from what I've been told.' Inspector Jones stopped, withdrew a handkerchief, and mopped his brow.

Rhys took a few pulse-slowing breaths while he waited for the inspector to continue.

'You would know we've had a recent attempted murder at Featherwood Falls. The investigation is ongoing, leaving us with a problem.' He cleared his throat and tapped his fingers on the leather desk pad. 'How would you feel about relieving as officer in charge at the station until Stan's return?'

'Me?' Rhys straightened his back, his stunned gaze meeting the inspector's.

'Yes. You.' The inspector's mouth widened slightly, a smile tugging at his lips. He picked up a pen and held it poised above a document on the desk. 'You don't have to decide now. Think about it overnight if you like and let me know in the morning.'

Excitement burned through Rhys. It was his dream to be stationed in a small country town—an experience his father had often spoken wistfully. Rhys barely remembered the early days of their life in the Brisbane Valley. He had been five when his father was promoted to Stanthorpe, and he loved growing up there—playing sport, hiking in the National Park, and especially mucking around with his sister and parents on their hobby farm outside town. Featherwood Falls was one of the few one-officer stations in his favourite part of Queensland and, without another thought, he pushed his chair back and rose to his size-eleven feet. 'I don't need to think about it overnight. I'd love to give it a go ... sir.'

The inspector gave an approving nod. 'Good. I'll complete the paperwork and let District Office know.' He wrote on the document in front of him before turning it around for Rhys to read. 'Sign here.' While Rhys glanced over the form and signed the bottom, the inspector continued, 'You're now in charge of Featherwood Falls Police Station—for the foreseeable future, and we need you there as soon as possible. Besides community policing, you'll be catching up on a good deal of paperwork.' He drew a noisy breath and added, 'Stan Brennan was ... a little behind with reports and correspondence.'

Rhys noted the creased forehead on the older man.

'I realise you're only twenty-seven, but you've proved yourself to be more than capable and, if you're anything like your father, I have every faith in your competence.'

Letting out a silent breath, Rhys felt his heart dance in his chest. 'Thank you. I appreciate the opportunity and the chance to return to that part of the world.'

The inspector straightened, his stocky build still barely reaching Rhys's chin. 'Say gidday to your dad from me.'

Rhys smiled, his excitement obvious. 'I will. I'll be seeing them this weekend. They're not fond of town living—prefer their rural haven and don't come in unless they have to.'

'Huh. I'm with them. Roll on retirement so I can go somewhere quiet where the fishing's good.' They moved toward the door and the inspector held his hand out.

After quickly running his sweaty palm down his trousers, Rhys took it.

'Congratulations, Acting Senior Constable Morton —and good luck.'

Rhys nodded before turning away and striding back to his desk.

A smile crept across his face before fading quickly as his thoughts raced. His heart skipped a beat.

What will Evie say?

~

SHE WAS SITTING on a bench under the shade of a tree, watching him approach. A shiver of apprehension gripped him, and he steeled himself. Slim and attractive, her dark hair hung over her shoulders in a glossy tumble. No-one had been more surprised than Rhys when twelve months before, Evie Thurgood, the most beautiful young woman he had ever seen, asked him for a date at a friend's birthday party. She could have invited any of the young, single men. But she'd chosen him—despite his over-large nose and floppy brown hair that never did as it was supposed to. He had been flattered. Trouble was, with her love of fine dining, movies and fashion, there was a limit to mutually agreeable places to be together, and the gap between them was widening. He'd taken on extra duties at work, unable to refuse his superiors, and loved nothing more than escaping before dawn on his days off to bush walk and forget about the scenes and events that occurred in his occupation. Evie didn't like that at all, and he ached with desperation for her understanding. He caught his breath to quell the butterflies in his stomach.

Smiling at him, she lifted her face to be kissed and patted the seat beside her. 'I've got a salad here for you —and a fresh fruit smoothie.'

He took the food from her perfectly manicured fingertips, grateful but wishing it were coffee and a meat pie instead. Slumping onto the bench, he stared at the children playing on the swings a short distance away, reluctant to face her.

Evie appeared not to notice, and he munched his salad without saying a word. While she waffled on about the new outfit she'd bought for a girlfriend's hen's party the following weekend and the demands her boss was putting on her to shorten her tea breaks and limit her personal phone calls, Rhys let his mind wander.

'Are you listening to me?'

His attention snapped back, startled by her flashing sapphire-coloured eyes, accentuated by the impossibly long eyelashes glued to her lids. Evie continued, seemingly without taking a breath. 'I mean, how dare he? I'm entitled to a fifteen-minute break for morning and afternoon tea, as well as my lunch break. And I can't help it if my friends need to tell me something important while I'm at work.'

Her petulant voice droned on while Rhys finished the smoothie. He stirred the crushed ice in the cup's bottom and braced himself. 'They have offered me a promotion. I'm leaving town—for a while, anyway.'

Evie stopped mid-sentence and stared at him. 'What are you talking about?'

'The officer in charge of the Featherwood Falls Police Station is in hospital, and they have selected me for the relieving position—if I want it.'

She snorted. 'I hope you refused.'

He raised his eyebrows, crossing his arms in defiance. 'No, I didn't.'

An icy change paralysed him as he waited for her outburst. When it didn't come, he took a sideways glance at her. A smirk hovered around her mouth, freezing him to the core. She turned away.

Eventually, she spoke, her tone brittle. 'Well, that's solved one problem.'

Rhys frowned, shaking his head. 'What do you mean?'

'You're not the only man in town who wants to be with me. I've met someone much more considerate.' Jumping to her feet, she took a few steps, halted, and turned to face him, pursing her bright red lips. 'Have a good life. I certainly will!'

His jaw dropped. *Really? Just like that. Was I nothing more than a convenience?*

She strode off.

Guilt sank like a stone in his belly. Dropping his head into his hands, he ran his fingers through his hair.

Seconds later, he lifted his gaze, catching the flash of a tight skirt and ridiculously high heels tottering around the corner.

Numb with shock, his gaze swung slowly back to the gracious sandstone police station over the road. It was barely visible behind the row of police vehicles, and a laugh rang out as a group of teenagers walking past flicked cigarette butts toward the building.

His mind cleared, and he let out a long sigh. Pushing himself to his feet, he shook his head.

Yep. Made the right decision. Time to move on—the last thing I need is a girlfriend.

2

Claire Shepherd was puffing by the time she reached the waterfall. Perspiration trickled down her back and she caught her breath.

'Coming in, Drum?'

She laughed at the little kelpie as he stared at the pool. After slipping her shorts and shirt off, she dropped them on a rock, breathing in the clean air as she tightened her bikini top.

Drum remained at her side, face tilted as though questioning her decision. She grabbed his collar and, leading him gently, waded into the sparkling water. Clutching him to her, she rested his front paws on her shoulders as she sank to her knees.

The water wasn't deep enough to swim more than three or four strokes, but it was cold despite the scorching January day and Claire's skin prickled with goose bumps. She released the dog and rolled onto her back, smiling as Drum swam anxiously in circles around her.

'It's okay, mate. I won't drown. And look at you— you're swimming!'

Reaching for the dog, she gathered him in her arms, then stood and walked back to dry ground.

'You're still not keen, are you?' The kelpie wagged his tail and licked her as she lowered him to the rock. Water ran down Claire's slim, pale body, darkening the granite beneath her. Drum braced himself and shook, spraying a three-metre diameter with droplets, wetting her clothes with a liberal dose of dog-scented spray.

Claire squatted and ruffled his ears.

'You're doing well, little mate. I don't know what you saw that day Dad died, but I have a suspicion you believe the creek had something to do with it.' She placed a hand on either side of his face and looked him in the eye. 'He didn't drown. It was the head injury that killed him ... so, you can stop seeing water as a threat.'

She patted him again and sighed, snatching up her shorts as she remembered the phone in the pocket, her mind on her beloved father. It was nearly two years since his death, and they had charged a man with manslaughter. With the mystery of his passing solved, they had all moved on—sort of, anyway. Her mother even had a new man in her life, who both she and her sister Briony approved of. But the dog accompanying her dad that day seemed unable to forget and helping him overcome his fear of the water had been Claire's major project while she was home.

Plonking herself on a warm rock, she threaded her arms through the shirt sleeves, jumping as the phone pinged. *Nathan?* Her heart leapt, disappointment taking hold as she saw not Nathan but Jasmine, her best friend's name, light up. Shaking her head, she swallowed the doubt that had plagued her since leaving Sydney.

Her intention had always been to return straight after new year, but with the new satellite dish she and Briony had organised for their mother's Christmas present, she'd discovered the internet connection was more than adequate for her to continue working from the farm. Mobile phone reception was still unreliable and weak, but, here at the falls, today her phone displayed two bars.

Swiping the icon, she read Jasmine's text.

Hey. How're things? Ring me—please?

Friends for over three years, Claire and Jasmine had met at the after-party following their university graduation. They'd moved into their current flat soon after, relishing its proximity to Centennial Park, so Claire didn't miss her life in rural Queensland as much as when she'd been studying.

Grinning, she hit the phone icon followed by the speaker and waited for her friend to answer, continuing to hold the phone in the air to maintain a good signal.

'Hi, girlfriend,' Jasmine said.

'Hi, Jazzy. What's happening?'

'Not much.'

Claire frowned at her friend's nonchalant tone. "Not much" sounded more like "quite a lot".

'Are you still coming back tomorrow?' Jasmine asked. Her voice held none of the excitement of her usual calls.

The hairs on Claire's arms rose. 'That's the plan. I'm looking forward to seeing Nathan. I'm all packed. Just having a last swim with the dog up at the falls.'

'Oh.'

The line went silent, and Claire squinted in the sunlight, checking the call was still connected before lifting her gaze to the valley in front of her.

Summer storms had freshened the land, turning the grass from taupe to green almost overnight. Stone fruit orchards, dotted with colour, sat neatly between open paddocks and clusters of bushland, and in the distance, the corrugated roofs of houses in the village shone. Beside the ancient timber woolshed of Featherwood Station, the deep green lucerne waved in the sunlight, beckoning to be harvested. She sighed again. It was a vista she never tired of, making the return to Sydney more difficult every time she climbed this hill.

'Why do you say that?' Claire answered cautiously. 'Is something wrong?'

'We've always told each other everything.' Disappointment filled Jasmine's voice.

'Yeah. We do. What's this about?'

'Why didn't you tell me you and Nathan had split up?'

Claire froze, unsure she had heard correctly. 'Did you say split up?'

'Yes. I ran into him last weekend at the beach, and he had a pretty tight hold on a rather attractive brunette. He didn't see me at first, so I bowled up to them both. I mean, I was sure you would want to know?'

'I see. And?'

'I said hi and asked who his friend was. He looked a bit, well ... shocked, I suppose. Anyway, he introduced her as Lisa someone-or-other—his new girlfriend! I said "hi" to her and then asked when you two had split up. He said at Christmas.'

Claire stiffened. Nathan had told her he had a two-week stint out west in the mines, which was why she'd stayed a little longer on Featherwood Station. So that was a lie? When had he planned to tell her the truth? Or did he think he could play the two of them? In a daze, she recalled their last date before she left Sydney. Tension had filled the tiny flat as she sliced the perfectly cooked, rare beef and tossed the salad before laying them decoratively on the table. It had just been Nathan and Claire—and Claire had hoped for a romantic, candle-lit dinner followed by a night of love that would sustain her for the duration of her Christmas trip home. However, things hadn't panned out that way. Nathan was late arriving—not just a few minutes, but by more than an hour. Claire had been furious, dissolving into tears when he refused to explain why and instead chastised her for being immature, controlling, and petty. So ... instead of coming home to the farm wrapped in a cocoon of love, a lump had gnawed at the pit of her stomach, and she'd struggled to keep her mind on anything other than her evasive boyfriend.

'What else did he say?'

'Nothing. I didn't give him the chance. Left straight away. I wasn't sure if I should tell you or not, but then I decided you wouldn't keep something like that from me ... would you?'

Claire drew a deep breath as the truth sank in. 'Of course, I wouldn't, Jazz. This is news to me—but it explains why he hasn't called me for a while—and why his last call was mysteriously short and to the point.'

Disenchantment flowed through her veins, and it took her a few seconds to realise she was more distressed about the secrecy than the prospect of no longer having Nathan in her life.

'I'm sorry to be the bearer of bad news, Claire.'

Jasmine's voice was soft and compassionate. 'When you get back, we'll commiserate together over a bottle of wine.'

Claire huffed, and a hint of a smile tweaked at her lips.

If that's the way it is, then I'm better off without him.

'Oh, would you mind if my cousin came to stay for a while? She's moving up from Melbourne and hasn't been able to find new digs yet,' Jasmine asked.

Claire raised her eyebrows. 'I guess not.' She didn't want to talk—her head felt thick with confusion, unanswered questions and, most of all, the realisation that everything Jasmine had said rang true. 'Hey, I've gotta get back to the house now. How about I call you in the morning before I leave? I need to get my head around this news, or Mum will worry about me. You know what mothers are like—they've got an inbuilt radar to sense when their precious daughters have had their feathers ruffled.'

Jasmine laughed. 'Sure. Talk tomorrow. And honey, don't worry about Nathan. He's always been a drop kick.'

'Huh. And you're telling me this now? Not what you said when you met him a few months ago.'

Jasmine giggled. 'Yeah, well. Just goes to show looks are not everything.'

Yeah, a Chris Hemsworth look-alike—but apparently not much else.

'Talk tomorrow, Jazz. Bye.'

'Bye. See you soon.'

Claire raised a hand to touch her burning cheek. Brought on by too much sun? No, by anger and shame at her own naivety—and the sensation of having been gutted.

3

*C*laire's head spun as she marched toward the homestead. It wasn't only the news Jasmine had shared that bit at her. The whole returning to the city thing had been gnawing at the back of her mind, even if she hadn't wanted to admit it. Now—well, there was no boyfriend, another flatmate moving in who she didn't know, and the painful thought of having to say goodbye once again to everything she loved about Featherwood Station. Did she even want to return? What was in Sydney for her she couldn't have here? *A man?* She snorted. *Nope, don't need one.* Her job? *Maybe I can keep working from here?* A vision of her workplace loomed.

The three-kilometre bicycle ride took her through busy roads, requiring dodging nerve-wracking traffic, breathing in exhaust fumes, and risking life and limb at every intersection. All just to reach the poky graphic design office crammed between an Indian super-market that constantly emitted a range of spicy fragrances, and an old-fashioned barbershop with a never-ending stream of middle-aged male customers.

'Are you alright, love?'

Greeted by her mother's concerned expression as she stomped up the steps onto the veranda, Claire let her shoulders slump. 'Yeah. Just processing a few things—stuff I should have worked out before now.'

Ginny pulled a cane chair toward her and lifted the black cat from its curled sleep. She snuggled it against her and pointed to the empty seat. 'Sorry, Oscar, Claire needs that.' Plonking herself on the wicker couch opposite, she met Claire's eyes. 'Sit and tell me what's going on.'

Blowing out a long breath, Claire relayed the content of the phone call with Jasmine. 'So, now I don't know what to do.'

Squeezing her daughter's hand, Ginny hesitated for a few seconds before speaking. 'Do you want to go back to Sydney? I mean, do you have to return for your job ... or would they let you continue working from home?' She leaned forward, her thick, brown hair falling over her face, and her hazel eyes filled with compassion.

Claire shrugged. 'Don't know. I told Jasmine I'd

ring her in the morning, so she's got an idea of when I'll be back. But ... I'm not at all sure I want to go.'

Ginny shifted the cat to the other end of the couch before standing and hugging her daughter. 'I understand. You know you can stay here as long as you like —forever if you want to. Your father always hoped one of you girls might be interested in continuing his legacy here in time.' She grinned and sat again. 'I think we both knew it wouldn't be Briony.'

A fond smile crept across Claire's face. She and her sister were close—inseparable during their teenage years. Then Briony had moved to Brisbane and qualified as a chef before embarking on a working holiday in Europe. As the northern spring morphed to summer, she had found a position on the Isle of Skye, met Alex soon after, and the rest was to be history— they had hoped. It had been after her father's death and the subsequent outbreak of COVID-19 that Briony felt the loneliness distance can bring—and finally got on a flight back to Australia before Christmas. Now, travel restrictions and the sparse number of available flights left her filling in time at a girlfriend's café in New South Wales. She fiercely declared her future lay with Alex and Scotland, and both Claire and their mother understood her frustration.

Claire's attention returned to her mother as hope crept through her.

'So ... with your interest and love in the farm and animals, there's always a place here for you.'

'What about Kirk?' Claire asked, her optimism falling again.

'Do you mean how involved is he in Featherwood Station?'

'Yes.'

'You needn't worry about Kirk taking your father's position if that's what you're thinking. While our relationship is deepening ...' Ginny hesitated and shot Claire a shy smile. 'He has his own home and hopes to buy land soon. Meanwhile, he has plenty of building work around the district to keep him busy but is here to help me whenever I ask.' She shrugged. 'Maybe down the track things will change, but, for the moment, we're both happy with our arrangement.'

Claire took a deep breath, pulled the band from her hair, and scooped the straight, wayward strands of gold into a ponytail. 'I could give you a hand with the farm-stay side of things too. I know you've only had one couple so far, but once we're all able to move around the country again and go on holidays, it could get quite busy.'

Ginny rose to her feet and patted Claire's bare knee. 'You're right, and I would love to have you around—and not just to help either. I believe we would make excellent business partners.'

Relief swept across Claire's face as Ginny continued.

'I suggest you forget about packing and go for a ride. Think about what you want and not only what you can do around this place to help.' She smiled at her daughter. 'Akela would love an outing and the worst of the heat has gone. I thought we'd have a barbeque for tea—okay with you?'

'Thanks, Mum. I wouldn't mind a ride actually … Nothing better than blowing a few cobwebs away. How about a cuppa first?'

'Sounds great.'

Claire laughed as Ginny reached out and pulled her to her feet. 'If I decide to stay here—and my boss approves, of course—are you sure Kirk wouldn't mind?'

'Of course not!'

'Well, you know … I don't want to cramp your style.'

Ginny chuckled. 'We're not teenagers, and this is a big house. Now, let's put the kettle on.' She wrapped an arm around her daughter's thin waist, and they stepped inside.

FEELING the contained energy in the mare, Claire urged her into a canter, rising in her stirrups as Akela's speed increased. At a gallop, they covered the distance from the yards to the Glenrowan boundary in a few minutes before Claire drew rein and leaned over the horse's neck, breathing as heavily as the mare.

'That feels better, doesn't it?' A wide smile covered Claire's face.

Dropping the reins, she kicked her feet free of the stirrups. Gazing around her, she noted the neglected appearance of Glenrowan, the neighbouring property. Although partially hidden by a ragged hedge, long grass reached almost to the only visible house window and around the shed, weeds danced in the breeze. She swallowed the bitter taste in her mouth as her thoughts turned to Nigel Ward—the owner of the farm and the man charged with her father's manslaughter. With a shiver, she turned back to the neat, carefully managed paddocks of Featherwood Station. Ice ran through her veins as she relived the lengths their selfish neighbour had gone to in terrorising her mother and jeopardising the future of their home farm.

'How dare he?' she said indignantly.

Akela flicked her ears and lowered her head to snatch a mouthful of grass.

Claire lay forward on Akela's neck, her arms hanging loosely either side of the mare's withers and her head resting on her mane. The horse grazed, swishing flies with her tail as she mooched along, until

Claire straightened and slipped her feet back into the stirrups. She took a deep breath, gathered the reins, and nodded.

'Yep. I know exactly what I am going to do—and no matter what the boss says, it doesn't include returning to Sydney.'

4

The air was clear and oppressive under the shimmering sun. Patches of melting bitumen glistened in the heat. Rhys turned his Isuzu utility into the police driveway and parked beside the station four-wheel drive in the carport. He paused for a few minutes, studying the official quarters leading from the back of the station, and sighed. Living onsite where he could relax in his own lounge room, watch television, and eat when he wanted to appealed far more than the dingy-looking hotel down the road. However, he understood the quarters were Stan's home and his possessions filled the rooms. So ... until advised otherwise, it appeared he would have to make himself comfortable at the pub—and hope the publican could cook. While he was happy knocking up a pan of bacon and eggs or steak and a pre-prepared salad, he knew his limitations and they included fancy cooking.

Squaring his shoulders, he slid the key into the lock of the front door before glancing at his phone to double-check the security alarm code. He punched the numbers in and waited for the beep, confirming he was safe to move around the building without the entire town knowing.

The floor squeaked, the timber boards beneath the standard, government-issue linoleum protesting against their age. On his left, a solid, timber-panelled door butted against a wide countertop with a sliding toughened glass window panel rising from it. The counter and doorway created an efficient divider between the reception area and the main body of the station.

A quick inspection of the office revealed all he had expected. Two small desks—one supporting a phone, computer, and printer, and the other laden with folders, loose papers, and books. Several filing cabinets lined the rear wall next to a gun safe. Picking through the bunch of keys in his hand, he unlocked the safe and stowed his firearm inside before locking it securely again.

A relatively modern office chair and an ancient padded seat stood haphazardly in the room. Muddy heel prints on the leather showed someone used it as a footrest more frequently than to sit on.

Rhys opened the door on the far wall of the reception area and entered the hallway to explore the rest of the building. An interview room, fitted out with recording equipment, ran off the hallway, and beside it was a small kitchen. Near the back entrance, a bathroom containing the toilet hid behind a blue-painted door. Opposite was yet another solid door, suggesting a narrow room directly behind the main office. *A butler's pantry?* Rhys attempted to open it, to no avail. He picked through the bunch of keys again, trying each one before he gained success.

'Ah-uh.'

The lock required more force than expected, and he took a few seconds to inspect it. 'Hmm, a squirt of WD40 should fix that.' He sneezed and switched on the light. Dust motes floated around him, and he wrinkled his nose as the musty smell of aging paper filled his nostrils. He studied the steel framework lining one wall.

'Geez. It's the storeroom—and it looks like no-one's been in here for years.' He wiped a finger over the shelves before pulling one of the many containers toward him. Faded ink labelled each box on all but the closest two. Squinting, Rhys removed the lid and inspected the contents. Old beige folders stood like a row of soldiers inside, their plastic tags yellowing and brittle. The label on the front of the first folder read 1975—1980.

Rhys raised his eyebrows. *Does it take a five-year period here to fill a single, thin folder?* 'Cripes. Now I understand Inspector Jones's comment about Stan not being great with paperwork. This stuff should have been archived years ago!'

Sneezing again, Rhys closed the box and backed out of the room before locking it behind him.

He ignored the door marked "Private", dismissing it as the entrance to Stan's quarters, and returned to the main office. A weekly planner beside the computer caught Rhys's eye, and he flicked through the previous few weeks. Very little had been documented except *collect mail* on each weekday and *rubbish bins* on Sunday evenings. One or two names he recognised as being other officers in the district were mentioned with the word *'lunch'* next to them. Presumably, if traffic branch or another police officer was passing through, they called in to have lunch with Stan?

The wall calendar with its photo of a large green tractor dominating the smaller, tear-off months indicated it was now Tuesday. It had been more than a week since Stan was whisked away in the ambulance.

'Right. First job appears to be collecting the mail.'

He locked the station again, resetting the security system, and strolled up to the post office.

'GIDDAY, young fella. Don't worry about Boris. We pretend he's a guard dog but it's all a ploy. He couldn't chase a chook off its nest these days.' The thin, white-haired man behind the counter nodded toward the ancient blue heeler lying across the doorway of the post office before raising his gaze to Rhys. 'What can I do for you today?'

Rhys held out his hand. 'Gidday. Senior Constable Rhys Morton. I'm standing in for Senior Constable Brennan while he's off on sick leave.'

'Oh!' The older man straightened, a wide smile across his wrinkled face, and clasped Rhys's outstretched hand. 'Pleased to meet you.' He narrowed his eyes a little. 'You're younger than we're used to around here.'

'Perhaps. I'm pleased to have this opportunity— and am looking forward to getting to know everyone.'

'Very good. Well, I'm Frank Brown. Me and the wife, Lola, run both the general store and the post office. Been here for yonks, so if you need to know anything, just ask.' He chuckled, his wrinkled face becoming even more creased.

His friendly warmth put Rhys at ease, and he let his shoulders drop. 'I don't officially start until tomorrow, but thought I'd pop up and collect the mail and get some coffee and stuff for smoko and lunch.'

'Good plan.' Frank turned to the row of private boxes on the back wall and dragged out a pile of white envelopes and a thin, yellow package. He slapped them on the bench and reached for a rubber band to bundle them together. 'There ya go. Now, if you nip through that side door, you'll be in the store and Lola will fix you up with whatever groceries you need.'

'Great. Thanks.' Rhys shot Frank a smile and pushed through the adjoining door to be greeted by the delicious aroma of hot savouries. His mouth watered and he glanced at his watch. Eleven-thirty. *Close enough.*

A short, grey-haired woman in a brightly coloured apron looked up from the kitchen and called. 'Won't be a tick. Just getting these pies out.'

He hovered at the grocery shelves while he waited, tossing up between the box of Coco Pops or the smaller, more expensive packet of muesli. A rush of guilt flowed through him as his thoughts flew to Evie and her insistence on eating all things healthy. He picked up the muesli.

I suppose I need to look after myself. Can't go having sick days here when I'm the only one in the station.

'Sorry about that, love. Now, what can I get you?' The woman stepped toward him, her round, pink face beaming and her bright, chunky earrings swinging as she moved.

'Hi. Umm ... I'm Rhys Morton. You must be Lola?'

'I certainly am. You met Frank in the post office I take it?'

'Yeah. I'm here for a while—relieving at the police station.'

'Ooh! Lovely.' She huffed, her smile fading. 'I might have said we were fine without a copper in town a little while ago, but ...' She stepped closer, tilting her head back to meet him eye-to-eye, and whispered conspiratorially, 'I guess if they've sent you here, you will have heard all the dramas that have happened over the past few months?'

He gave her a small nod. 'Yes, I've heard.'

'Right then. Well, welcome to Featherwood Falls. If there's anything you need or want to ask, Frank and I can probably help you out. Are you staying at the station?'

He shook his head. 'No. Unless Senior Constable Brennan retires or cannot return for whatever reason, the quarters are not available. So, I'm staying at the pub.'

'Hmm. In that case, you'll be needing something tasty for your lunch each day because Ned only does dinner. I bake fresh pies and pasties daily and can make you a burger or salad roll if you prefer.' She smiled again, and the stress leached out of him.

Ten minutes later, laden with groceries and munching a spicy meat and vegetable pie, Rhys ambled back to the station. He packed the food into the fridge and cupboard above the sink, switched on the electric jug to make himself a cup of tea, and removed the band from around the mail.

After thumbing through the advertising junk, community notices, and what appeared to be invoices, he picked up the yellow business envelope. Turning it over, he read the simple address:

OIC Police

Featherwood Falls

'Hmm?' He slipped his thumb into the corner of the envelope and carefully ripped it open.

The contents were wrapped in a layer of brown paper. With no note, Rhys unrolled the wrapping, his eyes widening as the wad of hundred-dollar notes fell onto the table.

'Wow!' He inspected the envelope again, confirming there was no name of the intended recipient—other than the officer in charge. Staring at the stack, he rubbed a hand over his face. Alarm bells rang, and he reached for the packet of disposable gloves sitting on the kitchen bench. He quickly donned a pair before counting the money. Then he re-wrapped it, slipped the bundle back into the envelope, and locked the package in the safe.

A thousand dollars?

He sat for a few moments, his mind racing. What was the money for? A regular gift for Stan from an old aunt? Repayment of a fine by someone? His stomach flipped.

Or is this part of something illegal?

THE SUN WAS LOW, and shadows crept across the road when Rhys followed the overweight, arthritic man up the worn staircase. He flinched with each phlegmy cough that erupted from the publican's bearded throat.

'Name's Ned, by the way. Been here for most of m'life,' the old man rasped. 'So, you don't know how long you'll be standing in for Stan ... or staying?'

'Not yet. I guess District Office is waiting on a medical report first. For the time being, I'll do my best to serve Featherwood Falls efficiently and reliably.' Rhys released a silent sigh, smiling inwardly at his response. *God, I sound like I'm reciting a boy scout oath.* His gaze swung to the tongue and groove boarded walls, high ceilings, and ancient, creaking fans struggling to cool the musty corridor. Lingering scents of cleaning fluids and cigarette smoke clung to the curtains and threadbare carpet. 'Been a while since you had guests?'

Ned coughed again, and Rhys grimaced.

'Yeah. A fella from the Snowy Mountains stayed a few weeks last year, but, other than that, this place mostly sees locals come for a drink in the evenings. Got a girl comes in to clean for me. Keeps suggesting I offer meals on a Friday and Saturday night.' He shook his head and shuffled along the hallway, throwing open a door to a room overlooking the main road. 'Good idea if it wasn't for this bloody pandemic. Too old for this caper now—but can't afford to change it.'

He let out such a deep, strangled sigh that Rhys stared at him. His forehead creased with worry that the old fellow was about to collapse in a heap on the floor beside him.

He didn't. Instead he reached for the door handle of the room at the end of the corridor, throwing it open. 'Here's your room.'

Rhys nodded appreciatively, caught by surprise at the beautiful timber French doors opening onto the veranda and the bright doona cover on the double bed.

'Great, thanks. I was told you can do meals?' He looked at the publican dubiously. 'Is that correct?'

Ned grunted. 'We-ll. I cook for myself every night. Got my poor, deceased wife to thank for that. I can knock up a tasty stew—that's Mondays, Wednesdays, and Fridays. Chops or steak with salad or vegetables on Tuesday, Thursday, and Saturday, and a roast on Sunday. That do you?'

Rhys grinned. 'Sounds great, thanks.'

'I'm not an early riser, so you'll have to sort yourself out in the morning. Kitchen's downstairs, behind the lounge room if you need it.'

'Thanks for the offer. Apart from the evening meal,

I'll probably eat at the station. Got a kitchen there with a fridge and microwave.'

'Righto. I'll leave you to it. If you fancy a drink, you know where to find me.'

Rhys waited until the sound of the man's rubber thongs slapped into the distance before throwing his suitcase on the bed and opening the French doors. He leaned on the veranda railing, absorbing the peaceful main street with its avenue of jacaranda and silky oak trees and its quaint buildings, and breathed deeply.

Who would think a pretty little town like this could ever need a police presence?

*S*leep evaded Rhys, and he tossed and turned. Thoughts of a local citizen languishing in jail and a vision of the cash rotated in his mind.

A cool breeze drifted through the open veranda doors, and he pulled the doona over his chilled limbs. Minutes later, golden rays spread across the hills ahead of the five o'clock alarm. Abandoning all hope of rest, Rhys slid out of bed, pulled on shorts and a singlet, and laced up his runners.

The pub was deathly quiet, exaggerating the squeaky floorboards as he tiptoed down the stairs and let himself out the front door.

He jogged along the main road before veering up a street beyond the school. A row of houses lined each side of the bitumen strip, and he paused in surprise. From the pub, the town appeared small—although the welcome sign outside Featherwood Falls showed the population was eighty-three. He shrugged.

Who knows how up-to-date those figures are?

Increasing his pace, he ran toward the bush-clad hills, the houses becoming more widely spread, interspersed with crops and orchards. His breath caught as the rise increased and he stopped and leaned forward, hands on his knees.

A goshawk hovered overhead, and he shaded his eyes against the rising sun, studying its flight. Circling closer to a patch of freshly ploughed earth, it dived suddenly before quickly rising again with a tiny creature in its talons.

Nature can be so beautiful—and so brutal.

His gaze drifted down the hill to the wide red roof of the general store. Behind it, a row of mesh cages merged into a large, tree-filled paddock. From where he stood, he could just make out several different-sized kangaroos and wallabies grazing. His interest piqued. A lover of Australian wildlife, memories flooded back from his childhood when his mother had been a registered wildlife carer. He set off again to where the road petered out into a series of private driveways and glanced at his watch. Six o'clock. The summer sun was already hot on the back of his neck as he trotted steadily back to the village.

Drawing near the paddock of kangaroos, Rhys slowed to a walk, allowing his smile to widen. As he reached the fence, the back door of the house adjoining the store slammed and Frank appeared, carrying a bucket in each hand.

'Good morning!' Rhys called.

'Gidday, mate. You're up and about early.'

Rhys rested his hands on the high exclusion wire netting and waited while Frank poured the contents of the buckets into the many feed dishes dotted around the paddock.

After dropping the containers on the ground, Frank sauntered over to the fence. 'Been for a run?'

'Yeah. It's a habit—and a good way of having a look around.' Rhys grinned and pointed to the animals. 'I'm guessing you guys are wildlife carers?'

'Yeah. Lola started years ago when someone hit a roo up the road and brought the joey in to her. Didn't know what to do for a start, but soon got organised— and as you can see, things have grown since then.' Frank laughed as he lifted his battered, wide-brimmed Akubra and wiped a hand across his forehead.

'What do you do with them all once they're adults?' Rhys inclined his head toward the bush. 'Release them up there?'

'Yep. You've got it. Most of them have been brought to us from around this district anyway—the majority after a car has hit their mother. Because of regular wild-dog control around here, it's a pretty safe area to let them go.'

Rhys nodded appreciatively.

'And if you're wondering, yes, we have the appropriate licences to foster native animals.'

'I'm sure you do.' He chewed on his lip for a moment before continuing. 'Frank. I'd like to ask about the police mail.'

Frank raised his eyebrows. 'Sure. Fire away.'

'The yellow envelope that was in yesterday's pile … would you know if that was a one-off?'

Frank grunted. 'Nope. Stan's been getting one every three months for a while now. I presume it's some kind of quarterly report that some poor bugger has to spend hours completing just to appease the powers that be.'

Rhys breathed deeply. 'Right, okay, thanks for that.' Glancing at his watch again, he nodded. 'I'd better get cracking. See you later.'

'No doubt. Lola's lamington day today.'

Rhys frowned. 'Pardon?'

'Wednesday. Every Wednesday, Lola bakes a tray of fresh lamingtons and the standard pies and pasties. I reckon the locals can smell them cooking cause they line up for them about ten o'clock.' He grinned at Rhys's lanky frame. 'Looks like you could put a few away yourself.'

Laughing, Rhys agreed. 'Nothing nicer than a fresh-baked lamington. I reckon ten o'clock sounds like a good time to collect the mail—agree?'

'I'll tell Lola to put a couple aside for you.' He gave

a wave, picked up the buckets, and ambled back toward the house.

For a few seconds, Rhys's mouth watered before his mind rested on Frank's comment.

The yellow envelopes arrive every three months. They could be nothing—a perfectly innocent regular payment for something Stan has sold.

His stomach churned. He should talk to someone about it—but who?

AT EIGHT-THIRTY, ensconced in the station's main office, Rhys sorted through the piles of random paperwork on the desk. The phone rang, its tone shrill in the silent room. After dropping the papers, he snatched up the receiver.

'Featherwood Falls police station. Senior Constable Morton speaking.'

'Hello, Senior Constable Morton.'

Rhys frowned at the speaker's hint of a chuckle. Had his phone-answering voice been too official?

'It's James Avery here, Rhys. Warwick CIB. How's it going down there?'

'Gidday, James.'

'I hear you're the new officer in charge.'

'Yeah ... while Senior Constable Brennan's away.'

'Great.'

Rhys relaxed a little at James' familiar tone.

'Good to know the place is being looked after,' James continued. 'No doubt you've heard about the manslaughter charge against one of the Featherwood Falls locals?'

'Yes. A little. I haven't familiarised myself with the file yet though.'

'Of course. I'll give you an overview.' James listed the charges against Nigel Ward before elaborating on the manslaughter of Lyndon Shepherd and the subsequent attempts at frightening his widow, the resident of the historical sheep and cattle property, *Featherwood Station*. As he relayed the events leading up to Nigel's arrest, Rhys listened intently, warming to the detective. His matter-of-fact tone contained empathy and a passion for his work, jogging memories of a much younger Rhys eavesdropping on his father's telephone conversations.

'Ginny Shepherd had a pretty tough time in the year or so after her husband's death. I've let her know the case has been finalised, and they have sentenced Mr Ward to ten years.'

'Oh.' Rhys blinked.

'So ... as you're now the community cop in the area, I thought you might call in and visit the Shepherd family. Perhaps you could see if someone has been taking care of the Ward farm while the trial has been going on. I'll email you the contact details of Mr Ward's solicitor.'

'Right. Of course. Thanks for the information.'

'If you need a hand with anything, call me,' James said.

'I will. Thanks again.'

Rhys put the phone down, remaining motionless for a few moments.

Geez, a local farmer in jail. It probably won't be ten years, what with parole and what-not, but even so ...

It was one thing to be part of a large and busy police unit, quite another to be the sole officer in a small town. Slumping in the chair, Rhys booted up the computer and logged on. James' email had already arrived.

He dialled the solicitor's office, tapping a pen on the desk while he waited for his call to connect.

'Murdoch-and-Smale-Solicitors-Cassie-speaking. How may I help you?' The girl's gabbled, chirpy tone startled him. In his limited experience, legal reception-ists were mostly middle-aged women, very often with stern, efficient voices and decades of experience.

It took him a second or two to reply. 'Senior Constable Morton from Featherwood Falls police station here. May I speak with Mr Murdoch please?'

'I'm very sorry. Mr Murdoch is not in at the moment. Can someone else help you?'

Rhys silently cursed his lack of experience in these

matters. Should he involve someone else? He cleared his throat. 'Umm. Please have him call me when he's available.'

'Of course. May I tell him what it is in relation to?'

'Yes. The property owned by Mr Nigel Ward.'

'Certainly. I'll have him call you. Goodbye.' The bright voice was gone, and Rhys frowned. Should he wait for the solicitor's call?

Shaking his head, he spent the rest of the morning sorting out the paperwork piled on the desk before dragging the dust-covered mower out of the tiny shed beside the old watch house. It took several attempts before it started, and Rhys frowned.

Apparently, Stan wasn't exactly a maintenance man either.

By two o'clock, the lawns around the building were tidy and Rhys admired his work, breathing in the smell of freshly mown grass. The solicitor had still not returned his call, so he removed the keys from his drawer, locked the station, and slid into the Toyota LandCruiser. He wasn't certain where the Shepherd place was, but, from the store, had glimpsed a sandstone building on a rise a couple of kilometres away. With the little information he had, and a good deal of guesswork, he followed the road out of town.

6

On the crest of the gentle rise, he slowed as a large sign came into view announcing, *"Featherwood Station"*. Carved into a slab of timber about half a metre off the ground, the sign was surrounded by red geraniums.

Turning in, he followed the long gravel driveway to a large and gracious homestead constructed of a mix of sandstone and honey-coloured timber with white trim. To the left of the picket gate, an enormous shed was filled with a variety of vehicles. To the right of the entrance, green lawns led to a hotchpotch of smaller farm sheds, a fowl run, and a long row of dog kennels.

He switched off the engine, opened the door, and stepped out.

A whistle sounded from the direction of the kennels. Two black and tan kelpies raced toward him, followed closely by a young woman in a wide-brimmed Akubra hat, her long legs encased in jodh-purs and her checked shirt flapping.

She whistled again, and the dogs dropped on their bellies a few metres from his feet.

'Sorry about that. I didn't see your vehicle arrive—but these two did!'

Ragged wisps of gold-blonde hair blew around her face, with the rest tied in a ponytail that hung over one shoulder. Freckles dusted her slightly turned-up nose, and a smile widened on her clear complexion.

Mesmerised, his gaze fastened on the sparkling grey eyes that met his. A jolt raced through him. 'U-umm. Are you Ginny Shepherd?'

The woman laughed—not a girlish giggle, but an unaffected explosion of amusement.

'No, I'm Claire.' She held out her hand. 'Ginny's my mother.'

Aware of her gaze sweeping over him, his pulse raced. He took her outstretched hand. 'Sorry. That's rude of me. I'm Rhys Morton, Featherwood Falls' new "temporary" police officer.'

'Lovely to meet you Rhys.'

One kelpie had crept forward and was sitting at Rhys's feet. 'Hello, little fellow. What's your name?'

'That's Drum, and this one is Harp. She's Drum's mother.' At her name, Harp looked at her mistress, waiting for a nod before moving close enough for Rhys to pat her. Claire inclined her head at the house and stepped toward the gate. 'Come in. Perfect time for a cuppa.'

As he followed the slim, straight back into the house yard and along the paved pathway to the veranda, he exhaled.

Remember—you don't need a girlfriend!

THE SCENT of freshly baked peanut brownies wafted in the air as Rhys slipped his boots off at the door. His mouth watered.

'Mum. This is Rhys, our new copper.' Claire waved toward the woman busily transferring cookies from a tray onto a cooling rack in the kitchen. 'This is my mum, Ginny.'

Shorter and curvier than her daughter, Ginny tucked a lock of wavy brown hair behind her ear and wiped her hands on a towel before grasping Rhys's outstretched palm, her wide smile mirroring Claire's. 'Hi there. Come and sit down. Perfect timing. Tea or coffee?'

'Umm. Coffee please?'

'I'll get the coffees, Mum. You make the tea,' Claire said. 'Where's Kirk?'

'He nipped home to shower. He'll be here in a tick.'

While the women busied themselves in the

kitchen, Rhys eased himself into a dining chair. A sense of warmth and homeliness engulfed him, and he stretched his legs out under the table. It had been years since he'd lived with his parents and, until now, he hadn't realised how much he missed the familiarity. *Who's Kirk?* As the thought crossed his mind, a car door slammed, and a minute later, a gigantic figure strode up the steps onto the veranda.

'Hello. Kirk Meyer.' He approached Rhys and extended a hand to wring Rhys's in a finger-crushing grip before dropping a gentle kiss on both Ginny's and Claire's heads.

Rhys stared wide-eyed at him. Kirk was a good-looking middle-aged man with curly black hair and a bushy beard. Piercing blue eyes twinkled and deep lines formed on either side of his mouth as he smiled. He smelled of soap and shampoo, and although shabby, his worn jeans and navy work-shirt appeared to have been ironed. Beside him, Rhys felt insignificant despite their similar height.

With the introductions over and tea and coffee served, the four of them chatted inconsequentially about the weather, Stan's health, and the dogs. Eventually, Rhys broached the subject of the Ward farm next door, Glenrowan.

'Is someone caring for it at the moment?'

Ginny answered quietly, a tinge of sadness in her hazel eyes. 'I've seen a vehicle come and go a few times, but to be honest, we've mostly stayed away as much as possible. Nigel didn't have a dog or any animals, and his staff seem to have left. Someone must have arranged for the crops to be harvested after his arrest —but since then, the place has been abandoned.'

Kirk added, 'I had to fix one of the boundary fences a month or two back, but, as Ginny says, other than that, we've stayed well away.'

'I see.'

Ginny offered the plate of biscuits to Rhys, and he took one, biting into the roast peanut and chocolate. Momentarily distracted by the crunchy sweetness, he savoured the mouthful before returning his attention to the others in the room.

'I've contacted Mr Ward's solicitor and am waiting for him to call me. Hopefully, someone will take responsibility for the place while he's ... not around. Once I find out who that is, I'll let you know.'

'Thank you, Rhys. That would be great.' Ginny frowned before continuing, 'As long as it's not my brother-in-law, we'll be happy. We haven't had a lot to do with Glenrowan over the years, but it would be nice to change that—and at least offer our friendship.'

'Good point.' Rhys nodded. 'Mrs Shepherd—'

'Please, call me Ginny.'

'Ginny.' A smile flickered across Rhys's face. 'Your brother-in-law ...?'

Before Ginny could answer, Claire piped up, rolling

her eyes. 'Uncle Donald is Dad's brother. He and his wife and son live about forty-five minutes away on their own farm. Last year, Uncle Donald hassled Mum to let him take over this property and ... well, let's just say he's not our favourite person.'

'I think you described him as wanting to be "Lord of the Manor". He's a ruthless and greedy operator who has done nothing but belittle me since Lyndon's death,' Ginny finished bitterly.

'Oh, okay.' Rhys took a slow breath, absorbing this information. 'How are you feeling now the trial is over? I mean, is there anything I can do for you?'

Ginny shot a glance at Kirk. 'We're fine now, thanks. Glad it's all over. What about you, Kirk? Can you think of anything we need to tell Rhys?'

The big man leaned back in his chair in quiet contemplation.

'Actually,' he said slowly. 'You should probably know about the mines, and the stash of rocks containing tin ore that I found around the time of Nigel's arrest.'

Rhys leaned in to rest an elbow on the table, his thumb and forefinger supporting his chin. 'Go on.'

Kirk relayed the story of his discovery of the old mines, neglected since the depression. 'The locals believed the place was haunted, so no-one has been near them for years. But, as I discovered, Nigel must have found something he knew was valuable—and stopped at nothing in an attempt to purchase that piece of land from Ginny without divulging to anyone why he wanted it.'

'And is whatever he found valuable?' Rhys narrowed his eyes.

'We're not sure yet. I took some samples to the Department of Resources. Their report confirmed there are a few minerals there. However, they consider the area too small and inaccessible to be worth mining. I've been up there a few times. I hiked up there again yesterday morning and camped overnight—which was why I was cleaning up when you arrived.' He shrugged. 'It's a pretty dirty job, especially in the heat we've been having, but I have an interest in prospecting as a hobby and look at it as being a retreat when I'm between other jobs.'

'Sounds interesting. I wonder if I might take a look myself while I'm here?' Rhys asked.

'Sure.' Kirk studied him intently. 'You look pretty fit.'

Rhys laughed. 'I try to be. I do a bit of bushwalking and play tennis when I can.' He stole a glance at Claire, catching her gazing at him. She ducked her head and turned to face Kirk.

'Me too,' she said. 'I mean, I'd like to come with you next time you go up there.'

A flush of pink rose up her neck, and Rhys's heart

leapt. Was the spark mutual? He struggled to focus on the man sitting opposite him.

Kirk nodded. 'Of course. That's settled. As soon as you get a day or two off, Rhys, we'll take you hiking to the back of Featherwood Station, and you can see for yourself. Are you okay with that, Ginny?'

Ginny nodded. 'Sounds like a good idea. Perhaps you could see if you can find the old burned-out hut?'

Rhys sat up straight, tucking his feet under the chair. His gaze swung from Ginny to Claire before resting on Kirk. 'Burned-out hut?'

Ginny answered. 'There's a local tale that years ago, before World War Two, a bushfire went through the hills behind us and sometime later, the remnants of a hut were found containing the bodies of a woman and a child. Gossip suggests they were the Chinese-born wife and child of a miner—a wild, violent man who was never found.'

'Wow!' Rhys raised his eyebrows. 'If only these hills could talk, eh?'

Ginny grunted. 'True. Apparently, he came from Ireland and, according to some of the old people who'd worked in the mines, they called him Wild Willy. The area used to be called Turtle Ridge, but after the fire and the gruesome stories that followed, the locals changed the name to Camel Hump. As Kirk said, no-one went near the place until recently.'

'You've got me intrigued now,' Rhys said with a smile. 'I'm keen to have a look myself.'

Perhaps it won't hurt getting to know Claire?

'Who's for another cuppa?' Ginny asked.

'I'd love one, but I need to get back to the station,' Rhys said resignedly. It was his first week on the job and the past hour had disappeared in a flash.

He caught Claire's glance as he rose from his seat, his feet heavy and reluctant.

Does she feel it too?

Claire, Kirk, and Ginny accompanied him to his vehicle, their friendly banter warming his soul.

'Thanks for calling in, Rhys,' Ginny said. 'We look forward to hearing who's going to be taking care of Glenrowan.'

'Of course.' Distracted by the mobile phone ringing inside the vehicle, Rhys reefed open the door. 'Excuse me, please. I'd better get this. Talk again soon.'

He started the engine, waited until the call switched to the vehicle, and clicked the answer button on the steering wheel. Then, waving goodbye to Kirk and the women, he drove away.

'Hello?'

'Senior Constable Morton?'

'Yes.'

'Michael Murdoch here from Murdoch and Smale Solicitors. I believe you wanted to speak with me?'

'Yes. Thank you for calling back.' Rhys quickly explained his position as relief officer as he motored down the drive. The call crackled, suggesting he was losing reception, and he braked, pulling to the side of the road beside the sign he had admired earlier. His gaze roamed over the vista as he asked Michael about Glenrowan.

'This morning I've received an application to manage the property for the next five years with the option to extend if required,' Michael said.

'I see. And ... is this application acceptable?'

'Very much so. It appears the candidate has an excellent knowledge of both Glenrowan and the general area.'

'That's good. Is it possible for you to send through the details?'

'Of course. I think in the circumstances, it would be a good move for you to monitor the property while Mr Ward is ... indisposed. I have been instructed to act on his behalf. However, being located a considerable distance away, I would appreciate any information or updates you feel are appropriate.'

'Not a problem. Send me the details and I'll pop out and introduce myself once they're settled in.'

'There's just one thing—if you don't mind?'

'Sure. What is it?'

'There's a key to the house hidden in a pair of boots on the back porch—and yes, I know that's not exactly wise, but that's irrelevant. If you wouldn't mind letting yourself in and boxing up the personal papers that are in the drawers of the desk in the dining room, I would be grateful. Mr Ward is happy for the property manager or his staff to live in the house, but requested I remove his personal papers for privacy reasons.' He harrumphed. 'I'm sure I can trust you to perform the task?'

'Not a problem. Should I keep the key at the station?'

'That would be appreciated. I will provide the new manager with the keys Mr Ward has left in my charge.'

'Will do.' Rhys was about to finish the call, but hesitated. 'It sounds as though you've made your decision already. Can you tell me the new fella's name?'

'Donald Shepherd.'

Rhys blinked rapidly. 'Did you say Donald Shepherd?'

'Yes—evidently, he is a cousin of Nigel Ward's.'

7

*A*s the dust settled behind the police vehicle, Claire meandered to the kennels and fed the dogs, unable to tear her mind from the young man who had, minutes earlier, sat at the dining table. He bore no startling features apart from an oversized nose in a thin face, brown hair with a tendency to flop over his forehead, and eyes that were neither blue nor green but somewhere in between, but something about him had commanded both attention and respect.

Telling herself she had no interest in him—especially if he was only here temporarily—she acknowledged that the community would be grateful for his presence. She latched the cage doors, a wry grin touching her mouth. *Let's face it, anyone will be an improvement on the worse-than-useless Stan.*

'Good dogs. See you in the morning.'

The late afternoon sun beat down, its burning rays only marginally cooler than two hours earlier. Claire wiped the sweat from her brow and squinted at the mown lucerne drying on the bottom paddock. She heaved a sigh. The joys of being with Nathan and her life in Sydney had faded over the past few days, her fury at his deception—and her naivety in not reading the signs–quickly overrun by her excitement of being able to work from their beloved home. Within minutes of receiving approval from her boss, she and Ginny had begun cleaning out the enclosed western veranda. Then, with Kirk's help, they'd shifted an ancient wooden table from the back shed to the lawn, which Claire spent hours sanding down and painting with a thick white gloss. Cane bedroom chairs had been whisked out of both her room and Briony's, their cushions washed and set at one end of the new office-come-lounge, and the small low table that had served as the girl's craft bench many years earlier, repainted to match the desk.

Although her work responsibilities would take priority, continuing her design work and meeting deadlines, during busy periods on the farm such as hay-making and shearing, she would shelve all but the urgent projects. She adored the stock work, and the endless circuits on the old blue tractor flinging wind-rows of drying lucerne into the air with the wide-angled hay-rake still filled her with a sense of achievement and happiness. But the smell, hustle, and bustle of the shearing shed in full swing was her favourite activity of all.

'Only one more rake and I reckon that lot will be ready for baling.'

Trudging past the chook pen, she refilled their water dish and put out fresh grain. Then she wandered around the back of the house and entered her new workroom from the sturdy stone steps. A sense of peace enfolded her as she stepped inside, and she smiled at the tabby cat curled up on a chair. With thick sandstone walls and a shelterbelt of trees along the south and western sides, the house remained cool all year round, requiring little more than a slow-moving ceiling fan in the summer and the wood fire in the lounge during the coldest months. The cats weren't the only ones to relish their surroundings.

She flicked her computer on and attempted to continue creating a book cover for her newest client—an author living only an hour away. Her attention drifted, and after twenty minutes of procrastinating, she gave up and strode to the kitchen. Voices murmured outside the window, followed by her mother's laugh. She smiled. Having Kirk in their lives after the trauma of the previous year had been a blessing. Her mother trusted him—and both she and her vivacious sister agreed their dad would have approved. With her mother's confirmation that he had no intention—as yet—of moving into the Featherwood Station homestead, she welcomed his presence and was relieved he and her mother were taking things slowly. Of course, there was the occasional night when he stayed over at the homestead or when her mother gave a coy smile as she said goodnight, after which Claire would hear her car driving down the road to the cottage Kirk had purchased before Christmas.

She filled the kettle as she called, 'Do you two want another cuppa?'

'No thanks.' Their responses came in unison, followed by Ginny's giggle.

'We're having a glass of wine while Kirk gets the barbeque going,' Ginny called, sticking her head through the door. 'Okay with you if we have dinner early and then get on with the hay?'

'Sure, Mum. I'll rake it again as soon as the sun has set.'

'Thanks, love. I'll do the moisture testing, and Kirk said he'd bale as soon as I give him the okay. Baler's all greased and ready for action.' Ginny chuckled. 'We should have asked that new cop if he'd like to come and load a few bales tonight. Would've been a good workout for him.'

Claire grimaced. 'Sure. And a great way to welcome him to the district—not!'

'Oh, I don't know. He seemed to have trouble keeping his eyes off you.'

Heat flushed up Claire's neck and onto her cheeks. 'Don't talk rubbish, Mum,' she snapped. 'You've had too much wine.'

Ignoring her mother's knowing gaze, Claire grabbed her tea and stomped back to her room.

She wrapped her hands around the mug and lowered herself into a chair.

Really? He made it clear he was here temporarily ... and there's no way I'm going through another breakup. Better to not start.

Despite telling herself that, a smile hovered around her lips and her heart danced in her chest.

RHYS TURNED onto the road leading to Glenrowan, mulling over Michael Murdoch's announcement. After hearing Ginny and Claire's opinion of Donald Shepherd, a sense of unease hung over him, growing as he neared the house. Long grass and weeds on either side of the road, burned by the blistering sun, swayed, their seeds drifting in the breeze. Khaki burr dotted the unused driveway, the property wearing an air of melancholy.

He stepped out of the vehicle carefully, avoiding the burrs as best he could, and made his way to the house yard. From where it sat, jammed open in a jungle of kikuyu grass, the gate refused to move.

Picking his way across to the porch, he nudged the pair of cobweb-covered work boots with his toe. A skink ran out of one, and a large red-back spider flashed under the laces to hide. Rhys kicked the boots over again, and a key fell onto the worn timber floor.

After a brief hesitation, he bent and scooped up the key, grasping it gingerly between thumb and finger as if it were coated in toxins or something worse. He took a deep breath, slid it into the lock, and opened the door. A stale, unlived-in smell greeted him, and dust caught in his throat. He coughed, wrinkling his nose in disgust.

Geez. Someone's got a dirty job ahead.

A mouse leapt out of an open kitchen cupboard, scuttling behind the fridge at such a speed Rhys did a double-take. After taking a few steps inside, he stopped, allowing time to absorb the filth and squalor before him. Shuddering, he retreated to his vehicle and extracted a pair of disposable gloves. Grabbing the cardboard box he'd brought with him, he tucked it under one arm while stretching the gloves over his long, narrow fingers.

Inside, with his back to the dirty, junk-filled kitchen, he opened the desk drawers one by one and tipped them into the box. Layer by layer, papers, folders, pens, a calculator and stapler fell into the carton. Rhys set the container on the floor and picked his way across the tiny lounge to the hallway. Two bedrooms, one with a narrow single divan and the other with a saggy double bed, opened from the narrow passageway while a bathroom the size of a dining table fitted neatly between them. No toilet? Rhys returned to the living area and glanced through the window, noting the outbuilding a couple of metres from the back door.

Huh, toilet and laundry.

A man's coat and a dirty pair of overalls hung on hooks beside the back door, and in the far corner of the backyard, a garden shed leaned against the old wooden fence. Between the laundry and shed, a single wire decorated with an assortment of coloured clothes pegs stretched across the yard, propped up with a long, forked stick.

After turning to lift the carton of papers, Rhys locked the door behind him and slipped the key into his pocket before stripping off the disposable gloves and hurrying outside to his vehicle. A magpie sat on the bull-bar.

'What a depressing place,' he murmured to the watchful bird. 'It's all yours.'

As he drove slowly back to the police station, questions swirled in his mind and his stomach rumbled with hunger.

8

*I*t seemed the word had spread that a new police officer was in town. Over the next few days, Rhys had answered call after call, responding to cattle wandering on the road, urgent domestic disputes that were magically resolved by the time he found the properties, and an accident involving a utility whose brakes failed and ended up shrouded in fencing wire in a paddock full of cattle. To top the week off, a stolen red BMW had flown through the village at a terrifying speed, involving hours of frantic communication between the neighbouring police stations and PolAir before they caught the offender.

Rhys collapsed at the desk on the following Tuesday afternoon. The adrenaline he'd been running on for days was now spent, leaving him tired but elated.

He took the opportunity to phone James Avery.

'Gidday, Rhys. How are you settling in out there?'

'I think you call it jumping in at the deep end,' Rhys replied. 'It's been a lot busier than I expected—and definitely not boring.'

James snorted. 'Keeping you on your toes, then?'

'Yep,' Rhys replied.

'Good. Did you have time to find out what's happening with the Ward farm?'

'That's why I'm ringing, actually.' Rhys gave a rundown on his visit to both Featherwood Station and Glenrowan. 'Um. I wonder if you could advise me on another issue?'

'Sure, fire away.'

'I've received—make that the station has received–a mysterious package.' Rhys spoke hesitatingly, half-expecting a reprimand for not reporting it earlier.

'Hmm. And you say the mailman reckons these envelopes turn up regularly?'

'Every three months. Says it's been going on for a couple of years now.'

'Okay,' James said crisply. 'I'll pop into the hospital and see how Stan's going. If he's well enough, I'll ask a few questions and see what transpires. It could be perfectly innocent—a debt being repaid to him or something equally minor.'

Rhys let out a long breath. 'Thanks. And you could be right—it's probably nothing.'

'If there's anything else you're worried or need to chat about, call me.'

'Will do. Thanks again.'

Frowning, Rhys slowly replaced the phone in its cradle.

If the money was a personal issue meant specifically for Stan, wouldn't it be addressed to him and not to the officer in charge?

THE FOLLOWING WEEK BEGAN QUIETLY, giving Rhys the chance to catch up on his reports.

Early one Thursday afternoon, two weeks after his arrival in Featherwood Falls, he lingered at the table, devouring a fresh salad roll, courtesy of Lola, and reflecting on the conversation he'd had with Kirk at Featherwood Station. Intrigue nibbled at him, coupled with a touch of sadness. His brow creased. The deaths of a miner's wife and child? A bushfire?

Rising to rinse his plate and mug, he then placed them in the dish rack and pulled on a pair of disposable gloves as he strode toward the storeroom.

It took more than an hour to sort through the containers and arrange them in chronological order. Having located the box dated "1930s", Rhys carried it into the kitchen, wiped away the accumulated cobwebs and dust, and gently sat the box on the spare office desk.

After removing the lid, he groaned at the pile of fragile, yellowed papers, faded ink covering the top few sheets. He leafed cautiously through them, finding only copies of statements from long-dead community members. Returning them to the box, he then lifted out a pile of station logs, their covers tatty and delicate.

In the quiet old building, time evaporated as Rhys read through the diaries, marvelling at the elegant script in black or blue ink. Most days bore only brief comments such as *Joseph Bond—driver's licence issued*, or *McNally's cows on the road. Assisted with fence repair and reminded the owner of financial responsibility should anyone collide with an animal.*

Boredom was kicking in as he reached for the 1937 book. He flicked through the first few pages, pausing at the heading of "Bushfire" on the page dated 23 January 1937. Slowly, he deciphered the thin, spider-like script.

- *Turtle Ridge fire out of control. All available help deployed.*
- *Report from Robert Henderson, Pikedale Station advising of an encounter with a miner several weeks ago. 'Miner and family believed to be living in a hut near one of the abandoned tin mines in Turtle Ridge area.' Concern expressed for their safety.*

- *Local farmers joined forces to clear fire breaks. Strong winds predicted. Country a tinder box after months of drought.*
- *All hands called to help fight fire. Brigades from Stanthorpe and Warwick pushed to capacity.*
- *Report from property near Silver Spur advising fire now contained.*

Rhys's pulse thumped as he turned the page and read the 24 January 1937 entry.

- *Firebreak successful, aided by an unexpected thunderstorm putting most fire out. Unknown losses of stock. Further search to be conducted to locate missing family.*

He continued thumbing through the pages, pausing on 26 January, where an entry in capital letters made his blood run cold.

- *SEARCH PARTY FOUND REMNANTS OF MINER'S HUT. INVESTIGATION TO PROCEED.*

'The hut Kirk mentioned,' he whispered. Footsteps thumped outside, and the door swung open, making him jump. He slid a scrap of paper into the logbook to mark the page and laid it on the desk. Raising his eyes, he met Claire Shepherd's level gaze.

'Gidday.' Claire closed the door carefully behind her and stepped closer to the counter. 'I was picking up a few things for Mum from the store ... and she asked me to call in and see if you'd like to come to our place for dinner on Saturday night. If you can spare the time, of course.' She pointed to the pile on the desk. 'You look busy.'

'Umm. Y-yes, sort of. Well, not really.' He fumbled to straighten the pile, causing several books to fall on the floor.

Claire winced. 'Sorry. I didn't mean to interfere.'

'It's okay.' Rhys ignored the tumbling pile and moved to the counter. 'I had a couple of quiet hours, so was going through a few things that need to be archived.'

'Sure.' An awkward silence hung in the air for a few moments, and her eyes dropped to stare at his hands resting on the bench. She lifted her gaze. 'Settling in?'

'Yeah.' He gave a wry snort. 'Getting used to Ned's cooking, if that's what you mean.'

Her smile widened, and she rolled her eyes. 'I get it. So ... dinner Saturday?'

His heart leapt. 'I'd love to. What can I bring?'

'Just yourself. Frank and Lola will be there too— they often come for a barbeque on the weekends. And

Mum's recently had one of the young steers killed, so you'll be offered more than baked beans.'

'Sounds great. Thanks very much. I'll be doing a couple of hours of random breath testing in the late afternoon. Will five-thirty work?'

'Perfect.' She returned his smile and stepped toward the door. 'See you then.' And she was gone.

Rhys grinned to himself, buoyed with excitement. Although his days had been busy, the nights were long ... and he had been feeling a little out of sorts. Usually content with his own company, here in Featherwood Falls, he wanted to be part of the community. *Though this isn't the best career for that.* With Ned's passion for watching sport on television, and the ongoing restrictions because of the pandemic, socialising was limited, and Ned certainly wasn't much of a conversationalist. So ... with nothing else to keep him occupied, Rhys had been heading to bed early and progressively working his way through the pile of Dan Brown and Jack Reacher novels he had found in the pub's lounge.

The afternoon dragged, and Rhys struggled to concentrate. His mind darted between his attractive young visitor, who had filled the reception area with sunshine—albeit briefly, and discovering if the story bandied around the district regarding the fires and hut was true.

The thin, black hands of the wall clock ticked by

while Rhys tidied up the pile, leaving only the diary marked 1937 on his desk. At three-thirty, he filled the electric jug and switched it on. He was spooning coffee into a mug when the shrill ring of the phone startled him, sending grains scattering over the table.

With a click of his tongue, Rhys hurried to the office, snatched up the receiver, and opened his mouth. But before he could say "hello", a frantic male voice launched into a report about a car running into a ditch three kilometres north of Featherwood Falls township. The caller hung up. Rhys frowned, picked up his hat and keys, locked the door, and strode to the Toyota.

He pulled up behind a farm truck and switched on the flashing lights. A small silver hatchback perched precariously on the verge, its crushed nose pointing toward the roadside drain and a dead kangaroo on the grass in front of it.

A grizzled man in dirty overalls and a battered, oil-stained Akubra leaned over the open driver's door of the little car. He looked up as Rhys approached, his wrinkled face pale and his faded eyes wide.

'It's Madge Puglisi! She's not hurt. I've called the ambulance and her son is on his way. She swerved to avoid the kangaroo. It didn't work,' he said.

I can see that.

Rhys gave a curt nod of acknowledgement before squatting beside the driver. Switching to professional mode, he spoke gently to the elderly woman, confirming the details shared by the farmer, who then introduced himself as Merv.

Reassuring both Mrs Puglisi and Merv they were not in danger, Rhys whipped out the notebook from his top pocket and documented the details of the accident while they waited for the ambulance. He was constantly interrupted though by Merv's tales of all the accidents he had "happened upon" in the past.

'I'm a busy man,' Merv said, and Rhys's lips twitched at the irony.

'Thanks for your help. You can go home if you'd like to.' Rhys drew a long, silent breath, lifting his gaze at the approaching sound of a high-powered vehicle.

His eyes narrowed as a black Falcon utility approached with a rumbling purr. He stood while barely fifty metres away, the vehicle braked hard, spun around, and sped back the way it had come. As it turned, Rhys focused on the registration plate, cursing quietly. Too far away to read the number, he could only note that the plate was yellow, revealing a New South Wales registration.

At the distant sound of a siren wailing, Rhys returned his attention to Mrs Puglisi. The ambulance drew up in front of the silver hatchback and the paramedics swiftly assessed the patient while a dirty Holden sedan screeched to a halt on the opposite side of the road. A middle-aged man jumped out, and without casting a glance in either direction, tramped across the bitumen, leaving muddy boot prints as he hurried to Mrs Puglisi's side.

'She's my mother,' he called to Rhys, as if his statement explained everything.

More sedately, a woman got out of the passenger seat and followed, ducking her head to peer anxiously at the woman almost hidden by the men surrounding her.

Facing Rhys, she nodded, a quavering smile touching her lips. 'Hello. I'm Barbara, Mrs Puglisi's daughter-in-law.' Turning to point to the new, gum-booted arrival, she announced, 'That's Peter, my husband.'

Half an hour passed before the paramedics declared the elderly woman well enough to be driven home.

'You take her,' Peter said to Barbara. 'I'll wait for the towy and catch a lift with him.'

While a paramedic escorted Mrs Puglisi to the car, Merv finally climbed into his truck and drove off.

Within a few minutes, the scene was quiet as Rhys and Peter dragged the dead kangaroo clear of the road and checked its gender.

'A big buck. No wonder your mother's car has so much damage.' Rhys gazed sadly at the well-muscled animal. 'Such a shame.'

They waited for the tow truck in companionable

silence as the heat of the day dissipated and dark clouds built in the western sky.

An ominous flutter stirred in Rhys's gut at the memory of the black utility speeding away from the scene. It was the second car he'd noticed in the past few days that didn't quite fit with the agricultural area. Then again, he hadn't been in Featherwood Falls long enough to familiarise himself with local vehicles. And besides, the tiny town was on a road that adjoined Queensland and New South Wales, albeit a minor road, so random low-slung cars and motorbikes were bound to traverse it, despite the poorly maintained surface.

'Looks like we're about to cop it,' Peter announced, pointing to the thunder cloud almost directly above them.

'Quick. Hop in.' Rhys opened the passenger door for him before hurrying to the driver's seat as the deluge arrived.

Heavy, deafening rain pounded the roof as the tow truck approached.

Rhys groaned. 'That'd be right. Will he wait until the shower's over?'

Peter grunted. 'I doubt it. You know what these guys are like. They wait for no man ... or weather event.' He laughed and opened the door, stepping into the torrent.

Ignoring the conditions, the truck driver reversed

to the little car, lowered the tilt tray, and leapt out of the cab.

Rhys sighed and reached into the back seat for his raincoat. Peter and the truck driver may not care about getting wet, but he had his utility belt to protect, and the last thing his radio and gun needed was a good soaking. He struggled into the coat as the rain blew sideways, saturating his trousers in seconds. Peering through the curtain of water, he could barely make out the driver's face. He wore shorts and a navy-blue singlet, a cap pulled low over his eyes. With a dismissive shake of his head as both Peter and Rhys attempted to assist, the man quickly and efficiently locked chains into place and wound the hatchback onto the tray, fastening it to the bolts in minutes. Lifting his arm in a brief wave, Peter climbed into the truck's passenger seat as thunder clapped overhead. With its cargo anchored forlornly on the tray, the truck moved off.

Rhys flicked the water from his face, shivering as a trickle flowed down the back of his neck, soaking his shirt. He jogged to the Toyota and started the engine. Wet, cold, and hungry as he was, he experienced a flash of doubt for the first time since arriving in Featherwood Falls.

Have I made the right decision in accepting this position?

He snapped to attention, chiding himself. Of

course, he had ... Being the officer in charge of a small country police station had been his dream since he joined the force—and he wasn't about to give it up.

9

*A*nticipation of the weekend visit to Featherwood Station buoyed Rhys through the following two days, and by lunchtime on Saturday, he was counting down the hours with the excitement of a child.

Despite his plan to conduct a three-hour random breath testing session during the late afternoon, he cut it short after two, relieved that he had encountered no problems. Twenty-one vehicles had been intercepted, mostly parents bringing children home from sporting activities, and although he wanted to get to know the residents of the town, the divide between being a community member and law enforcement made that a bit hard. The last thing he wanted was a delay in arriving at Featherwood Station.

He polished his R.M. boots and hunted for the iron

in the shabby laundry at the rear of the pub. After pressing his blue checked shirt and moleskin trousers, he showered, dressed, and headed for the car, liberally scented with musky aftershave and with a six-pack of beer and a bottle of Chardonnay under his arm.

As he drove toward the gracious old home, Rhys's gaze roved around the property. Glimpsing a long, low building with a veranda across the front behind a row of trees, he braked gently.

Shearer's quarters, I suppose.

He reached the yard, surprised at the number of vehicles parked nose into the house fence. Drawing to a halt behind the tractor in the machinery shed, he strolled toward the house gate, drinks in hand. A burgundy Prado stood next to a sleek black V8 Ford utility with New South Wales registration plates. Rhys arched an eyebrow. *Is that the one that sped away to avoid me?* He hadn't seen the Prado around town. *Is this a celebration of some sort?*

Tentatively, he opened the gate before closing it quietly behind him. Parties had never been his cup of tea. He preferred small groups where conversation was easy and the music volume moderate. Despite wanting to fit in—and get to know Claire a little better—today was no different.

He had only taken a few steps along the flagstone path when Ginny approached, her lips clamped in a tight line and her expression thunderous. The two men strolling behind her both wore amused smirks on their faces. One was stout with a florid complexion and small piggy eyes. Rhys estimated him to be in his early fifties. The other was much younger, tall, well-muscled, and with the whitest hair Rhys had ever seen. Colourful sleeve tattoos covered his arms and neck and the large roman nose protruding from his clean-shaven face reminded Rhys of a picture of Captain Hook from a childhood book.

Ginny stopped suddenly, her frown disappearing. 'Hi, Rhys. Lovely to see you again.'

'Hello, Ginny.' He glanced at the men behind her, and she cleared her throat.

'These gentlemen are just leaving. I won't be a moment..'

He gave a frowning nod, as the older of the two men extended a hand in greeting.

'You must be the new cop I've heard about. Donald Shepherd, Ginny's brother-in-law.' A sly sneer spread across the man's face as he spoke, despite the friendly greeting. He turned to his companion. 'And this is Lars, my new employee—foreman. He'll be living on Glen-rowan and taking care of the crops for me.'

Rhys grasped Donald's work-roughened hand and squeezed it hard. He may not have been a farmer but, after experiencing the strength of Kirk's grip, this time he was ready. 'Good to meet you both. No doubt I'll see you around town.'

Ginny swung the gate open, her frown returning. 'Goodbye, Donald, Lars.'

'Our visit wasn't welcome, apparently.' Donald shot a glance at Rhys as he passed through the gateway. 'Never mind. We'll call again when Ginny's in a better mood.'

They ambled to the vehicles where Donald climbed into the burgundy Prado and Lars, the flashy black ute.

Something about the younger, snowy-haired man triggered alarm bells for Rhys. He stood next to Ginny until both vehicles had turned onto the road at the end of the driveway.

'Phew!' Ginny met his gaze, her expression apologetic. 'I'm sorry about that. Now you've met my brother-in-law, I'll let you make your own judgement. I didn't invite either of them, and they are not welcome —despite my plan to be friends with my new neighbours.'

'I understand. It must have come as a shock to hear they had appointed Donald as manager?'

'You're not wrong.' Ginny shuddered. 'It was nice of Nigel's solicitor to let me know, though. I'm not usually so negative about family, but that man bears no resemblance to my poor, deceased husband. I'm sure Lyndon would turn in his grave if he knew Donald was taking over Glenrowan.'

Rhys said nothing, merely digested the information. *What occurred in the past to create such divisiveness within the family?*

'Even though they're cousins?' he asked.

'Who are cousins?' Ginny stared at him as though he'd spoken in a foreign language.

'Donald and Nigel Ward.'

She shuddered. 'I don't know who told you that, but I assure you, there's no blood connecting those two. If there was, Lyndon would also be a cousin, and that's something we all would have known about.'

Rhys raised his eyebrows. 'And Lars? Have you met him before?' he asked.

She shook her head and breathed a sigh. 'I know I shouldn't judge a book by its cover. He has only just moved in, so who am I to comment?' Pausing, she narrowed her eyes and shrugged. 'But I don't think I'll be playing tea parties with him.'

'I get it. Remember, I'm here. Any time you have any concerns, please call me.'

Ginny took his arm. 'Thanks, Rhys. Now, let's forget about those two invaders and have a drink. Kirk and Frank have the barbeque going and I think Claire and Lola are putting the final touches on dessert.'

She led him up the veranda steps, where Kirk and Frank welcomed him and offered a drink.

'What did you think of that Lars fella?' Kirk asked. 'Certainly doesn't look like your average farmer.'

Ginny screwed up her face. 'Those turquoise eyes of his give me the creeps.'

'We'll see how he goes.' Kirk turned to Rhys and handed him a beer. 'Settling in okay?'

Rhys nodded. 'Yeah. Been busier than I expected—but I guess that's a good way to be.'

Frank grunted, the lines around his twinkling blue eyes stretching to his white hair. 'I was talking to the school principal the other day, and he said he's hoping you'll be able to pay a visit to the kids. You know, get to know them and increase their confidence in the police. It's been a long time since we held those blue-light discos.'

'What made the discos stop?' Rhys recalled the fun nights when he was at high school in Stanthorpe. His dislike of sizeable crowds meant he hadn't attended regularly, but he had helped his father occasionally, and had witnessed the relationship between the police and the youth of the town improving and strengthening. His father had a knack for remembering names, and the respect between him and the children had been mutual.

'I dunno about the bigger towns, but here, our population dropped. Families moved away to seek work and a better education for their children. When Stan arrived here, he wasn't interested in continuing anything to do with kids.' Frank snapped his mouth shut as though he'd said too much.

'So, Stan wasn't a family man?' Rhys asked.

'No. He had a wife, but they were always arguing. One day, she must have had enough because she packed her bags and left. Dunno where she went, but for the last umpteen years, Stan's been on his own. I reckon that's what caused him to lose interest in his work—and life,' Frank said. 'Probably didn't help his health, either. He smoked, drank too much, and from what we could see, rarely ate anything you could call healthy. I reckon the only friend he really had here was Ned—and even then, it was an odd friendship.'

A wave of compassion for the man flooded through Rhys. Although determined to do everything he could to serve the town well, so far, the community vibe he'd hoped for in Featherwood Falls was slow in revealing itself. Probably because of the many pandemic lockdowns and restrictions, he reasoned optimistically. The loneliness he had experienced already must have been similar for Stan—and he reserved judgement of a man he had never met.

Claire stepped through the doors onto the veranda, carrying a tray of assorted nibbles. Her yellow and white striped shirt and wide smile brought a sunny presence and something surged in his chest.

'Hi, Rhys. Welcome. I hope you're hungry?'

He smiled at her, his concern for Stan forgotten. 'Starving.'

She thrust the tray at him, and he helped himself to a spring roll. 'Yum. This sure beats Ned's stew.'

Lola and Ginny appeared, each carrying dishes which they laid on the long table at one end of the veranda.

As soon as she put the platter down, Lola made a beeline for Rhys and enveloped him in a bear hug, her chunky purple earrings swinging against his chest. 'It's nice to see you out of your working environment—although you do look rather smart all dressed up in a uniform.' She gave a giggle, and Rhys fidgeted.

He turned his face toward the evening breeze to cool the heat radiating up his neck.

'Come and sit down, Rhys.' He met Claire's sympathetic grin as she pointed to a chair. Pulling out the one opposite him, she raised her glass to touch it against his. 'Cheers.'

Glasses clinked and they ate as the sun sank lower on the horizon.

Warm and replete with good food, beer, and the enjoyable company, Rhys relaxed, stretching his legs out under the table. He was glad of the small group. *Six people are perfect.*

When Kirk once more raised the subject of Glenrowan's workforce, he raised an eyebrow.

'What do the rest of you think of Donald's plan to grow tomatoes and corn instead of carrots and celery? Kirk asked. 'Seems weird to me. I would have thought tomatoes would be a lot more labour intensive than carrots and celery—and it's the wrong season to be planting corn.'

'I haven't thought about it,' Frank replied. 'They mentioned building poly-tunnels. According to Donald, they're planning to grow the tomatoes both hydroponically and out in the open.' He shrugged. 'I only hope they can find enough staff to harvest them when the time comes, cause the way he was talking, there'll be tonnes of produce.'

'I think Donald's got a lot more contacts than we realise,' Kirk said. 'We know he wanted Featherwood Station so he could run more cattle. I suspect he's simply a greedy man who wants to be king of his castle —and be able to spout about being a big landholder. I can't imagine why, though. No point being the richest person in the cemetery.'

Ginny stood up and kissed him on the cheek before gathering the dirty plates. 'Not like you, eh? Enough to live comfortably and see what tomorrow brings.'

Kirk laughed and wrapped his arm around her. 'Something like that.'

Rhys met Claire's gaze across the table.

She smiled. 'Want to help me with the dishes, Rhys?'

'Love to,' he answered, pushing his chair back as his heartbeat increased a notch.

SCRAPING the plates into the chook bucket, Claire paused to glance at Rhys.

'I was wondering if you'd like to come to the falls with me next time you have a day off?'

'The falls?'

'Yes. We have a couple of springs up in the hills at the back of Featherwood Station, and they form the creeks that flow through the property. Years ago, Dad built a dam out of rocks at the bottom of the granite outcrop where the waterfall cascades down, making a nice pool below the falls. It's surrounded by a patch of rainforest that makes it pretty special.'

'Sounds lovely. So, you can swim there?'

'Yeah. It's not huge—more of a plunge pool, I guess. It's a pleasant spot on a hot day, though.'

'Sounds great. I've got a day off next Wednesday if that works for you.' Rhys's enthusiasm for the plan was obvious in his voice. So far, he had spent his one and only day off walking the back roads for three hours to familiarise himself with the area, and then lying on his bed reading a book. A day spent with Claire Shepherd was a *much* more enjoyable prospect.

'I'm sure we can make it work. My job's pretty flexible. Except for zoom meetings, I can work whatever hours I like, provided the jobs are done.'

'So, what exactly do you do?'

'I'm a graphic artist.' Claire briefly outlined her life in Sydney.

'Life must be pretty quiet here then, compared to Sydney.'

She laughed—that delicious, hearty laugh he'd heard the first time they met.

'It is—and I love it.'

Her blonde hair swung in a glossy veil around her shoulders and her clear, makeup-free skin glowed.

Rhys caught his breath as she smiled at him.

'I noticed a building a hundred metres or so down the side track as I drove in. Is that the shearer's quarters?' he asked.

'It used to be. That's the track to the woolshed. Mum and Dad started renovating it before Dad died, and then Kirk helped Mum finish it. It's now the accommodation for farm stays. Mum always wanted to do something like that. We're so lucky to live in such a beautiful place, she wanted to share it with others.' Claire shrugged. 'Then Dad died, and Covid arrived—so, it's been slow in taking off, but we've all got a good feeling for the future.'

'Sounds like a great idea.'

Claire swiftly packed the dishwasher while Rhys followed her instructions, filling the kettle and setting out six mugs.

They dawdled, chatting idly about their jobs and families before beginning the tea-making process.

'Are you two making the tea or still picking the leaves?' Ginny's call brought a grin to Claire's face.

She turned her gaze on Rhys. 'Looks like we'll have to wait until Wednesday to finish this conversation.'

He nodded, his long, thin face flushed with anticipation. 'I can't wait.'

10

*S*till dwelling on Saturday night and her chat with Rhys, Claire sang along with the radio as she drove to Stanthorpe the following Monday.

Having ordered a new printer, she'd decided that rather than wait until the carrier made his weekly trip to Featherwood Falls, she would make the journey herself and have a look for a new swimsuit while she was there. Of course, the coldest town in Queensland was probably not the best place for beachwear, but it had some lovely shops full of surprises—and Claire had often found exactly what she wanted there when she couldn't find it in Sydney or Brisbane. *Worth a look, anyway.*

Coming into town via the back roads took her through lush orchards and past picturesque wineries. After the worst drought in years, which coincided with the tragic death of her father in 2019, the welcome rain over the past eighteen months had transformed the country. Fresh growth filled ditches and fields and the branches of trees hung low with orange, purple, and green fruit. Birds flittered across the road in front of her, darting for insects while fat cattle and sheep rested contentedly in the paddocks, chewing their cud.

She parked behind the computer shop, collected the printer, and stowed it in her car. Then she strolled up the main street, window shopping as she went. Diving into an attractive-looking boutique filled with eclectic garments, she browsed the racks, a little surprised to find not only a pretty if limited range of swimwear, but a soft cotton top in a dainty floral pattern with a lace-edged neckline. Its vibrant shades of blues, pinks, and greens were the exact colours that looked good on her, and without hesitation, she bought it. Although very much a jeans-and-shirt girl, she liked to dress more femininely occasionally. Of course, Wednesday's date with Rhys had nothing to do with her choice of purchase.

Excited by her acquisitions, which included a royal blue bikini, she stepped out of the shop wearing a smile. Meandering along the paved pathway, she glanced across the road at the coffee shop. It was already bustling with customers—a good sign. She waited for the traffic to pass before crossing. With every table occupied, she collected her coffee, savoury muffin, and chocolate slice when they were ready and began strolling toward the park.

The sun was strong, beating down on her fair skin, and she increased her pace, rounding the corner opposite the pub and pressing close to the buildings and their blessed shade. Along the front of the hotel, small tables and chairs hugged the wall, allowing patrons to enjoy the glorious day.

She drew level with the pub on the opposite side of the road as four men set their drinks on a table and pulled out chairs. Claire glanced at the group, narrowing her eyes as the back of a white-blond head caught her attention. *That looks like Lars.* She frowned. Not wanting him to recognise her, she spun away, and stared into the shop window in front of her. Its reflection allowed her to study the mirror images and she was certain now it was Lars. That physique and the profile of his nose as he turned slightly confirmed it. Her gaze then roved over his drinking mates. All three were muscular, in denim and leather, and wore beards, tattoos, and sunglasses. She didn't recognise any of them, and for that or some other equally worrying reason, a nerve on her temple twitched. They looked like the bikies she'd seen—and carefully kept her distance from—in the big cities.

A shiver ran up her back and she hurried to the park, where she plonked herself on the seat under a tree and stared, brow deeply furrowed, at her lunch.

Are those men potential workers for Glenrowan? Is that what the "new-look" farm assistants will be like now Covid has put a stop to the usual backpacking fraternity?

Her reservations deepening, she brushed the crumbs off her lap, swallowed the last of the coffee, collected her shopping bags, and headed to her little Subaru.

They certainly don't look like farm assistants to me.

As she drove away, her eyes widened at the sight of three Harley-Davidson motorcycles parked against the kerb. *Lars's friends', no doubt. Guess I was right about them.* She blew out a long breath through pursed lips and turned up the music on the car radio.

A queasy sensation had crept into her stomach, refusing to dissipate. It had been her uncle Donald who had recruited Lars for the foreman position, and she dearly hoped there would be no more trouble. Her thoughts drifted to Andrew, her cousin, and the only child of Donald and Sarah. Although a few years younger than her, the two of them had always been close, spending holidays on Featherwood Station as children, riding, swimming, and playing in the woolshed. During Donald's recent surprise visit to Featherwood Station, he had announced Andrew was enrolling to study agronomy. Claire found it strange that her cousin hadn't told her himself, although she and Andrew talked or messaged each other irregularly. If Donald hadn't sufficient time to do the job, why hadn't he appointed Andrew to the foreman position, assuming he wanted to learn more about farming? A vision of Lars and his companions flashed across her mind, and her spirits rose a fraction.

I hope that means whatever dodgy activities Donald has planned for Glenrowan, Andrew has no part in them.

Pulling to the side of the road, she switched off the car, snatched up her phone, and got out.

He answered on the first ring. 'Hey, cuz. What's up?'

'Hi, Andrew. I was thinking about you and thought I'd give you a call—you know, a long overdue catch up.' She spoke lightly. 'I hear you're diving back into studying.'

'Yeah. My decision. Kept the plans quiet though cause it's taken a while to talk Dad around.'

'Oh. He sounded happy about it when he visited us recently.'

Andrew snorted. 'He would. Got no choice. Mum and I've been talking about it for a while. You know Dad. Thinks he can control us all but doesn't give a shit about what we want.'

Claire blinked hard. Despite the family's opinion of Donald's methods, Andrew had always defended his father—until now. 'Oh. Bit of a row then?'

'Nah. Not really. I'd already been accepted at uni and Mum's supporting me financially now she's had a chance to squirrel away a good chunk of her wages. I told him he could take it or leave it but if he wanted me to come home and work like a slave, he could think again.'

Claire grinned, picturing her uncle's red-faced expletives. 'I bet that got a frothing-at-the-mouth reaction"?'

He laughed. 'Yeah, you know him well.'

'That's good. I'm sure you'll love uni and having a life of your own.'

'You're not wrong. I really enjoy farming but have had a gutful of Dad's greed and am looking forward to the change.'

They chatted for a few more minutes before Claire swiped the red icon and breathed a sigh of relief, certain that the future of Glenrowan had nothing to do with Andrew.

RHYS TURNED the air conditioner down a degree as powerful motorbikes roared along the road outside. He frowned and took a seat in the desk chair nearest to the cooler. It was hot—too hot for standing on the side of the road doing RBTs or even for strolling down to buy one of Lola's delicious salad rolls. He had made himself a ham sandwich instead. After reaching for the 1937 diary, he opened it on the page marked with the scrap of paper.

- *27 January 1937—Investigation of fire conducted. Findings:*
- *Timber hut located and inspected. Walls partially remaining but roof burned and fallen. Interior of hut filled with blackened timber.*
- *Removal of inside debris revealed remnants of a body.*
- *CIB requested.*

'Wow.' With his interest now well and truly piqued, Rhys turned the page, wanting more. On

the 28 January entry, the sloping script filled every centimetre of the delicate parchment.

- *Two bodies found at miner's hut on Turtle Ridge, believed to have been inhabited by the McMahon family. Suspected to be those of a woman and young child. Both skulls contained what appears to be a bullet hole. Homicide and forensic teams are now involved. Search of area failed to locate William McMahon, the miner referred to by other miners as Wild Willy.*
- *Mr Angus Shepherd from Featherwood Station contacted OIC advising a teenaged girl had turned up in a dishevelled state the previous night. Claims she has been hiding in the bush before making her way to Featherwood Station.*

CIB attended property to interview. CIB report
confirmed girl's name is Jo-Lee McMahon.

Leaning forward to rest his elbows on his knees, Rhys gripped the logbook in his hands as he trawled through the next few days. Among the tedious record-ings of day-to-day policing matters, the notes in small, neat writing continued.

Although the investigation reports were elsewhere —probably archived by now—someone had taken the time to keep the Featherwood Falls Officer in Charge abreast of the situation. He read on.

Two hours later, he straightened his stiff limbs and shivered. Goose bumps covered his arms, and he blinked, unsure if it was the room temperature or delving into the past that chilled him. Reaching for the remote, he switched the air-conditioning unit off and got to his feet.

He strode to the storeroom and hauled the 1930s container off the shelf before carrying it into the office.

Outside, the roar of an engine shattered the sleepy main street, and Rhys stilled. After dumping the box on the desk, he reefed the door open and peered down the road in time to see the tail end of a black utility disappear around the bend.

'Bugger. I hope that bloke isn't going to cause trouble here.'

His thoughts moved to the Shepherd family. Ginny

had clearly experienced both shock and fear at the goings on over the previous couple of years. The last thing she needed was a new neighbour who made matters worse. He glanced at his watch, surprised it was already past five o'clock.

After stowing his utility belt in the safe, he locked the door before heading to the pub. A restlessness consumed him, and he craved solitude despite having been alone most of the day. He called out a greeting to Ned as he passed the bar and ran up the stairs two at a time.

Minutes later, in shorts and runners, he struck out along the back road and headed for the bush.

As evening drew in and the scrub surrounded him, Rhys slowed his pace. Birds cheeped and squawked as they settled for the night while a family of kangaroos grazed peacefully in a clearing.

He smiled at them, relaxing now as his mind cleared. There was so much more to discover about this little town. So many secrets hidden or forgotten. He guessed many more were yet to be revealed. Turning back toward the village, he exhaled noisily.

What concoction will Ned be offering for dinner? Stew, of course! He gave a wry huff and broke into a jog.

11

*R*hys woke before sunrise on Wednesday.
'Yay. Day off,' he whispered.

But it wasn't really having the day off he was so looking forward to. He grinned as a vision of Claire formed in his mind and he shook his head.

I don't want a girlfriend.

Stepping through the French doors onto the veranda, he breathed in the cool morning air. Above the bush-clad hills to the east, shades of pink and purple mingled in the soft light of dawn, and across the road, perched on the power line, a magpie warbled.

His phone pinged, and he walked back into the bedroom and picked it up.

Claire!

Panic surged through him. Was she cancelling their date—if it was a date?

He tapped the screen and read the message, his smile widening.

Good morning. Thought we might take a picnic with us and go for a hike before our swim. Sound okay?

He responded immediately. *Sounds great. Will come prepared!*

He hit send before realising they hadn't arranged a time. He added, *What time?*

Dots waved on the screen, showing her answer was about to arrive.

7:30?

Great. See you then.

The sun peeped over the horizon while Rhys dressed and gathered his gear. After stuffing his towel, spare clothes, and sunscreen into a backpack, he grabbed a pair of socks and hiking boots before slipping his feet into thongs. Then, picking up the book he was halfway through reading from the bedside table, he trod quietly down the stairs.

Tense with excitement, he drove the short distance to the police station and unlocked the door. The decision to eat all but his evening meal in the station kitchen had been a good one, offering him familiarity and a private place to enjoy his food. He switched the electric jug on and glanced at his watch.

Five-thirty. He sighed. Two hours seemed forever. While he waited for the jug to boil, he opened his book and continued reading. The town was quiet, with only the occasional bleat of a sheep in the distance and a crow cawing in a tree on the roadside. Rhys dallied over his bowl of muesli, drinking two cups of tea and re-reading the same page several times before giving up. Fidgeting with the buttons on his shirt, he meandered around the building, checking his watch every few minutes. At seven o'clock, he filled his water bottle, stuffed two apples and a block of chocolate in his backpack. Then, cramming his wide-brimmed Akubra on his head, he strode to his ute.

Whistling softly, he loaded the backpack into the vehicle's tray and dropped his boots onto the passenger seat floor. Before backing out of the drive, he lowered his window, allowing the gentle breeze to flow into the vehicle, and glanced at the clear skies overhead. *Another beautiful summer day.* Tapping his fingers on the steering wheel as he drove away, he looked around the sleepy township. Frank was putting the sign outside the shop, and he lifted his hand and waved.

'Morning Frank!' Rhys called through the open window, slowing as he passed.

Minutes later, he turned onto the Featherwood Station road and sped up the hill. Ahead of him, the sun shone on the hills, accentuating their shades of blue and mauve. He passed the neat, white-painted cottage he now knew as Kirk's place and slowed as he approached the driveway to the Shepherd farm. He was early—by almost fifteen minutes—and he hoped Claire wouldn't mind.

A cacophony of barking welcomed him, and Claire yelled, 'That'll do!'

She strode toward him as he stepped out of the ute, her face flushed under the wide-brimmed hat.

'Hello,' she said breathlessly. 'I saw you coming up the road while I was shifting the electric fence.'

He nodded, smiling. 'Hi.'

'Come inside. Everyone's having a lazy breakfast this morning. Fancy bacon and eggs?'

Despite his bowl of cereal, Rhys's mouth watered at the thought. 'Thanks. Sounds delicious.'

She smiled and swung the gate open.

Following Claire along the paved pathway, his heart lurched. A blonde ponytail hung down her back. As she trod onto the bottom step, she removed her hat and the morning sun lit up the shimmering gold threads woven through the pale strands of her hair.

'Good morning, Rhys.' Ginny's voice rang out before he reached the veranda.

'Gidday.'

The smell of bacon greeted his senses. 'Smells pretty good.'

Kirk stood in front of the barbeque and cracked an egg on the hot plate. 'Gidday, mate. Two eggs for you?'

'Yes please.' Salivating, he surveyed the tantalising mushrooms and tomatoes piled in one corner of the barbeque and the plate of fried potato slices beside the hot plate. 'Wow. This looks great.'

Ginny laughed. 'We've all got a big day ahead of us and you never know when you'll get a break, so we like to start with a full belly on these occasions.'

'Mum and Kirk are getting the stud ewes in today to crutch and drench them,' Claire explained, 'and you and I have a few hours walking to do.' She smiled as she pointed to his thongs. 'So, I hope you're not planning to go hiking in those?'

'No.' He grinned. 'My boots are in the ute—along with my backpack.'

'Where are you going to take him, Claire?' Ginny asked.

'I thought we might go up that access track the electricity mob used to use, up to the back of the farm where it joins the old rabbit-board fence. From there, we can walk along the ridge to Fletcher's boundary where the spring comes out, then follow the creek down through the bush until we get to the waterfall. I reckon after that, Rhys will be very glad of his swim.'

'Geez. I hope you're feeling energetic, Rhys. What distance would that be, Ginny? Ten kilometres? Twelve?' Kirk asked as he scooped up the food from the barbeque and layered it on the serving tray.

'Thanks, Kirk,' Claire answered. 'I haven't done it for months, but it only took about four hours the last time Briony and I did it.'

Ginny rolled her eyes at Rhys. 'In that case, you'd better allow longer. I don't think the girls have been that way since they were teenagers.'

'Help yourselves before it gets cold.' Kirk set the food on the table while Claire spread out the plates.

Savouring every mouthful, Rhys's spirits rose. What more could a bloke want? Beautiful weather, a full stomach, and the whole day ahead of him to spend with a gorgeous young woman who apparently enjoyed exactly the same type of activities he did ... even if she wasn't his girlfriend.

AT HALF-PAST EIGHT, Rhys hoisted his backpack on, slipping his arms through the thick straps and blinking at the added weight. Insisting they be prepared for any eventuality, Claire had stuffed a first-aid kit into her pack before adding a towel and a change of clothes. The container of food rested neatly on top, but there was no way the enamel mugs and thermos of coffee would fit. Rhys gallantly offered to slide them into his larger backpack, along with the snakebite kit, two extra litres of water, a torch, and the emergency blanket Kirk insisted they carry.

'I know you reckon you'll be back by midafternoon,

but in this part of the country, you never know what the weather will do,' he said.

Claire raised her eyebrows and grinned wryly at Rhys. 'He's a mountain man from the Snowies. Can't you tell?'

'All good. I admit I'm a bit the same.' He shrugged. 'Guess I mostly hike alone, so I'm used to taking everything but the kitchen sink myself. Oh, better grab the climbing tape.'

He raced back to his vehicle and returned with a thin cloth bag.

'What's climbing tape?' Claire asked.

Rhys unwrapped the parcel and opened it, displaying a thick roll of soft, tubular webbing.

'It's lighter and stronger than rope and useful if we find ourselves on the edge of a cliff and need to lower ourselves down,' he explained.

'Geez, I hope that won't be the case,' Claire said. 'So, how do you get the tape down if we're all at the bottom of the cliff and it's tied to something at the top?'

'There's forty metres of it. We loop it around a tree at the top, lower ourselves using the twenty-metre doubled strength, then when we reach the base of whatever we're climbing down, we release one end and pull it around with the other.'

'Oh, I see.' Claire looked at Rhys with renewed admiration.

'Come on then. We'll drop you at the gate. It's on

our way to the sheep.' Ginny jumped into the farm ute and switched on the engine.

Using the side step, Claire hoisted herself onto the tray back ahead of Rhys. He climbed up after her and faced the front over the roof of the cab, feeling her warmth as they stood side by side, gripping the top rail of the frame. Exhilaration burst inside him as the ute jerked forward and his arm brushed against Claire's. Rattling past the cattle yards and on up a track that ran alongside the fence into the hills, they continued until, at the top of a rise, Ginny halted the vehicle.

'This is your stop.' Ginny stuck her head out the driver's window, and Rhys jumped down before reaching up to help Claire.

Shaking her head at his offered hand, she turned her back to him, slipped her foot onto the step, and lowered herself to the ground. She pointed to the barely visible dirt road beside them. 'We're going that way.'

'Have a good day, you two,' Ginny said.

Claire gave her mother a wave and smiled at Rhys. 'Thanks. We will.'

They stood for a few moments as Kirk and Ginny drove away, drinking in the vista spread before them. All thoughts of work, the logbooks, and the money in the safe drained from Rhys's mind while Claire's presence and the anticipation of the day ahead filled his soul.

Although wiry, Claire strode off at a fast pace, surprising Rhys. His long legs stretched out to keep up with hers and they were both puffing heavily by the time they reached a crest a kilometre or more away. Pausing two steps behind Claire, Rhys noted her pink cheeks and sparkling grey eyes.

'You must be fitter than me,' he laughed.

She shook her head. 'I doubt it. Apart from going to the falls with the dogs and riding, I've done little exercise since I've been home—oh, except for stacking hay bales, if that counts.'

'I reckon it would.' His admiration for this woman soared. He had stacked hay for his father many times when he'd been at home and it was every bit as strenuous as a tough gym workout.

'Actually, I'm really only trying to cover this section of our walk quickly, so we have more time for the more interesting parts of the day,' she continued.

'Okay.' Intrigued, he dragged his gaze from her to the view down the valley and whistled softly. 'It certainly is a pretty part of this country.'

'Yep. Even better from the top.'

She turned away, and they continued tramping along the narrow dirt-wheel tracks that ran between rows of grass and tangled weeds.

They chatted intermittently as another hour passed, sharing snippets of their work life and childhood until Claire halted again and unbuckled the waistbelt of her pack. 'It gets easier from here, I promise. I reckon we're due for some of that coffee.'

He slid his pack to the ground before extracting the mugs and thermos flask.

Claire perched on a rock, removed her hat, and wiped the sweat from her forehead. 'So, we've covered the polite bits.'

He glanced at her as he squatted on the ground, pouring the coffee. Frowning, he tilted his head to one side. 'Do you mean the easy bits of the hike?'

She shook her head. 'No. Conversation. I was wondering if you have a girlfriend.'

'Oh, I see.' He screwed the lid back on the thermos and handed a mug to her. 'No, I don't. You?'

She shook her head. 'I had a boyfriend—at least, I thought I did.' She shrugged. 'Thanks to my flatmate in Sydney, I heard he was seeing someone else while I was here for Christmas. So ... that's history.'

Rhys moistened his dry mouth with a swallow of coffee, determined to keep his inner joy in check. 'Were you upset? I mean, are you still grieving?'

She grunted. 'Not now. I was pretty gutted to begin with—but then I realised it wasn't as unexpected as I first thought. He worked in a fly-in, fly-out job, so was away a lot, and sometimes he would ring me regularly, but other times I wouldn't hear from him for days.' Claire studied the contents of her mug 'I guess sometimes we know things will not work out long term, but we don't like admitting it to ourselves.'

'You're not wrong.' He inhaled deeply. 'I also had a girlfriend before I came here. I don't know why, but when I got the offer—that is, the temporary promotion—I thought she would be happy for me. Turns out she wasn't.'

They shared a laugh, drawn together by common understanding.

'Did she like bushwalking?' Claire asked.

Rhys let out a guffaw and shook his head. 'Far from it. Hated getting her shoes dirty almost as much as her hands. So, no, hiking was not on her agenda. She loved dining out, parties, and fancy clothes, and was—is—a beautiful and nice girl. Just not for me.'

'So, it's all over now?'

He looked up, realisation dawning—he had barely thought about Evie since arriving in Featherwood Falls. Nodding, he said, 'Yep. All in the past.'

Their eyes met, and their smiles spread like a languid wave.

12

*T*he following two hours passed in a flash as, having unburdened themselves of their personal statuses, an easiness bonded them—a mateship that grew with every step.

After trudging through spiky melaleuca and admiring the glossy green leaves of the random lilly pilly, they paused at the top of a ridge. Looking down on Featherwood Station and the surrounding farms and hectares of forestry, they slipped their backpacks off and sat, leaning against a tree and watching the variety of finches and brown honeyeaters flitting in and out of the surrounding shrubs. While they rested, they ate the sandwiches and Claire elaborated on her plans to remain working from home.

'I've always loved the farm and now I can help Mum whenever she needs it.' She gave a small giggle.

'Actually, I think it's me who needs it more than Mum does—especially now she has Kirk in her life.' She gazed at him. 'Tell me more about your work.'

He shrugged. 'It has its moments, but most of the time, I enjoy it. Shiftwork is hard going—and some situations we have to attend are pretty confronting—but most of the time it's a friendly environment to work in, especially in a nice place like Featherwood Falls. I just wish I could stay here permanently.'

'So, you don't want to get to the top?'

'Not really. I know some guys who'll go all over the state chasing promotions. But me ... I think I'd be happy to remain in a place like this.'

They shared a grin.

'I'm glad you're here,' Claire breathed.

For what felt like an age, their gazes locked on each other again and time stood still. Claire was the first to break the moment, jumping to her feet and reaching for her pack. 'Come on. Not far to go now to the falls—and it's all downhill.'

Rhys huffed out a groan, creases forming at the sides of his eyes as he smiled. 'Slave driver.'

Claire hauled him to his feet before dropping his hand and hoisting her backpack on. She stilled, squinting into the distance, and Rhys followed her gaze, concern creasing his forehead.

'What is it?' he asked.

She pointed. 'Can you see that patch of white behind the trees—in the clearing?'

He stepped closer to her and peered toward the rolling hills that led to the flat land along the creek. 'Is that on Glenrowan?'

'Yes.'

'It looks like it could be the poly-tunnel or tunnels Donald mentioned they were putting up,' Rhys said. 'Pity we don't have binoculars. Those specks around it are moving. Could be workers?'

Claire sniffed as though a foul smell had assaulted her senses. 'Probably. To be honest, I didn't realise they'd be doing everything so quickly.'

'I suppose they have to get a move on if they want to get a crop harvested before winter. I mean, it's already February and it won't be long before the first frost hits.'

Claire sighed. 'You're right. I'm being unreasonable … it's just, the Ward's have done the same thing all my life—growing vegetables like carrots and celery—and it's strange to see so many changes happening—especially when the property owner is in jail.'

Rhys switched his gaze to her. 'It's probably better that than lying idle and having the buildings vandalised.'

Her jaw dropped, and she stared at him for a moment. 'Gosh, I hadn't thought of that. You're right.' She shrugged. 'Come on then. Let's forget about the neighbours for the moment. We've got a much more pleasant place to visit.' Then, striding through the undergrowth, she led the way toward the valley.

The sun beat overhead as early afternoon passed. It was the sound of rushing water that greeted Rhys before he saw it.

Leading the way across flat sections of granite and around boulders, Claire stopped and turned a smiling face toward him. 'Voila. Our very own oasis.'

His mouth dropped open, and his skin tingled. It was the most glorious spot he ever remembered visiting. Water cascaded over a staircase of rocks before plummeting through the air to land in a pool below. A clump of native rainforest surrounded the pond, while its edges were decorated with numerous flat stones of varying sizes, perfect for sitting on. A thick wall of granite formed the lower boundary, allowing the stream to continue more gently as it sought the valley. From the clearing on the eastern side, the small village of Featherwood Falls was visible in the distance.

'Wow. When you mentioned the waterfall, I imagined nothing like this.'

'It's pretty good, isn't it? You can see why we keep it to ourselves.' Claire rifled around in her backpack and pulled out her bikini. 'Won't be a tick. I'm ducking behind those bushes to change.'

He slowly withdrew his boardshorts from his bag

before removing his boots and socks, reluctant to shift his gaze from the vista below.

Throwing her clothes in a heap on a rock, Claire darted past him in a flash of royal blue against pale skin. Jolted by her movements, he stood, unbuttoning his shirt as he walked cautiously behind a wide-trunked tree to change.

The water was icy, and he sucked in a breath as Claire scooped up handfuls to splash him with. She giggled at his yelp.

'Brr—it's freezing!'

He plunged under the water and grabbed her around the waist, picking her up and tipping her over. Her hair spread like a fan before she stood again, uttering a spluttering laugh.

'Okay, you got me.' Subdued now, she lay on her back and let herself drift the few metres to the other side. 'It's cold when you get in, but you have to admit—it's refreshing.'

Rhys chattered his teeth together and laughed. 'Yeah, sure.' His body was adjusting and, after a couple of minutes, the water provided both a cooling and soothing relief to his weary muscles, renewing his energy. He stroked across to Claire and leaned his back against a rock, his feet stretched out in front of him. It wasn't deep, coming only to his hips at the deepest point, but he could imagine how much fun it must have given the Shepherd family over the years.

He pointed to the patch of native bush. 'I'm amazed that's still standing. Look at that red cedar. It's huge!'

'I know. And see that smaller tree with the green leaves beside it—that's a Featherwood tree. Apparently, there were heaps around this area years ago and I guess that's how Featherwood Falls got its name.'

Lulled into silence, he narrowed his eyes to focus on the trees, letting his arms float apart. His hand touched Claire's and, as though on autopilot, she glided closer. Wrapping his arm around her, he drew her into an embrace. Euphoria consumed him as she lifted her face toward his and he pressed his lips to hers.

Heat ravaged his body as he held her against him, her skin silky and cool. Savouring the moment, he closed his eyes, willing it to go on forever.

Gasping, Claire drew back, her cheeks flushed and a shy smile on her mouth. 'I think we'd better get out of the water before we turn into prunes.'

He chortled, the enchanted spell broken but not lost as, hand in hand, they floated quietly back to the side where they'd left their clothes.

It was late afternoon before they reached the homestead and the aroma of something delicious wafted onto the veranda to greet them.

'Are you in a hurry to get back to town?' Claire asked. Her nerves jangled, torn between wanting him to go and hoping he would stay. *You don't need a boyfriend—especially one who's only going to be around for a short time.*

He shook his head, and the skin around his eyes crinkled.

'Okay. Mum and Kirk aren't back yet, but it looks like they've got enough in that slow cooker to feed an army. Do you want to stay for dinner?'

'I'd love to. Thanks.'

'Right.' Her efficient tone hinted it wasn't quite time to flop on the couch. 'I'll make us a cuppa and then, if it's okay with you, we'll feed the horses and dogs and I'll give you a tour of my office?'

'Sounds good to me.' He slid his pack off and dropped it on the veranda.

'Come and wash up while the kettle boils.'

She led him along the polished timber floor to the enormous bathroom where they both washed their hands. Returning to the kitchen, Claire opened the cake tin on the bench and held it toward him.

'Hungry?'

He shot her a wry grin, looking down at his thin body and legs. 'Always.'

She laughed. 'Me too.'

A serene atmosphere filled the room as they demolished two cups of tea and a sizeable chunk of cherry and coconut cake. Two tabby cats lay on the hearth rug in front of the empty fireplace, despite the warm day.

Rhys replaced the empty mug on the table. 'What are the cats called?'

'Sassy and Kimba. There's a black one called Oscar around somewhere too—he's Mum's special friend so is probably on her bed.' She laughed as she pushed her chair back, arching her back. 'Crikey. I think I might be stiff tomorrow.'

Relieved he wasn't the only one feeling the effects of an active day, he too stretched and bent from side to side. 'Hmm. It's been a few weeks since I've done a big walk, so I reckon I might be the same.'

She giggled softly and linked her arm with his. 'Come on, Grandpa. Let's get these jobs done so we can put our feet up.'

THREE HORSES WERE WAITING by the stable yard as they approached and nickered their welcome. Claire pointed to the bay mare, tossing her head up and down.

'That's Akela, the one we mostly ride.' She swung her gaze to the two chestnuts. 'And these two old guys are Flash and Rusty. They were mine and Briony's ponies and are more or less retired now. Poor old fellas are full of arthritis, but as long as they get their gummy-nuts and chaff every night, seem pretty happy.'

Rhys stepped closer and rubbed each one's face. 'Hello, old boys—and girl.'

'You seem pretty confident with them. Have you had horses?' Claire's eyes widened as she spoke.

'Yeah. My sister and I both had horses when we were growing up in Stanthorpe. She rode a lot more than I did, though. Like lots of other young fellas, the motorbikes became more attractive,' he finished with a grin.

'Great. It's a pity these two boys are getting too old to ride.' She chewed her lip, her focus drifting to Akela. 'We really could do with another horse now I'm home again permanently. Mum still likes to ride, and she and Akela seem to have a good relationship.' She met his eyes. 'If we do get another horse, you could come for a ride with me—if you'd like to, that is?'

He smiled. 'Of course. I would love to.'

Trailing around together, Claire introduced Rhys to the feeding routine of the horses, dogs, and chooks before they returned to the house. Leading him along the side of the homestead, she stepped aside to usher him up the old stone steps.

The white-painted door opened into a long, cosy room furnished at one end with two simple cane chairs strewn with brightly coloured cushions. Rhys looked longingly at the television in the corner before the

bookshelf and the array of framed photos on the wall
caught his gaze. He stepped toward them and pointed
to the picture of Claire with her arm slung around the
shoulders of another young woman.

'Is this you and Briony?'

'Yes. That's my sister. We don't look like it though,
do we? Briony's like Mum and I'm more like Dad
—apparently.'

'Where does Briony live?'

'Ahh. Well, at the moment she's in Yamba working
in a café with a friend. She mostly lives in Scotland—
her boyfriend is Scottish. Anyway, she came home for
Christmas and now, with all the lockdowns and Covid
issues, can't get back to be with Alex until the
international airlines return to normal.'

Rhys frowned. 'Poor girl. I bet she's frustrated.'

'She is ... but, hopefully, life will return to some
sort of normality soon?' She opened her hands, palms
up, and huffed.

Moving toward her desk at the other end of the
room, Claire switched on the computer.

'Sorry, do you mind if I quickly check my emails? I
never know what jobs will be thrown my way next—or
what the timeline will be. I can work my own hours,
provided I meet the deadlines.'

'Sure. Go for it.' He collapsed onto a chair and
leaned his head back.

'You can have a look through that folder on the

coffee table if you like. It's full of the jobs I've done, so you'll get an idea of what fills my days while you're running around apprehending drunk drivers and breaking up domestic fights.' She peeped around the large computer screen as she spoke and grinned.

He returned her smile and picked up the folder.

Rhys leafed through the myriad of colourful graphics, advertisements, company logos, and book covers while she tapped away at the computer keys, his fascination and admiration growing with every turn of the page. Although he lacked knowledge of the industry, he recognised talent—and a plethora of beautiful work.

The two of them remained silent for the next twenty minutes, carried away in the world of art and design. Eventually, Claire rolled her chair back and rose to her feet at the exact moment voices drifted across the yard outside.

'Sorry about that. All done now. Sounds like the others are home.'

Rhys closed the folder and placed it carefully on the table. 'Wow. These are outstanding.'

She tipped her head to the side, dismissing his comment shyly, and beckoned. 'Come on. Dinner time.'

He followed her through the bedroom next to the study and into the dark hallway that ran through the centre of the homestead. The sun had faded behind the belt of trees on the western side of the house, casting long shadows through the side windows.

'Hello, you two. How was your walk?' Ginny smiled as she met them in the hall.

'Great, thanks,' Rhys answered.

Ginny glanced down at her filthy clothes as the smell of sheep manure reached Rhys's nostrils. 'Won't be long. Kirk's gone home to shower and change and I'm doing the same. Will you open a bottle of wine please, Claire? There's some cheese and pâté in the fridge too if you want to take them out onto the veranda.'

THE EVENING PASSED TOO QUICKLY for Rhys. Fighting back a yawn, he reluctantly rose to his feet a little before nine o'clock, thanked Ginny for the delicious meal, and said goodnight to her and Kirk. Accompanying him to the ute, Claire touched his hand.

'Thanks for today. It was great.'

He looked down at her and smiled softly. 'It was a fantastic day. I hope we can do it again.'

She raised her eyebrows. 'So, you won't blame me if you wake up stiff and sore tomorrow?'

He slung his backpack on the ute tray and reached his arms out to her. 'Of course not,' he whispered as he wrapped them around her.

They kissed then, a gentle kiss that spread warmth through Rhys's veins and bliss through his soul. 'See you soon?'

'Sure,' she said.

The ute puttered slowly out of the driveway, and Rhys turned toward town. Despite his weariness, he burst into song and sang at the top of his voice all the way to the pub.

13

*S*till buoyed with pleasure from his previous day's activities, Rhys entered the police station soon after sunrise, dressed in full uniform and with his boots polished.

He switched on the electric jug before marching into the office and pressing the answerphone button.

It crackled before rasping breaths sounded. 'A-are you there?' a deep male voice asked, then went quiet for a few seconds. 'It's Bruce Taylor from the dairy farm on Dingo Gully Road.'

More silent seconds.

'I'm sick to death of those bloody motorbikes racing up and down the lane past my place. The cows don't like it and you need to do something about it.'

There was a crash, and the phone went dead.

Hmm. Seems a bit upset.

Rhys returned to the kitchen and ate breakfast before opening the map in the office. He located Dingo Gully Road, a narrow council lane on the southern side of Featherwood Falls.

'Might as well get it sorted out first up,' he muttered.

After strapping on his utility belt, he folded up the map, locked the doors, and got into the police vehicle.

Clouds hung over the hills surrounding the town, and an oppressive stillness filled the air.

Rhys lowered the window and breathed deeply. 'Yep, I reckon it'll be raining before the day's out,' he said aloud. Turning off the bitumen, he slowed where the road forked. A sign lay in the long grass, its post buckled as though a truck had whacked into it. He pulled on the hand brake and got out to inspect it—relieved to read *Dingo Gully Road*. The trouble was, which way? Both looked well used, however, one had new gravel on it while the other was predominately hard-packed dirt. Tracking slowly, he took the newly surfaced one, reasoning that if the Taylor property was a dairy farm, the milk tanker would traverse the lane regularly, ensuring it was well-maintained.

The road dipped, crossing a stony creek bed where a trickle of water flowed. Rhys glanced left and right, noting the willow trees clinging to the banks. He accelerated up the damp rise to where it straightened, leading through lush green pastures on either side before disappearing again into a patch of bush. He had travelled almost five kilometres, slowing outside each property to read the names on the mailboxes, before he reached a well-worn and potholed entrance.

A white-painted sign swung between two steel poles with *B. Taylor and Son* painted in blue. Below the name was a picture of a black and white cow with the words *Purebred Holstein Friesians* beside it.

He followed the short drive and parked next to a pristine dairy with extended concreted yards around it. Before he stepped out, a small, withered man appeared from the bowels of the shed, a cloth hat pulled low over his round, florid face.

Snatching the hat off his head, he wiped his forehead with it and strode toward Rhys.

'I've had enough of these motorbikes!'

Rhys nodded and held his hand out in greeting. 'Rhys Morton. Good to meet you, Mr Taylor.'

The man grunted, 'Bruce.'

'So, tell me about the problem. Are they kids on trail bikes?'

'No. They're those great big things that you see bikie gangs ride on the telly.' He threw his hands in the air. 'The cows don't like them, and we've never had trouble before. I can't afford for the milk yield to drop. God knows we get paid little enough for it now!' Spittle frothed around his lips as he spat the words at Rhys. Shaking a finger, he shouted, 'Do something!'

'Okay, Mr Taylor. Do you know where they are going to?'

'We're the second-last farm this side of the forestry and I've got no idea why anyone would come this way when they can access the other side of the plantation from a bitumen road. A bloke from Brisbane runs cattle in the bush block next door. Don't see him much though—probably fallen off his perch by now.'

'You mean he died?'

Bruce shrugged. 'Dunno. Once upon a time, we knew everyone in the district. These days, we can go to our own little town and hardly see a soul we know.'

'When did you first notice these motorbikes?'

He rubbed his chin with a work-roughened hand. 'W-ell. A couple of groups have been coming through Featherwood Falls on a Sunday for years—you know, day-tripping bike enthusiasts out for a run. We can hear them roar along the main road from here, but they never came up our road so didn't bother us. Since all this pandemic stuff's been going on, things have settled down a good bit and we've enjoyed having peace and quiet. I thought when this started, someone just got lost, but over the past couple of weeks, they've been roaring up and down most days.'

'Up and down? Do you mean several times every day—or just in the morning and again late afternoon?' Rhys pointed to the cows mooching their way down a farm lane behind the dairy. 'I'm guessing that would coincide with milking?'

Bruce nodded ferociously. 'That's it. Morning and evening, right when I'm milking.'

Rhys shot him an understanding smile. 'Leave it with me, and I'll do some investigating.'

'Right. Good—you do that.' And he turned on his gumbooted heel and marched to the dairy.

After returning to his vehicle, Rhys drove back to the road. He turned left, in the direction Bruce had indicated the bikes were travelling, slowing where the graded road became rough and dusty.

Bush closed in around him as he continued, opening here and there to small glades where an assortment of different-coloured cattle grazed.

With the window down, the sound reached him before he saw them. Two motorbikes—and, as Mr Taylor had said, definitely not the average trail bikes he would expect to find out here.

He pulled to the side of the road and stepped out of the vehicle, raising a hand to bring them to a stop. They braked, spraying dust, and skidded to a halt. Each rider planted a booted foot on the ground to steady the Harley-Davidson. Rhys flinched internally at the black helmets and leathers as a memory of an unpleasant encounter from a previous time and place flashed through his head. These riders both sported long beards, one straight and brown and the other a thick bush of black with silver streaks through it. Tattoos covered the bare, well-muscled arms of one man, and someone had thoroughly decorated both their necks in dark ink. The rider with the brown beard scowled, his broad back stiffening.

A shard of concern gripped Rhys, but he plastered a smile on his face. 'How're ya going?'

'What are you doing here?' brown beard growled.

'Might I ask the same of you? Got a complaint about the noise these bikes are making coming up and down this road.'

'It's a free country—and a public road,' he snarled.

'True. So ... what's your business?'

The man leered closer, his face barely a metre from Rhys's.

'You're not supposed to be up here,' he said slowly, shaking his head.

Is that a threat? Steeling himself, Rhys remained calm.

The rider peered at Rhys's nametag. 'You're not the cop from Featherwood Falls.'

'Yes, I am.'

'Where's the old bloke?'

'Time off. Now, can I see your licences please, gentlemen?'

Both men dallied for a moment, and Rhys gritted his teeth, staring at them and lifting his chin a notch. For a few seconds, he half expected them to roar off, ignoring him, but they fished in their pockets and handed over their driver's licences.

'Your addresses please?'

They reeled off Gold Coast addresses while Rhys jotted the details in his notebook. Then he walked around each bike and added the registration number and description while questions jangled in his head. Them asking where the old bloke was had come as a surprise. Had they been here before? What contact had Stan had with them?

'These registrations up to date?' Rhys asked.

'Yep,' they answered in unison.

Glancing in the direction from where they had come, he asked again, 'What brings you here?'

One man gave him a belligerent stare while the other shrugged and said, 'Helping a mate with some cattle.'

'What's his name?'

He huffed. 'Dougie.'

Rhys raised his eyebrows. 'Dougie?'

They both stared at him in silence, but Rhys stood firm, regarding their bulky frames. Both would have outweighed him by a good bit and knowledge of their isolation, and his vulnerability, gnawed at him.

'Righto. Hang on a tick while I run a check on these licence numbers.'

Pressing his lips together, he glanced around the hills as he opened the vehicle door. The chance of having radio and internet reception out here was slim, but he punched the licence number into the iPad just in case. *Bugger*. There was nothing. Snatching up his mobile phone, he checked the reception bars. The "no service" message headed the screen. He photographed each licence, ensuring the faces were clearly visible then turned back to the bike riders.

The man with the grey-streaked beard had remained straddled across his seat while "brown beard" had his back to Rhys. He turned as Rhys approached, chewing a stalk of dry grass, his eyelids drooping in apparent boredom.

Handing their cards back to them, Rhys nodded. 'How about you take it steady past the dairy farm in future? The cows are worth a lot of money and don't appreciate being frightened. I'm sure you wouldn't want to see them getting hurt—and there's no point in upsetting the locals.'

"Brown beard" shot a glance skyward, but both remained silent.

'You're free to go,' Rhys said.

Without another word, they roared down the road, leaving Rhys staring after them.

He drove back to Featherwood Falls slowly, remembering the words his father had instilled in him from a young age. *Trust your gut, son. It's rarely wrong.*

The encounter with the bikies had provoked suspicion—and raised more questions about the residents of this peaceful little valley than Rhys had been prepared for.

He would follow procedure and check the licence details as soon as he returned to the station—but deep inside, he knew there was a strong possibility the names and addresses supplied would not exist.

14

_T_here was no time to check anything or return to the station as, just as he approached Featherwood Falls, an emergency call came over the radio.

"Farm accident near Macintyre State Forest. Serious. Possible fatality. All units in area to attend."

His knowledge of the area remained sketchy, so he punched the details into the GPS, spun the vehicle around, and accelerated away.

Adrenaline fuelled his journey, while dread sat deep in his belly. Possible fatality. The words sent an ache through his heart and filled his mind with despair.

A vision of Claire's lovely face flashed in front of him, and he was relieved the accident was well away from Featherwood Station. Over dinner the previous night, she and Ginny had discussed the need to mow a paddock of lucerne—one with proximity to the creek. They had joked about an occasion when Lyndon, Claire's father, had gotten too close to the edge and the tractor had slid down the bank into the water. It had given them all a scare, although no damage was done. Rhys was painfully aware of the dangers involving farm machinery—and the thought of Claire being exposed to any form of danger sent terror through his heart.

It took more than forty minutes to locate the accident, by which time two police vehicles from the Stanthorpe office, an ambulance, and an emergency response truck had arrived before him. Guilt wrestled with relief as they delegated him to conduct traffic control on the road next to the farm while they extracted the patient from under the upturned tractor and cleared a pad for the approaching helicopter.

Midday came and went, and rain clouds weighed heavy above him as he drove back to Featherwood Falls. He was still fifteen minutes from home when the first big, fat drops hit the windscreen. Within seconds, the deluge arrived, and Rhys slowed to a crawl as the rain fell in swathes, obliterating his vision. He continued into town, stopping at the store to pick up a hot pie for his lunch.

Although it had only been two days since he'd seen

Lola, anyone visiting the store might have thought he was a long-lost son, so fervent was Lola's greeting.

Reaching up chubby arms, she pulled him to her, the ever-present earrings brushing against his chest as she exclaimed, 'I'm so pleased you're alright.'

He withdrew from her embrace, his forehead wrinkled in confusion. 'Why wouldn't I be?'

'Bernice Taylor was in here earlier. She said you'd had to deal with some nasty bikies that had been annoying them and she was worried they might have … done something awful to you.'

Rhys burst into laughter, shaking his head.

Of course—the old bush telegraph.

'Nothing to worry about. Just asked them to go steady when they pass the dairy, so they don't frighten the cows.'

He was still smiling as he splashed his way through the rain back to the station. Despite the pace at which the news seemed to spread around these tiny towns, he felt a kinship with those residents he was becoming familiar with. Lola reminded him of his maternal grandmother, a beautiful, caring soul who had died suddenly of a heart attack at sixty-two. The same considerate, gentle concern bestowed on him by Lola seeped through him, and contentment filled his heart.

WHILE MOWING the police station lawn a few days later, Rhys's mind flicked between the brief but becoming-more-frequent texts between him and Claire and the frustration of the encounter with the bikies.

It had come as no surprise when he'd returned to the station and booted up the computer to discover his searches on the various platforms were fruitless. The riders' names were non-existent and the licences false. Both registration plates were also unlisted, leaving Rhys with a sense of hopelessness. It was a common frustration within the service, along with the challenges of spending long hours accumulating evidence and arresting criminals and then watching them being given a telling off with no repercussions by the justice system.

He had sent the completed report from his visit to Mr Taylor and the discussion with the motorcycle riders to District Office with a copy to the intelligence section. *Better cover all bases—just in case those vehicles and riders turn up again.*

His mobile phone rang, sending a vibration through his chest, so he switched off the mower and answered.

'How are you getting on down there, Rhys?'

It took him a few seconds before he recognised the gravelly voice.

'Inspector Jones. Umm, everything's going well, thanks.'

'Good. I thought you'd like to know we've received Senior Constable Brennan's resignation.'

Rhys straightened, flushed with hope for a split second before his heart sank. Did this mean his relieving position was over already? He understood the employment procedure. A permanent replacement could now be gazetted—however, it would be weeks if not months before the position was filled, so where did that leave him?

'I see.'

'Are you happy in Featherwood Falls?'

The question surprised Rhys. He'd only been in the village two months, so it was a bit early to tell ... until the memory of the previous Wednesday flashed through his mind. His lips twitched.

'Yes, I'm really enjoying it.'

The inspector's tone changed, and Rhys could feel his smile through the invisible communication line. 'I thought you might be—so I suggest you get onto the personnel department and find out when the position might be gazetted. Stan will arrange for the removal of his furniture within two weeks and once that has occurred, you're welcome to move into the police accommodation. It's my intention to leave you in your current position until a permanent appointment has been determined. How do you feel about that?'

Rhys's hopes leapt again. 'That would be great, sir.'

'I know you've only been there for a couple of months, but I encourage you to apply for the position.'

'I certainly will, sir. Thank you very much.'

They exchanged a few further pleasantries and ended the call.

Does this mean the chances of getting the permanent position are greater for me than someone else?

Nothing was guaranteed—but he dismissed the thought and looked forward to living in the onsite residence.

With a smile plastered on his face, he finished the mowing and was stowing the machine in the garden shed when he remembered his conversation with James Avery about the package of money languishing in the office safe. Had he talked to Stan? He hurried inside and rang him.

'Hi, James. Rhys, from Featherwood Falls.'

'How are you, Rhys?'

'Great, thanks. Um, I'm not sure if you know, but the inspector rang me earlier and mentioned Stan Brennan has retired. I was wondering if you talked to him about the money?'

'Oh, I'm sorry, Rhys. I meant to get back to you on that and it completely slipped my mind—had a busy few weeks.'

'I understand,' Rhys said and waited for James to continue.

'I had no luck, mate. When I popped into the

hospital, Stan was in the middle of having tests and I couldn't talk to him. Then, with the spate of youth crimes that've exploded around here, I've been up to my neck ... and now he's been discharged and gone to Perth to live with his sister. I've tried contacting him by phone, but he won't take my calls.'

Rhys groaned in surprise. 'So, what do we do now?'

'I'll keep trying and will talk to the inspector. He'll let you know what to do, but for the moment, keep the money locked in the safe.'

'Okay. Will do.'

'Thanks. Catch up again soon.'

'Yeah. Bye.'

Rhys frowned. He'd been in the service long enough to understand the difficulties of extricating a suspect from interstate. With Stan Brennan now unwell and retired from the force, the chances of having him questioned would be slim. Frustration burned through Rhys. No matter how many excuses he made, he was quite sure the regular packages of money had something to do with the long-standing cop.

He pushed his chair back, opened the safe and checked the yellow envelope was where he had left it —tucked inside a beige folder underneath the petty cash tin.

While he devoted the rest of the afternoon to preparing notes for when the position was gazetted, his mind kept drifting to the money. If it had been intended for Stan, wouldn't he have come back to Featherwood Falls before he left for Perth?

He pinched the skin around his Adam's apple while he pondered the issue. Eventually, in an attempt to ease his frustration, he wandered into the kitchen and switched on the jug.

There's got to be a reason for these packages being delivered. If we receive another one, I will follow it up if no-one else will.

*M*ounted on Akela, Claire trailed the mob of steers up the track to a fresh paddock after spending the morning drenching and vaccinating them. Grateful for the cooler days, she zipped up her jacket and breathed deeply, rolling her shoulders. A magpie warbled on the fence post nearby and she faced it, smiling, as she did with every magpie she met. Her father had always said, "If they know you, they will never swoop or frighten you during nesting season". He was right. The only time a bird had swooped her was in Sydney, on her bicycle, when she'd taken a different route to work.

She was approaching an open gate, and she whistled the dogs. With a wide sweep, Chime and Drum galloped around the leaders, urging them through the open gap. A black wave of rushing bovine bodies bucked and frisked into the new paddock.

After unhooking the gate, Claire guided Akela behind it, encouraging the mare to push the steel bars with her chest until it reached the strainer post from which a length of chain hung. Claire leaned over the mare's shoulder and wrapped the chain around the post before securing the ends together with a heavy-duty lock-tight clip.

Straightening, she sat for a moment while Akela dropped her head and snatched at the grass on the side of the track. Above, thick, fluffy clouds dotted the blue sky, and Claire turned her face up to the sun, soaking in the warmth. A flash of white caught her eye as she picked up the reins. She studied it for a few minutes.

'Yep. Definitely poly-tunnels on Glenrowan now.' She spoke aloud, and Akela flicked her ears back and forth and snorted as if in agreeance.

The vision jogged Claire's memory, and she pulled her mobile phone out to check for service. 'Two bars. That should do it.' She touched Rhys's name and waited for the call to connect.

'Featherwood Falls Police Station, Senior Constable Morton speaking.'

'Hello Senior Constable Morton speaking,' Claire said.

'Hi. How are you?'

'I'm fine. I smell like cow poo and chemicals, but that's par for the course, I guess.'

He laughed. 'Could be worse.'

Her tone lowered, serious now as she answered, 'Yeah. Hey, I thought I'd let you know I've seen the poly-tunnels next door again—just a snippet of them, but we were right. That's what they have built on Glenrowan.' Before he could comment, she rattled on. 'I know I'm probably sounding a bit paranoid, but I saw Lars in Stanthorpe the other day, talking to some bikies. I presumed he was recruiting staff, but it seemed weird to me that if that's the case. Why is he using bikie friends to help on the farm? Do you think you should pay them a visit—you know, to check they're not growing more than just tomatoes?'

A huff echoed over the phone. 'I can't do that, Claire. Unless there is evidence to suggest something illegal is going on, I would be trespassing and could be accused of harassment.'

'Oh.' She slumped in the saddle. 'I didn't think of that.'

'I know what you're thinking, but they have to be given the benefit of the doubt—unless evidence suggests otherwise.'

'Okay. I understand,' she said, deflated.

Changing the subject, Rhys asked her what she had been doing with the cattle and they chatted for a further couple of minutes before saying goodbye.

It was while Claire was brushing Akela an hour later that the conversation replayed in her head. She straightened, and, leaning on the mare's back, she grinned.

Rhys might not be able to pay Glenrowan a friendly visit, but there's no reason I can't.

TWO EVENINGS LATER, Claire marched past the woolshed, across the flat paddock to the creek, and with sneakers on her feet, waded through the ford that marked the boundary between the two properties. Reflections of the moon glistened on the water and a soft, silvery light filled the evening air.

She'd mulled over the best way to investigate the contents of the poly-tunnel. Pretend she was calling to say hello? Show an interest in tomato growing? Neither excuse seemed to fit and, in the end, she'd decided a surreptitious visit when no-one else was around would be the easiest. After all, her brief encounter with Lars had done nothing to endear him to her and her own uncle was the manager—so if someone saw her, she could use the excuse that she thought she'd seen his vehicle there and wanted to speak with him.

Her heart thumped in her chest as she sauntered along the grass beside the driveway, keeping within the protection of the thick row of trees and shrubs that edged Glenrowan's boundary. While most of the farm comprised flat, open fields filled with a thick plantation of corn reaching over Claire's head, the balance was native scrub and trees, providing shelter from the strong winds and frost that frequented the area.

Claire was grateful for the cover as the house came into view. A single light shone through an uncurtained window, and she skirted around the back of the dwelling, staying well away from habitation and giving thanks for the lack of a dog or security system. A boobook owl called, and she jumped, her heart racing.

Guilt flooded through her. *Rhys won't be too happy when he finds out what I'm up to.* Still, if her suspicions were unfounded, then there was no reason to mention her visit to anyone.

She reached the first of the long row of tunnels, their polyester covers shining ghostly white under the moon's beams.

Pushing the entrance flap to one side, she flicked on her phone's torch icon and shone the light around. Rows and rows of metre-high tomato plants filled tubes, their tops suspended by wires and their roots immersed in shallow troughs. The tinkling sound of liquids running through pipes, together with a hum of pumps, deadened the noises of night birds and bats outside.

Claire blinked rapidly. So, it was true! Glenrowan really was growing corn and tomatoes—on first appearance, anyway. She crept out of the tunnel and, treading silently, passed the next two before opening the entrance to the fourth. Again, her torch beam illuminated rows of smaller tomato plants. As she was about to take a closer look, footsteps sounded outside, and she froze, switching her phone off and dropping it into her shorts pocket.

Seconds ticked by and she didn't dare move. The footsteps retreated, fading into the distance. She waited another few minutes, taking slow, silent breaths. Then, grateful for her soft sneakers, she tiptoed out of the tunnel and darted across the cleared land to the shadows of surrounding trees.

Despite the cool night air, her skin was clammy, and Claire ran a hand over her face. She paused again, waiting for her pulse to slow before creeping back the way she had come.

'Funny time of day to pay me a visit.'

Almost level with the house again, she leapt in terror as the deep, heavily accented voice sounded right behind her.

She whipped around and stared straight into the glacier-blue eyes of Lars. Her jaw dropped and she tried to speak, but nothing came out.

'What do you think you're doing prowling around here? This is private property and you're trespassing,' he snarled.

He took a step forward, looming over her until she

could smell his stale sweat and see the insides of cavernous nostrils under his gigantic, bent nose.

'I-I,' she stuttered, then stopped and straightened her shoulders. 'Uncle Donald said you were growing hydroponic tomatoes and I've been wondering how you do it. I-I was going to ask him to show me around but haven't had a chance.'

'So why didn't you come over in daylight? I would have been happy to give you a tour.' He reached out and ran a finger down her cheek. 'A pretty little thing like you. We could have some real fun.'

A squeak emitted from Claire's mouth—a primal sound that electrified her. 'Sorry.' She twisted away and fled, her interest in the crops forgotten.

Resisting the compulsion to look back, she ran faster than she had in years, while the only sound following her was the echo of a raucous, evil laugh.

She had no memory of crossing the ford. It was only as she reached the back door of her studio that she looked down at her soaking feet and legs and slumped onto the stone step. Her whole body shook, and she fumbled with her wet shoes before falling through the door and closing it tightly behind her.

She turned the key, grabbed her dressing gown from the end of her bed, and hurried to the bathroom.

Thank goodness Mum's at Kirk's place tonight.

After a shower, Claire made herself a mug of hot

chocolate and retreated to her bedroom, while the events of the evening replayed in her head.

Her reflection looked back at her in the mirror—grey eyes as big as golf balls and a complexion so pale that the freckles stood out like miniature splotches of brown paint.

She climbed into bed and snuggled under the doona, grateful for the two tabby cats already asleep beside her.

Okay, so it looks like they really are growing tomatoes —but Rhys doesn't need to know I checked.

But no matter how much she tried to convince herself that nothing untoward was occurring on Glen-rowan, deep in her gut, something disagreed.

a few days later, Rhys received a call from the sergeant at Stanthorpe Police Station checking if Rhys would be in the office the following morning.

'Yes. Unless something untoward occurs, I'll be here.' He hesitated before asking, 'Is there a problem?'

'There's a matter we need to discuss, but I'd rather we did it in person.'

'Okay. See you tomorrow then.'

'See you around ten.'

Rhys hung up slowly as his eyebrows knitted together. The sergeant had sounded solemn. *What's this all about?* He'd been hungry prior to the call, but his appetite disappeared.

Rubbing the back of his neck, he attempted to distract himself by arranging the delivery of the furniture he'd left in a storage facility in Warwick. An answerphone message earlier in the day had advised a removal truck would arrive on Friday to collect Stan's furniture and belongings. But even the anticipation of moving into the roomier and more comfortable accommodation was not enough, and he stewed over the conversation.

Rhys was up early the following morning. By ten o'clock, he had given the kitchen and office a thorough clean and purchased two of Lola's gigantic lamingtons. His pulse thumped as the police vehicle drew up outside and parked under the shade of a tree. A large, middle-aged officer strolled through the gate and stomped up the steps into Featherwood Falls Station.

Rhys opened the door ahead of him. 'Good morning.'

'Hello, Rhys.' The man offered his outstretched hand, a smile on his rugged face. 'Aidan Chessop.'

Rhys took it, his face impassive. It was the first time since his arrival another officer had called in and he had thought that when they did, it would be for social reasons. Now he wasn't so sure. 'Tea? Coffee?'

'Coffee would be great, thanks. White with one.'

They settled in the tiny kitchen while the electric jug boiled, and Rhys placed the lamingtons on a plate.

'I'll get straight to the point.' Aidan cleared his throat, and Rhys's confidence dived.

This sounds serious.

'There's been a complaint laid against you,' Aidan said.

Rhys's jaw dropped, and he stiffened. 'W-what sort of complaint?' His voice caught. That was the last thing he had expected—especially with the possibility of a permanent position in the little town.

'It's anonymous—however, I imagine you'll have an idea who made it.' The Sergeant's voice was professional but contained a warmth to it that lifted Rhys's hopes a smidgeon. 'Evidently you intercepted two gentlemen a week or two ago. They claimed they were out for a pleasant country motorbike ride. Their grievance states you harassed them, demanding details they considered had nothing to do with the police. They also suggested they had to pay you cash to let them go.'

Rhys struggled to contain a curse. 'Are you serious?' he spluttered.

'Don't be alarmed. I've got a copy of your report and I just need to hear your side of things. I fully understand they were bikies who provided false names and all the details relating to their bikes and licences were also false. May I have a look at your notebook, please?'

'Certainly. He pulled it out of his pocket and flicked through to the recordings on the date he intercepted the motorcycles.'

Aidan took the book and read while Rhys made coffee for them both.

'All your notes match what you've written in the report. The question I need to ask is did you make demands of them to pay you money?'

'Absolutely not.'

'Do you have any other information that might help us identify these people?'

'No, sorry. I had no radio or internet connection there to conduct the checks. I had to accept what they told me … but I took photos of their driver's licences with my phone and attached them to the report I sent in.'

'Okay. And did the photos on the licences match the men you intercepted?'

'Yes, they did.'

'Would they have known you took the photos?'

'No, I took the cards to the car to do the checks, and when I realised I had no reception, I photographed them.'

'At least we know what the men look like. I see in your report they asked you why you were there and where the old fella was. What do you think they meant by that?'

'It seemed odd to me. Almost as though "the old fella"—who I presume is Stan—had some sort of arrangement with them not to bother them? I've got no proof of that. It's just a feeling'

'Hmm. That's interesting. Anything else?'

Rhys stared at him for a moment. Should he tell

him about the package of money? He took a deep breath. 'Did you hear about the package of money?'

Aidan frowned. 'No. What money?'

'It was amongst the mail the day I arrived. James knows about it and apparently someone's coming to collect it at some stage. I've got it locked up ... but I can't help but wonder if it's got something to do with Stan and those bikies.'

Aidan rubbed his chin, raising an eyebrow. 'Interesting.'

'Yeah, that's what I thought.' He shrugged. 'Apart from those thoughts—and they are just thoughts at the moment—everything's in the intelligence report.'

'You've done the right thing, Rhys. We just have to follow protocol. I can't think of anything more you could have done in the circumstances,' he reiterated.

Rhys hissed a quiet sigh of relief. Sitting back, they chatted amicably while enjoying their lamingtons and coffee.

Half an hour later, Aidan rose to his feet and picked up his folder. 'Thanks for everything. I suppose you've heard Stan Brennan's retiring,' Aidan said.

'Yes, I have.'

'Are you going to put in for the position?'

'Yeah, I like it here.'

'Well, good luck. I hope your application is successful.'

Rhys walked out to the car with Aidan before

returning to the office and slumping into a chair. He was exhausted, ragged—but a frisson of hope and energy filtered through him. He glanced at the clock.

The afternoon seemed to drag as he plodded through the emails and reports. At five minutes to five, he logged off the computer, his mind churning over the morning's conversation with Aidan. Would the complaint affect his chance of getting the permanent position? Stumbling to the back door, he checked he had locked it before returning to the office. He stowed his utility belt in the safe and switched the phone over to the emergency number, then, with no memory of the short walk, he strode into the pub and slid onto a stool at the bar. Ned turned a startled gaze to him and reduced the volume of the television.

'I need a beer, Ned.'

'Sure. Bad day?'

Rhys huffed. 'Stressful.'

The old man nodded and pulled two beers from the fridge behind him. He twisted the lids off and leaned on the counter. 'All in a day's work then, ay?' Ned inclined his head toward the kitchen. 'Stew's cooking. Be ready around six.'

Rhys's stomach heaved, and he gulped a mouthful of beer. Anything to wash away the vision of a stodgy brown mess heaped high on a plate.

'Going for a run, Ned. See you later.'

RHYS'S MIND cleared as fury took over. Swearing under his breath, he changed into shorts and T-shirt, tucked his mobile phone in his pocket, and walked outside.

Striking out on a back road, Rhys skirted the town, jogging around the hill that provided a peaceful view from his room until he could no longer see any sign of the village. Although private land, there was a narrow lane between what appeared to be separate farms. With his pulse pumping furiously, he continued up the rise. Gradually, his anxiety faded as he noted the diversity in the surrounding farms. On one side, the grass was short and grazed to dirt level with wide patches of foxtail weed and burrs. On the other, sheep and cattle browsed, but small in number, allowing a variety of native grasses to flourish. Plantations of half-grown trees filled the valleys, surrounded by fences to ward off the stock. He glanced to the other side again and grimaced at the overgrazed paddocks. Farming was not an easy life—his own parents' experience had taught him that—but a sadness washed over him as he compared the two properties. *I wonder what the future holds for my generation, and those to come.*

A rock jutted out of the narrow pathway, and he sat on it, taking slow, steady breaths and chastising himself for being morose.

His phone dinged, and he pulled it out of his

pocket, his heart thumping as Claire's name shone on the screen.

Hi. Roast dinner here tonight. Come and join us?

A smile spread across his face, and his lanky frame softened. He prodded the phone, stopping to correct typos while his mind ran ahead of his clumsy fingers.

Sounds great. See you soon.

Propelled by anticipation and gravity, Rhys reached the pub much faster than his uphill journey had taken. Ned had resumed his position in front of the television while three noisy road workers sat around a table beside the window.

'Ned!'

It took a few seconds before the old man registered Rhys's presence, and he turned slowly to face him.

'Sorry, mate. I'll have to cancel that dinner tonight.'

Ned grunted. 'Had a better offer, huh?'

Rhys smiled. 'Can I have a six-pack of four-X please, and a bottle of Chardonnay?'

Ned slapped the beer on the bar and took the fifty-dollar note from Rhys.

'No worries. I'll put your stew in the fridge for tomorrow night.'

Rhys struggled to keep the grimace from his face as he held his hand out for the change. He turned away and trod firmly up the stairs to his room.

17

*H*umming as he stepped out of the vehicle, Rhys's insides fluttered at the sight of Claire approaching. She wore jeans and a pale blue top, her loose, golden hair hanging around her face. He wasn't sure what was happening to him. He'd never felt like this before. The responsibility of manning a one-person police station had meant he and Claire hadn't been able to see as much of each other as he would have liked. But now, her clear, sparkling eyes and wide smile made the wait more special.

They hugged, clinging to each other for a few moments while Rhys drank in her scent. Freshly showered and smelling of citrus and flowers, her fragrance dizzied his senses.

They released each other, and their eyes met. She

whispered, 'It's good to see you. It feels like forever since you were last here.'

He laughed. 'I know. Hard to believe it's only been a couple of weeks.'

She grasped his hand, and they walked toward the house.

Both Ginny and Kirk were sitting on the veranda, a glass of wine in hand, and they rose to greet him.

'You look tired, Rhys.' Ginny frowned as she pushed a wavy brown lock off her face.

He dismissed her motherly concern with a shrug. 'I'm alright. Had a couple of busy weeks, I suppose.'

'Really? In Featherwood Falls?' Kirk huffed. 'I thought now that the Nigel saga is tucked away, the town would have gone back to sleep again?'

'There's always stuff that needs doing—and although it might be a small community, it's certainly not a boring one.'

Ginny raised her eyebrows. 'Oh? I hope that's in a good way?'

He twisted the lid off a beer and sat on the couch next to Claire, noticing her pallor. Concern gripped him. These people were friendly, but the last thing they needed were his problems. He was not ready to divulge his worries—to them or anyone else.

'Yeah. All good. Actually, I have some news that I hope you'll be happy about.' All three pairs of eyes remained glued to him as he continued, 'Stan's handed in his resignation.'

Ginny let out a huff and slumped back in her chair. 'Well, that's the best news I've heard for ages.'

Worry lines appeared on Claire's forehead. 'So, where does that leave you?'

'I can apply for the permanent position—and I'm just hoping like hell that my experience here puts me at the top of the list.'

'How long will it be before they decide?' Claire asked.

'Who knows? The good thing is I'll be staying until they choose the replacement and the due date for applications hasn't even been announced yet. Once it's gazetted, there'll be applications to read, short-listings, and interviews—then maybe in a few months, we'll know who's got the position. In the meantime, I'm to move into the police quarters.'

He looked at Claire, and they shared a secretive smile.

'You won't have to eat Ned's cooking any more then.'

'No.' He frowned. 'I'll have to cook my own tucker —and I admit I'm not very good at it.'

'You can eat with us at least once a week,' Ginny said with a smile. 'And we can send you home with a takeaway pack for the following day.'

'I'll teach you how to cook a few of my favourite

things—since eating seems to be a mutual hobby,' Claire added, and he grinned.

The conversation drifted on, discussing recruitment of private versus government jobs, lifestyle choices, and the farm. It was almost seven o'clock before Kirk sliced the lamb and they sat down to eat dinner. Rhys was relieved to see the colour had returned to Claire's face. Having a sister had introduced him to the trials of the female cycle and his initial concern for her dissipated as he reasoned that was probably the problem—female hormones.

Wiping his mouth with the napkin after a second helping of lemon meringue pie, Rhys leaned against the back of his chair and looked at Ginny.

'That was the best meal I've had since I was last here. Thank you very much.'

'Claire's responsible for that.' Ginny inclined her head toward her daughter. 'I've been in Warwick today visiting my mother, and Kirk was working over at Kallala.'

Dismissing Rhys's compliment with a shake of her head, Claire said, 'When do you have time off next? I'm looking forward to hiking up to the old mine site before the weather gets cold.'

'Not until the end of the month. I mean, I have a few days off here and there, but I'm still on call, so I can't go far.'

Claire glanced at Kirk. 'So, Kirk, do you think we

could plan for a night or two up there when Rhys has his next long break?'

Kirk smiled knowingly at her. 'Sure. Let's work toward that.'

'Count me out,' Ginny said firmly. 'I'm happy to stay here. Too many animals to expect anyone else to feed them.'

Rhys thought about the situation for a minute before asking, 'Do you ever have holidays—you know, get away from the place? And if you do, who looks after things here?'

Ginny shot him a wry grin. 'I haven't had a night away since before the girls left home—and that was a couple of years before Lyndon died.' She shrugged. 'It has never bothered me, though. Lola and Frank used to pop up and feed the animals years ago when we took the girls for a couple of nights at the beach, but I wouldn't expect them to anymore. They've got enough to do with their own wildlife babies and the shop.'

'And besides that, we're surrounded by restrictions at the moment with the pandemic—and who knows when that will end,' Claire added.

Silence filled the room for a few minutes as each of them digested the reminder. Then, in a cheery tone, Claire piped up. 'On the positive side, Mum, you've got all of us to help with the hay-making.'

Kirk roared with laughter, and the final shreds of Rhys's despondency floated out the window.

BUOYED with memories of Claire's goodnight kisses the previous evening, Rhys whistled as he bounced around the station, sweeping the floors, and wiping the counters and furniture with disinfectant spray and a cloth.

At ten o'clock, he locked the door behind him and drove the police car along the road to the school. It had been an odd beginning to life in a small town. On one of his daily visits to the store, Lola had mentioned that prior to COVID-19, and the subsequent enforced restrictions, the community would have held a welcoming get together for any new teacher or police officer in the town. Now there was nothing, and it had been Rhys who had phoned the principal to arrange a visit to the school—not only to meet more of the locals but also to introduce a friendly understanding between the children and himself, just as his father had.

Hopes of new friendships helped quell his nerves as he crunched his way along the gravel toward the solitary building. It was old and quaint but well maintained, with a veranda running along the front and a central staircase leading up to the door. In the vast school grounds, a covered, concreted play area and tennis court took up ten times the space of the classroom, and next to the far end of the school building, there was a toilet block painted in standard government colours to match the school—cream with a red roof and dark green trim.

Before he had reached the top step, a young boy with a shock of red hair stood beside the open door.

The child turned his head away and called, 'The policeman's here.'

A small smile crept across Rhys's face, and he followed the boy inside.

'Hello there. Quinn Alderton.' The slightly built man thrust a hand out to shake Rhys's, and he took it, absorbing the friendly beam below a thatch of tight, black curls and piercing blue eyes.

'Gidday. Senior Constable Rhys Morton. Good to meet you.'

'Come in.' Quinn beckoned him to follow, taking two steps across the tiny foyer.

Rhys glanced in either direction. A kitchen on one side and an office on the other. He paused in the doorway of the open classroom.

'We've got twenty-three students here, ranging from prep—that is four to five-year-olds—up to our senior pupils in year six,' Quinn said. 'Say good morning to Senior Constable Morton, children.'

'Good morning, Senior Constable Morton,' they drawled.

Rhys smiled at them, relaxing under the curious awe that oozed from the children.

Phew. This'll be fine.

Following a brief introduction, Rhys asked the children questions, drawing them into what quickly became a noisy talk-fest. After fifteen minutes, they trooped outside, and he let them take turns at switching on the flashing lights and siren in the vehicle before the bell rang and Quinn announced it was their morning tea break.

An efficient-looking woman, dressed in a neat skirt and plain cream top, walked up behind them and Quinn introduced her to Rhys.

'Emma Grey, our wonderful teacher's aide.'

Rhys presumed she had been in the office while he was in the classroom as he had noticed no adults other than Quinn.

She nodded politely at Rhys and faced Quinn. 'Enjoy your morning tea. I'll mind the children,' she breathed.

Rhys estimated her age to be around forty and was surprised he hadn't seen her, or Quinn, around town. Following Quinn back upstairs, he jumped as another woman's head popped out of the kitchen.

'Hi there. I'm Joanne, Quinn's wife. How lovely to meet you,' she gushed.

Rhys smiled at her, taken aback at the effervescence that bubbled from the tiny woman. Dark brown hair framed her round face, and thick, well-shaped eyebrows accentuated grey-blue eyes. Her lips parted in a smile, displaying a row of straight white teeth. She reminded him of a bird as she ushered him into the squashy kitchen and darted over to the bench to switch on the kettle. A plate of scones, smothered in jam and cream, sat on a small, cloth-covered table against the wall, while an old leather sofa and a single hard chair filled the rest of the room.

He lowered himself onto the sofa and offered the occasional smile as Joanne and Quinn chatted constantly. They divulged the story of their arrival in Featherwood Falls, only weeks before the pandemic took hold, and the subsequent chaos that had developed while trying to educate children via means other than allowing them to mix at school. He wolfed down three scones and a mug of coffee as the others talked, adding that Emma was a town local who had worked at the school her entire adult life.

By the time he slid into the driver's seat of the LandCruiser half an hour later, he'd eaten so much that lunch was out of the question, heard more about the locals than he'd managed in the several weeks since his own arrival, and had agreed that both he and Claire would play tennis with Quinn and Joanne on the school courts the following Thursday.

I wonder what Claire will think. Should I have checked with her first?

He chewed the inside of his cheek.

I'll ring her later.

It wasn't until he stepped into the station again that

he remembered the complaint—and his stomach sank. He had met another three Featherwood Falls residents and was feeling more settled in the little town. Despite Aidan's reassurance, the last thing he wanted was to be transferred somewhere else—especially if it was to a town hundreds of kilometres from Claire.

18

The project had been a tough one. With a hard-to-please client, the graphics for the company's new brand had finally been accepted after to-ing and fro-ing for days. Claire was over it. Her temper was frayed, and she felt mentally exhausted.

A ride is what I need.

Ginny pulled a tray of date biscuits out of the oven, their chocolaty fragrance filling the room as Claire wandered into the kitchen.

'Yum.' Claire reached out and removed one off the tray, juggling it from hand to hand as it cooled.

'Are you really that hungry?' Ginny raised her eyebrows.

Claire snickered. 'Always, Mum. You should know that by now.'

'How's the project going?'

'It's finished—at least, I think it is. They'll probably come back wanting yet another tweak somewhere but, for the moment, I'm taking a break.'

Ginny angled her head sympathetically. 'So ... what are you planning to do now?'

'I thought I might go for a ride.'

Ginny screwed up her face. 'On Akela?'

'Of course. The boys are really too old and stiff now to expect them to do anything.' Her heart ached, knowing that both geldings were aging quickly, their sway backs drooping lower while their gaits became more measured. Rusty's eyes were rapidly changing from deep pools of brown to cloudy blue, while Flash had developed a limp that no amount of painkillers or massage could improve.

'I'm afraid Akela might not be up to it today. I rode her pretty hard yesterday, mustering those cows and calves, and she needs shoeing again.'

'Oh.' Claire slumped onto the couch as she swallowed the last mouthful of biscuit. 'I wish the ponies weren't so old,' she added sadly.

While Ginny spread the biscuits out to cool, they said nothing for a few moments, each consumed with their own thoughts.

'When I talked to Grandma the other day, she mentioned her old friend, Mick, is looking for a temporary home for one of his horses,' Ginny said.

'Who's Mick?'

'You know. The fellow with the paddocks next to the racecourse. He's always buying and selling horses and apparently, he's got attached to one and wants it to go to someone he knows will give it a suitable home. Since he smashed his leg up a year or so back, he doesn't ride much—mostly lunges them in the yard. He asked Grandma if she knew if we needed another horse and Grandma said we didn't.' She shrugged.

'I suppose we don't actually need one ... but now that I'm home permanently, it would be nice, wouldn't it?' Claire shot her mother a hopeful grin. 'Then the two of us could go riding together again.'

Ginny nodded, her smile suggesting there was more to Claire's comment than just mother and daughter going for a ride. Spooning cocoa powder onto the bowl of icing sugar, she said, 'Why don't you give Grandma a call and get Mick's phone number off her?'

With more enthusiasm than she'd managed all morning, Claire leapt up and crossed the room to pick up the phone.

It rang for ages before switching to the answering service.

'Please leave your name and number after the tone.'

Claire smiled at her grandmother's soft, quavering voice.

'Hi, Grandma. Mum said Mick's looking for a home for a horse he has. Would you mind passing his number on to me when you have a chance? We could do with another one here and might be able to help him out. Talk soon. Bye.'

Ginny glanced at the clock. 'Oh, sorry. I forgot today is her bridge day.'

Claire grunted. 'Is there anything else you'd like me to do? I need to get outside for a couple of hours.'

Ginny's thoughtful expression met her daughter's. 'I haven't let the dogs out for a run yet. Why don't you take them to the falls to stretch their legs?'

'Great idea.'

TWENTY MINUTES LATER, Claire strode across the hill, the five kelpies milling around her as they sniffed the ground and raced back and forth, as though urging her to hurry.

A cool breeze blew through the valley and she zipped the front of her jacket up, thankful that she'd grabbed it at the last minute.

Before she reached the water, both Banjo and Chime had plunged in and were swimming in gleeful circles. Drum pressed against Claire's legs, and she ruffled his ears. 'It's okay, mate. Too cold for me today, too.'

Perched on a rock, she grinned as the dogs swam and played. Her pocket vibrated, and she jumped. She pulled her phone out and beamed at the name lighting up the screen.

'Hello,' she drawled.

'Hello, you,' Rhys responded, his smile palpable through the airwaves.

'How's your day going?' she asked.

'Okay. I've been to the school this morning to meet the kids and spread a bit of positivity in the community.'

'Great. I haven't met the new principal yet. I think he and his wife arrived about the same time I moved to Sydney.'

'Yeah. They seem nice. I met Joanne, too—and the teacher's aide. Umm ...' He trailed off.

'What's wrong?'

'I've dobbed you in to play tennis. Apparently, now the government is allowing us to move around and exercise outdoors, Quinn's keen to meet more of the community and get something happening in Feather-wood Falls.'

'Sounds great.' Claire brightened, tilting her face to the sky with a smile.

Before the pandemic, the school tennis court had held weekly practice sessions in the evening with a monthly tournament and barbeque. If she was staying in the area, revitalising the activity would be a welcome distraction from the daily workload—not to mention an opportunity to spend more time with Rhys.

'Righto. I'll let Quinn know.'

They talked for a further ten minutes, the occasional stab of guilt still surfacing over her secret visit to Glenrowan before Rhys said, 'Sorry. Gotta go. A call's coming through on the police line.'

'Okay. Talk later.'

'Will do.' And he ended the call.

'Come on, dogs. Let's go home.' A wavering smile sat on Claire's face for the duration of the hike back to the homestead, and after a cup of tea and a sandwich, her creative thoughts began to flow again. She sat at the computer and began her next design.

THE FOLLOWING MORNING, a shower of rain passed over Featherwood Falls, a rainbow stretching across the sky. The dogs barked, their tone indicating a stranger had arrived on the property, and Claire frowned. Ginny and Kirk had gone to the back of the farm to replace a section of fence, and the homestead was still and quiet, enabling her to concentrate on her new project.

Having not heard the vehicle, Claire muttered a thanks to the dogs as she rose from her chair and hurried to the veranda, her bare feet silent on the polished floor. A battered Toyota utility was parked in the middle of the yard with a dilapidated horse float behind it.

Curiosity hurried Claire. She jammed her feet into a pair of boots before striding to the gate.

A small, wizened man wearing a baseball cap stepped out of the vehicle, his bandy legs encased in baggy trousers and the torn pocket on his shirt hanging down his chest.

'You Claire?'

Taken aback at his gruff greeting, she nodded without opening her mouth.

'Good. I brought your horse.'

Claire's eyes widened. The man seemed familiar. 'Are you Mick?'

'Yep. Your grandmother said you'd give this fellow a good home.'

Claire was astounded. *But Grandma didn't return my call?* 'Oh. I didn't expect you to bring him to us ... but thank you.' She moved toward the float. 'I'll help you unload him.'

Mick hobbled after her, flicked the catches on either side of the ramp, and lowered it to the ground. Inside, a tall, speckled brown and white rump greeted her while at the front of the trailer a long, thin face and a pair of soulful brown eyes turned to face her.

The horse backed out onto the gravel driveway and looked around. He towered over Claire, and she had to stand on tiptoe to rub the whirl of hair between his eyes.

'Hello, horse.' She turned to Mick. 'Not a thoroughbred then? What's his name?'

The old man shrugged. 'Nah. He's a ring-in. First time I've ever had an Appaloosa. I call him Splash.'

Claire smiled as the gelding lowered his head and gave her a tiny nudge, as though asking for another pat. When she'd been a child, her father had owned a similar coloured horse, and she had loved the pretty spotted patches of brown and white on his rich bay coat. The name Splash was apt—and she'd heard many times that, for whatever reason, this colour mostly guaranteed the horse had a good temperament besides athleticism.

'What's his history, Mick?'

'He's an odd one, this fella,' Mick said. 'Came on a truck with a two-year-old mare I'd bought out of the dogger yard, but I've no idea of his story—only that I'm glad I saved him cause he's much too good to be put in a can.'

Claire recoiled in horror. It was common knowledge that they often sent underperforming and old horses to the abattoir to be made into dog food, but in her family, that never happened. All Shepherd horses were cared for until they either died naturally or had to be put to sleep to avoid pain and then were buried on Featherwood Station.

'Has anyone ridden him?' she asked.

'Yeah. I've been taking him down to the track, and two jockeys have given him a few rides. Seems gentle and doesn't pull.' He laughed. 'Actually, he's not keen on galloping either. Just trots or canters along as though he's enjoying the countryside. I reckon with a bit of love and riding, he'll help you on the farm.'

'Thank you, Mr ... Mick. I promise we'll look after him. Can I have your phone number so I can let you know how he's going?'

'Sure.' Mick handed the lead rope to Claire while he shuffled back to the ute and scribbled a number on a scrap of paper. Thrusting it at her, he gave a grin, and she flinched at the gap on one side of his mouth where teeth should have been.

I think you've had a tough life.

'Would you like a cup of tea?' she asked. 'I can pop Splash in the stable yard for the moment.'

He waved a gnarled hand at her as he closed the ramp. 'No. Better get back. Got plenty to do.'

'Oh, okay. Well, thanks again—and thanks for delivering him, too. Umm—if he settles in well, how much do you want for him?'

'Nothing. I got him for free and I just need him to go to a good home with someone who cares.'

She nodded, her eyes wide. 'Thank you. I'll look after him.'

Touching the front of his cap, he slid into the driver's seat and drove away.

She and the horse watched him go, incredulity at what had just occurred rendering her immobile.

Splash nudged her, and she smiled up at him. 'Come on, my friend. Looks like you're living with us now.'

The horse strode out beside her as they walked toward the stable yard, his head swinging in all directions as though soaking up his new surroundings with delight. She filled a hay net and checked the water trough was full, then, resting her hands on the top yard rail, she leaned her chin on them as he ate.

The gelding's long legs and protruding ribs reminded her of Rhys, and the edges of her lips rose as a vision came to her of the two of them riding into the distance—Rhys on Splash and her mounted on Akela.

'Perfect. Now there's no excuse for him not to come for a ride with me.'

19

*R*hys hammered the picture hook in place and secured the painting. He stepped back to stare at it, a smile creeping slowly across his face. He'd missed being able to lie on the couch and gaze into its depths while recovering from an extra-long shift or a traumatic event he'd had to attend. To others, the scene was nothing more than a young man and two children playing cricket on a beach—one a girl in a skimpy sundress, her skirt tucked into her knickers and a wide straw hat on her head, and the other a boy in shorts and a long-sleeved shirt, its sleeves rolled to the elbow. The boy held the bat like a club, ready to whack a tennis ball high in the air, while the man was poised with one leg off the ground, his body in forward motion and his arm straight as he released the ball. The little girl's attention appeared to be more on the shells around her feet than on anything else, least of all the game.

Rhys smiled as memories came flooding back—of holidays at his grandparents' house on the northern end of Rainbow Beach. Beyond the family, the sea was grey, with waves rushing in, edged with white froth. High above, seagulls circled against a patchy blue sky streaked with thin, pink-tinted clouds in front of the sun.

He had loved his grandparents, and his chest filled with pride. His grandfather had painted the picture, copied from a photo his mother had taken. The man and children were his father, sister, and him. When his grandparents had died in a tragic boating accident, it was the only item he asked for—and his parents had been happy to give it to him.

Glancing around the room, he nodded with satisfaction and moved toward the empty boxes. The living room was compact, and his extra-length couch filled the entire end wall. A bookcase, coffee table, and television took up the remaining space.

Moving house was not something Rhys usually enjoyed, but this time it was different. Filled with a sense of ownership and pride in the tiny station and, determined to prove he was the right person for Featherwood Falls, he pushed the possibility of anyone else getting the position aside.

After flattening the cardboard boxes, he moved to

the bedroom as the deep, throaty sound of a V-8 drove past—clearly over the speed limit. He dashed to the window, catching the rear of the black utility as it disappeared from view.

He had not worked on a commercial farm since his teenage years, when his school holidays were filled with hard work and laughter as he picked fruit alongside international backpackers. Now suspicion and instinct niggled at him. Donald may have employed Lars as the foreman, but he certainly wasn't the district's usual example of a vegetable grower and, if he wanted to live amicably in this community, Rhys expected him to follow the traffic rules at the very least.

Hmm. I can see you, Lars, and we need to have a few words.

THE FOLLOWING THURSDAY EVENING, Claire and Rhys joined Quinn and Joanne for an evening game of tennis.

With a good dollop of laughter and embarrassment, Claire dashed around the court, hitting the net or missing the ball altogether as often as she landed a perfect shot.

'Sorry, guys. I'm seriously out of practice.' She puffed as perspiration trickled down her face. Joanne had played little better for which Claire was secretly grateful, but both Quinn and Rhys seemed to have found a mutual streak of competitive spirit. While the girls gracefully bowed out after playing five sets of doubles, the men swallowed a quick beer and returned to the court for a game that rendered them both sweaty and exhausted. Eventually, Rhys hit the winning shot, and the men shook hands and left the court.

Rhys rubbed his face on a towel and slumped onto the bench beside Claire.

'Okay, Mr Kyrgios. Looks like I need to improve my fitness and ability if you expect me to play with you,' Claire said tartly.

He slung his arm around her shoulders and drew her to him. 'Don't worry. I just had more frustration to belt out than you did.'

Claire frowned. 'Frustration? Did you have a bad day?'

'No, not really. I've been getting my little home in order—which has been fantastic. I'm afraid I won't get the permanent job and I'll have to pack it all up again.' He smiled down at her. 'I guess I'm not very good at waiting.'

She leaned against him, her head resting on his shoulder for a moment before she pulled away, straightening.

You're not the only one.

'Hey, you guys. Come and join us for pizza,' Quinn called.

'I made them myself,' Joanne said proudly as Claire and Rhys stared at the three assorted pizzas on the table under the tree. The aroma of tomatoes, herbs, and melted cheese made Claire's mouth water, and she murmured his approval.

'You didn't need to do this, Joanne,' Claire said. 'I thought tonight was to be just a practice game and a drink?'

A beam swept across Joanne's flushed face, and she shook a hand dismissively. 'I love cooking and I wanted us to have a bit more time to chat and get to know one another.' She pointed to the plates and napkins. 'Dig in.'

'Are you a teacher, too, Joanne?' Claire asked.

Joanne tipped her head back and laughed. 'Heavens no. I'm an accountant. Before we moved here, I'd set up my business and was working from home, so things worked out perfectly for us really, despite the pandemic. I work school hours while Quinn is teaching.'

'And you don't mind the country life?'

'Love it.' She swept an arm around her. 'I know it's getting too dark to see, but I enjoy gardening, too—so in my spare time I've been cleaning up around the buildings and getting the children to help me plant vegetables and flowers.'

Rhys nodded admiringly.

'It's been lovely and quiet here compared to the city —until recently, anyway,' Quinn added.

'What's happened to change that?' Rhys frowned, helping himself to another piece of pizza.

'Oh, I suppose we've been spoilt. With the lock-downs starting soon after we arrived, the through traffic really slowed, and we got used to the peace and being able to wander across the road with barely a glance in either direction. Now life's returning to normal, there seems to be a lot of strangers passing through.' Quinn shrugged. 'Including some pretty rough-looking types.'

'Lola said the motorcycle groups are coming through again. Mostly they're the riders who used to do the weekend trips—but there are a couple who must live locally. Apparently, they've called in to the shop for food a few times,' Joanne chuckled. 'She reckons they look like bodybuilders who've come straight out of prison.'

Rhys studied his pizza, his eyes narrowing.

'Hmm. I haven't seen them in the pub,' Quinn added. 'Not that I go there very often, but I usually pop in for a chat with old Ned and to pick up some beer on a Friday evening.'

Swallowing his last bite, Rhys grunted softly.

'Is everything okay?' Claire squeezed his hand, and

he smiled softly. 'You haven't said a word since we left Quinn and Joanne's.'

'Sorry. I was remembering what they said about the strangers in town. It's my duty to keep the community safe, and I'd hate to think a criminal element was infiltrating this beautiful little place.'

Claire pressed against his side as her stomach cramped. 'What you need is a couple of days in the bush. Blow all these worries away and give you some time to appreciate nature.'

'You're right. Another week and I'm all yours.'

She grinned before that little voice inside her head interrupted her thoughts.

Don't forget—he's not here for long and the last thing you need is more heartbreak.

20

*C*laire was sorting out the camping gear when the familiar burgundy Toyota pulled into the yard.

'Uncle Donald,' she muttered churlishly while butterflies did somersaults inside her. Had Lars told him of her unexpected visit?

She continued brushing the cobwebs off the hiking tent as he strutted toward her.

'Hello there,' he called.

She gave a nod, forcing the glimmer of a smile onto her face.

'Your mother home?'

Claire inclined her head toward the house. 'She's cooking.'

'Perfect. I'll head on inside.'

Raising her eyebrows, Claire turned back to the

tent and gave it a ferocious shake. There was something about her uncle's demeanour that piqued her interest. A visit from him always had a reason. She hung the tent over the fence in the sun and tiptoed toward the house.

Standing out of sight beside the kitchen window, she fixed her attention on the polite but stilted pleasantries being exchanged inside.

'If you want coffee, I'm afraid you'll have to make it yourself. As you can see, my hands are full,' Ginny said tartly.

The pump sang as someone turned a tap on before Claire heard the familiar click of the kettle switch.

'Thought you might like to know what's happening next door,' Donald said.

His tone had an arrogant edge to it, and Claire smirked. *Mum will be fuming.*

Her uncle continued while regular thumps suggested to Claire her mother was kneading bread.

'Lars has had a bit of trouble getting labour for the farm—so he's got a couple of mates helping. You don't need to worry about your neighbours though—everything is in hand.'

Ginny grunted and Claire retreated quietly to the shed. She didn't need to hear any more. Lars had obviously kept the knowledge of her visit to himself, and she would, too. She blew out a sigh of relief and turned her attention to the camping gear. Preparing for their weekend in the bush was far more exciting.

WHILE CLAIRE BOILED THE KETTLE, Saturday morning broke with a pink blush creeping over the hills to the east.

A vehicle approached, and her heart leapt with anticipation.

As Rhys trudged up the veranda steps, Kirk ambled along the hallway, stretching and yawning like a black bear after hibernation.

'Morning, fellas. All bright-eyed and bushy-tailed, I see.' Claire smiled at them both.

'What time do you call this?' Kirk said. 'I thought we left at seven?'

'We did. And now it's six, so you've got an hour to get organised and eat breakfast. I've packed the food and distributed it into three lots.'

Rhys drew close and gave her a hug. 'Good morning, Ms Efficiency.'

She sagged against him for a moment before pulling away and pointing to the pan of scrambled eggs on the stove.

'Come on. Big day ahead, and it looks like it's going to be perfect for hiking.'

He grinned and dragged out a chair while Kirk meandered back to the bedroom.

An hour later, in a last flurry of gear swapping to balance the weight of their packs, Ginny appeared in her dressing gown to wave them off.

'Have you got your mobile phone, Rhys?' Ginny asked.

'Yes. And the first aid kit, snakebite kit, and climbing tape. Ready for every eventuality.' Rhys smiled at her and patted the bulging backpack lying on the tray of the ute.

Kirk tossed his pack next to Rhys's and reached for Claire's. 'Whatever we've forgotten, we'll manage without.' He strode back to Ginny and wrapped his arms around her.

Claire turned to face Rhys and raised her eyebrows. While delighted her mother and Kirk had developed a loving relationship, it still felt strange to see a man other than her father embrace Ginny with such adoration.

'See you tomorrow night, Mum. If we're going to be late, we'll ring as soon as we have reception.'

'Righto. Except for feeding the animals, I plan to catch up on housework and reading, so I should be contactable.'

They piled into Rhys's ute with Claire squeezed between the two men, her thigh pressed against Rhys's.

Then, with a last wave and beep of the horn, they drove out of the yard to the track leading them west.

ALMOST AN HOUR LATER, Rhys slowed and turned the vehicle parallel to the fence running alongside the bush.

After hoisting their packs onto their backs, Claire opened the padlock and chain on the gate into the hills while Rhys locked the ute and gazed over the valley. Morning mist hung in the hollows and a hawk circled overhead.

He sighed, smiling. There was nothing better than a weekend in the bush—away from the phone and responsibilities. Besides, he needed the distraction. Waiting for the applications to open for the permanent position was killing him.

'Come on, you two,' Claire called.

Kirk helped her secure the chain behind them, snapping the padlock tightly while Claire slipped the key in the back pocket of her trousers.

Half an hour later, Rhys grinned at the disappearing view of Claire's derriere for the umpteenth time. He lengthened his stride and drew alongside her.

'Are you always in a hurry? Not that I mind, of course.'

'Sorry. Briony hated walking with me—said I galloped when I should be trotting.' Claire slowed her pace and turned back to Kirk with a cheeky grin. 'How're you getting on, old man? Shall we slow down to help you?'

'Hilarious. Just wait until tomorrow afternoon— then we'll see who's the fittest around here,' Kirk retorted.

Claire laughed and marched on.

As the sun rose, the three hikers settled into a rhythm with Claire in the lead, Rhys a few metres behind, and Kirk plodding steadily in the rear. They stopped frequently to study the bird life and fresh growth on the shrubs and trees they passed. After two breaks for food and water, they arrived at the main mining site where Kirk had been working, lathered in perspiration and grateful for a few more hours of daylight.

'We'll set up camp here and I'll show you where I've been working before it gets dark.' Kirk slid his backpack off and unrolled a compact nylon tent.

With an open front and two flimsy poles to raise it off the ground, it was just big enough for one person and was an identical match for the shelter Rhys carried. Up here, where the night temperatures varied from cold to freezing, they all knew any form of protection from the elements was an essential piece of equipment.

He grinned at Rhys. 'Claire's tent is a flasher version than ours—even has a door.'

Rhys shot Claire a hangdog look, disappointed that having her body warmth a little closer appeared to be out of the question. 'Lucky you,' he said to her.

Thin inflatable mattresses and lightweight sleeping bags completed the cosy camp and, while Claire scooped water from the creek and filled the billy, Kirk and Rhys gathered wood and laid a fire.

Armed with head torches, the three of them wound their way along the creek bed to where a rocky overhang protected the entrance to a cave. Kirk's mining pick was hooked into one side of his belt, and in a padded canvas holster, he carried several small fabric bags.

'This is where I found the sacks of rocks last year—the ones I had tested to see what they contained,' Rhys said.

'And they proved to be duds?' Rhys asked.

'Not really. The testing confirmed they are cassiterite, the tin oxide mineral that's still the most important source of tin. The trouble is this area was heavily mined over a century ago and what's left would take more labour and money to extract than what it's worth.' Kirk grinned. 'It's still pretty good fun fossicking for it though—and you never know, we might make a few dollars here and there.'

While he was talking, Claire shone her torch

around the cavern, studying the walls with squinted eyes. 'It looks like this tunnel goes right in under the hill. Have you been to the end, Kirk—if it has one?' she asked.

Kirk cleared his throat. 'I have. Follow me and I'll show you.'

For the next fifteen minutes, they crawled and wriggled their way into the mine, pausing to inspect each pocket of grey-black earth, gouged out by diligent miners decades earlier—those who had slaved in the bowels of the earth, hoping to set themselves up for life.

As the roof narrowed to meet the dirt floor, Kirk shone his torch on a thin opaque line that glistened on the dark wall.

'This interests me most,' he said. 'I've chipped a few pieces off and am pretty sure there are tiny fragments of gold. Can't be sure until it's tested, but ... that's my current project.'

'Wow.' Claire's voice sounded hollow in the eerie setting, and she reached behind her for Rhys's hand.

He shuffled forward while Kirk carefully chipped pieces of rock from the wall, dropping them into the fabric bags. Inside the pale fragments of rock, threads of colour sparkled in the torchlight. Barely enough to cover the tip of a fingernail, Rhys narrowed his eyes, desperate to see what Kirk could.

'Do you really think this could be gold?'

'Don't get too excited, mate. Yes, I do—but I know that it's a costly process to extract, so I'm not planning to retire just yet.' Kirk drew a deep breath and smiled at Rhys and Claire. 'I enjoy the thrill of finding things though ... and I might find something even more exciting than gold.'

They remained in the cave for a further hour, exploring the bags of rocks Kirk had discovered and dragging some of the bigger ones out into the entrance.

As the sky turned a lavender colour and the sun dropped, shadows lengthened in the valley below and birds called as they nestled in the towering eucalypts and scraggy bushes around the campsite.

Claire mixed a batch of damper before dropping it into the well-oiled camp oven that Kirk had lugged up to the site on a previous trip. The chicken curry she had made the previous day filled their bellies, satisfying their hunger and restoring their strength. The meal was a leisurely affair, spread out over the next two hours with toasted marshmallows and a hot chocolate drink.

Rhys leaned against the tree and sighed with contentment. His mind a jumble of what he had read in the police diaries about this place, and his growing passion for Claire. She felt so close at times—but at others, her restrained responses confused him.

Kirk wandered off to a pool downstream where he announced he would bathe before bed.

Rhys reached out and lay his arm around Claire's shoulders. 'Next time we come, perhaps we could bring a tent big enough for both of us,' he whispered in her ear.

She slapped him on the arm playfully.

As the moon rose above them, its snowy face beamed a pale white light across the land.

21

The following morning, Claire woke to the sound of Kirk whistling as enamel cups and plates clattered while smoke from the fire drifted in the air.

Claire shivered and pulled the sleeping bag around her neck. Unzipping the front of the tent, she glanced over to the tousled head in the shelter next door. Despite the three-metre distance, she could see his long lashes resting on tanned cheeks and a stubble shadow darkening his jaw.

His eyelids fluttered open, and he rolled onto his back in a tangle of bedding.

Propped on her elbow, Claire turned away as her heart fluttered. She glanced at Kirk squatting in front of the fire.

Mist swirled, shrouding the hills in its damp cloak, preventing the sun from warming the rocks.

'Come on, you two. Breakfast will be ready in five minutes,' Kirk said.

An hour later, they were back in the cave, with Kirk and Rhys taking turns to chip enthusiastically at the seam of pale stone. Claire swallowed her apprehension as she gathered the tiny pieces and stored them in the cloth bags, leaping in fear as a bat fluttered close to her ear. The hairs on the back of her neck rose. She had adapted to the confined space a little, but the dark, narrow cavern with all its creatures brought goose bumps to her skin, and she battled with an urge to scramble back to daylight.

Hunger eventually drove them outside and Claire blinked, her rapid breaths slowing in the bright light. She glanced at her watch. 'We'd better get moving or we'll be tramping home in the dark.'

With a three to four-hour walk to where they'd parked Rhys's ute, they ate quickly and repacked their gear before striding back the way they had come.

They had only walked a few hundred metres when a wallaby hopped across in front of Claire. She paused, watching it disappear along a ridge to their left, and called back to the men. 'I think we should go that way. I remember coming up here with Dad when I was about ten and I reckon if we follow the fence, it'll bring us out directly above the gate we came through into the bush.

Kirk and Rhys caught up with her and, rubbing a palm over his beard, Kirk swung his gaze from Claire to the wallaby track. 'Are you sure?'

'Pretty sure.' Claire tipped her head back and shaded her eyes with her hand. 'There's still plenty of daylight, so I say, let's do it.'

Rhys shrugged. 'I'm happy with whatever you two want to do.'

'Okay then. We might have to do a bit of bush-bashing, but it's probably better for us to explore a different route while there's three of us, than for me to attempt it when I'm on my own,' Kirk said.

Claire grinned at them both before facing the track and waving her arm in a beckon. 'Righto. Follow me.' Then she marched off in her long, swinging stride, leaving the men to catch up.

The undergrowth thickened, and they had to slow their pace, stepping carefully to avoid being tangled by the hardenbergia vines and debris from the overhanging trees and shrubs. After an hour, they paused for a drink, and Claire studied her companions. The bland expression on both men's faces gave nothing away, but deep inside, Claire had doubts about her decision. She silently wished she'd kept her mouth shut and continued back the way they had come. Taking a long swallow from her water bottle, she started at Kirk's exclamation.

'Hey. Look at that!'

Claire rose onto her tiptoes and followed the direction of Kirk's outstretched arm with its dirt-engrained index finger. A small clearing. Surrounded by shrubs, it would have gone unnoticed had they not stopped. She glanced at her watch.

'It'll only take a few minutes. Let's check it out. You never know, it might be a nice place for us to camp next time we come this way,' she said.

Taking the lead again, she pushed through the low scrub, holding the thin, eye-level branches that threatened to whip her face to the side. She reached the edge of the clearing and took a hurried step forward, pitching to the ground as her boot caught under a strand of hardenbergia vine.

'Arghh!' With the weight of her backpack, she fell heavily, her outstretched palms desperately clutching at the empty air.

Both men rushed to her, and while Kirk removed her pack, Rhys slid his arms around her waist as though about to lift her up.

'Are you alright?' he asked, his face paling under the dark stubble. 'Can you move?'

'Yeah. I'm okay.' Claire accepted Rhys's help and struggled to her feet before attempting to dust off her hands. She narrowed her eyes. 'Look at that.'

Rhys glanced at her reddened palms, his brow furrowing. 'What's the black stuff?' He looked back at the ground where Claire had landed, kicking the undergrowth away with his boot. Diving forward, he pulled up a blackened fragment of timber and turned to the others. 'Old firewood? Someone might have camped here before—or it could be remnants of the last bushfire that went through here?' He turned to Kirk, as if seeking a solution.

The older man stood stock-still, squinting at something on the other side of the clearing. He slid his backpack off and trod carefully across the rough ground.

Claire brushed Rhys's protective arm, taking his hand instead and following Kirk.

A broad, round post stood tall and firm against the dark green foliage, its black surface appearing to be only the remains of a burned-out tree.

Kirk swept a heavy boot in a semi-circle, pausing as his toe caught under another piece of timber. He turned toward Rhys and Claire, his eyes wide and solemn. 'I think we've stumbled upon what was once a timber dwelling—a hut of some sort.'

Claire stiffened. 'Do you mean ... like something a family might have lived in?'

'Like Wild Willy?' Rhys added.

The three of them stared at each other before,

almost as one, they bent their heads and began combing the ground.

Minutes later, they had uncovered the remains of four corner posts and a stretch of wire netting.

'I think this might be the base of an old bed,' Kirk said. His tone was quiet with disbelief.

For a few moments, they stood in silence until Rhys pulled a notebook from his chest pocket. 'We need to take the coordinates. If this is the site of an old dwelling, we might have to take a closer look.' He glanced at the sun with a hand shading his eyes. 'And I don't think we've got time or daylight to do much more than that today.'

With renewed enthusiasm, they wrapped the piece of wire mesh and a small slab of burned timber in a spare garbage bag extracted from Kirk's pack. Then, while Rhys took photos of the site and transferred the location details into his pad, Claire and Kirk piled what they had uncovered against the tallest support post.

Retracing their steps to the wallaby track, they continued along the ridge, stopping as often as possible to chip a notch into the bark of a tree or build a small cairn of rocks to mark the path.

Engrossed in their discovery, they plodded on, each obviously consumed with their own thoughts, until they ran into a fence stretching as far as they could see in either direction.

Claire yelped with excitement. 'This is it. This is the way Dad brought me all those years ago. From here, we follow the fence down the hill until we reach the edge of the bush—and I reckon that's where we'll find Rhys's ute.'

'Are we still on Featherwood Station?' Rhys asked.

Claire nodded exuberantly. 'Yes. Dad was fastidious about fencing, and I remember him talking about him and Mum renewing the bush fences. They spent weeks up this way when Briony and I were at high school.' She ran her hand along the tight strand of barbed wire, clamped firmly to the dog netting below it. 'I don't remember them running cattle or sheep up here, but Dad liked to have all the boundaries clearly marked, anyway. I suppose it defined what was ours and what wasn't—and by using the dog wire, helped reduce the dingo and wild dog attacks over the years.'

She raised her eyebrows, and a wash of pride filled her chest. This was her family farm. Her father's legacy and his demonstration of how to manage this tough country in the best way possible for all. The bush areas could remain free of domestic stock and wildlife reigned supreme. Then her breath hitched as she recalled the patches of damaged undergrowth they'd spotted on their hike up into the hills.

As though able to read her mind, Kirk said, 'Once we get on top of those wild pigs and feral cats, I reckon your dad will rest easier.' He smiled at Claire. 'Don't worry. I'm working on it.'

She returned his smile. 'How about you, Rhys? Do you have any experience in pig hunting?'

He gave a wry grunt. 'Can't say I do—for the four-legged variety, anyway. I've met a few two-legged versions that cause as much trouble for us as the animals do for you—and that's still a work in progress.'

They shared a grin, took a few mouthfuls of water, and began the descent to where the bush opened to meet the grazing land.

22

A week later, Rhys trawled through the daily emails, highlighting those that needed following up and printing off allocated assignments from district office.

He was about to close the computer when a new message popped into the inbox. The subject provoked a burst of anticipation, and he opened it and read the contents twice.

It was from Inspector Jones and simply read, "Position gazetted today. Suggest you get onto it asap."

For the rest of the morning, a frenzy of anxiety propelled him through the first draft of his application. The selection criteria were generic, and his confidence grew as he drew on examples of events and emergencies he had attended over his brief career.

Disturbed only by a quick trip to collect the mail

and a fresh loaf of bread, Rhys worked on the application, saved a copy, and then, while he munched a sandwich, he rang his father.

'Hello, son. How're things going down there?'

'Hey, Dad. Really well. How was the trip?'

'Fantastic. Caught a lot of fish and had a good look around the area.'

His parents, Ron and Julie, had purchased a caravan the year before, and, although interstate travels were curtailed for the moment, they had used every opportunity possible to explore as they called it, "their own backyard". That Queensland was so huge gave them endless short trips and long ones, from the warm, tropical coastline to the outback desert and the rugged Cape York. On their most recent holiday, they'd put the dingy on the roof of the car and headed to the small, coastal town of 1770, close enough to return home in a day if they needed to, and not too far north so they could avoid the tail end of the cyclone season.

They chatted for a few minutes before the conversation returned to Rhys.

'So, how're things going in Featherwood Falls?'

'Great. Actually, I was wondering if you would mind looking over my application? As you know, I've been waiting for the permanent position to be advertised and that happened today.'

'Sure. Send it through. I'll go over it and send it back with any suggestions I can think of.'

'Thanks heaps, Dad.'

Rhys leaned against the back of the chair. He was lucky. The relationship between him and his family was a good one and his respect for his father had grown since joining the police force. There was no other person he would trust more than his dad for guidance.

'Do you want to have a chat with your mum? She's right here.'

'Sure. Put her on.'

The conversation continued for a few minutes more before they exchanged goodbyes and Rhys ended the call. Then, with renewed enthusiasm, he cast a final eye over his application and sent it to his father.

THE THRUM of a powerful engine roared past the station, and Rhys jumped to his feet, his glance through the window confirming the rear of a black vehicle highlighted with a yellow registration plate.

'Bloody Lars again,' he muttered. 'Time for that chat.'

He grabbed the keys and locked the station before driving to Glenrowan. He hadn't visited since gathering Nigel's private documents and was surprised to see how much the crops had grown.

'Maybe this guy knows his stuff?' He spoke aloud, his eyebrows knitting in doubt.

Two men emerged from the packing shed below the house. And now that they had slashed the weeds around the building, two caravans, surrounded by piles of pallets and old fruit boxes were visible.

He pulled up outside the shed and got out of the vehicle while the men stared at him. One wore a wide-brimmed hat and greasy overalls. A tattoo ran down the side of his neck, similar to that of one of the bikies he had intercepted out near the Taylors' place. There the similarity ended, however, and Rhys turned his gaze to the other man. Lars. Glancing around for the black V-8, Rhys nodded as the sun emerged from behind a cloud, shining down on the car partially tucked behind the shed.

'Gidday, fellas.'

Neither man spoke, and Rhys continued.

'Lars, I need to talk to you about you and your vehicle.'

Lars took a few lazy steps toward Rhys, a sneer curling the edge of his lip. 'What's wrong with it.' His heavily accented response was not one Rhys recognised.

Scandinavian? Russian? Rhys wasn't sure. 'Oh, nothing. You've got a very nice vehicle there. Only problem is, it's a little too powerful for our speed restrictions.'

Lars's sneer widened. 'So?'

'So, I'm asking you to respect the road rules and, especially when driving through the town, keep your speed to fifty kilometres per hour, like everyone else has to.'

Lars turned to the other man and sniggered, pointing to the police vehicle. 'I think Mr Policeman is jealous. He would love to be behind the wheel instead of in that chunky contraption.'

Before Rhys could answer, Lars stepped closer to him and leaned his head forward.

'Tell you what. I'll slow down if you tell that pretty little girlfriend of yours to keep off this property. Visiting Glenrowan after dark means only one thing to me—and I'm sure I'm not the first man to play games with that one.'

Rhys stared back at him with a straight, serious face. His insides churned as fury rose within him. The last thing he would do was to show this evil human how much his statement had rattled him.

'I don't make the rules, but it's my job to ensure they're followed. If I catch you exceeding the speed limit again, you'll cop a fine.' Rhys almost spat the words before turning on his heel and marching back to the LandCruiser. He threw the vehicle into gear, turned it around, and drove away.

What was that mongrel talking about? Claire?

An icy chill engulfed him. *Oh, no.* Upon reaching

the road, instead of returning to town, he swung to the left and headed toward Featherwood Station.

CLAIRE WAS behind the wheel of the farm truck when the police car approached. She smiled and waved at Rhys as she drew to a cautious halt and switched off the engine. Tiers of square hay bales teetered on the tray, waiting to be transported to the shed for winter feed.

'Hello,' she called.

Rhys walked around the front of his vehicle and met her by the truck, his face a solemn mask of disbelief. 'Hi.'

'Is something the matter?' Claire's stomach plummeted.

'I've just had a word with Lars about him exceeding the speed limit around the area. He mentioned you paid him a visit.'

She bristled, her pulse pounding in her ears. 'I did. You said you didn't have any evidence to check if he was doing anything wrong ... so I couldn't see any reason why I couldn't do it for you.' Justification fuelled her bravado, fading rapidly as she gazed into his eyes, now dark with anguish.

'You shouldn't have done that,' Rhys's tone was quiet, measured. 'Apart from trespassing, you don't seem to realise who you're dealing with.' He lifted his cap, shaking his head as he ran a hand through his hair.

She slumped onto the running board, her boldness spent. 'I wouldn't have called it paying him a visit. But I know I did the wrong thing. I was so sure they were growing dope in those tunnels, and I really wanted to be the one who tipped you off so you could get all the accolades. Only Lars caught me and ... well, I ran home.' She shivered. 'He threatened me—at least, that's the way I took his suggestion of playing games with him.' Shuddering again, she swallowed. 'I'm really sorry. That man's creepy. He scares the living daylights out of me,' she ended in a small voice.

Rhys sighed, his frustration obvious. 'You shouldn't have gone over there—but you know that. I agree with you, though. I wouldn't trust him, or any of his cronies. You could have put yourself in danger—with horrendous consequences.'

'I'm sorry,' Claire said again.

They were both silent for a few seconds.

'Feel like a cuppa?' Claire asked.

Rhys shook his head. 'Sorry. I've got work to do, and it's not even two o'clock yet.' He pointed to the hay on the truck. 'If you can wait until after five, I'll pop back and help you unload that.'

Claire shot him a wavering smile. 'Oh, that would be fabulous. Mum and I took turns to get it loaded, but we were hoping Kirk would be home from work early enough to help us get it in the shed.'

He squeezed her shoulder gently. 'I'll be back when I finish work.'

Side by side, they walked to his vehicle. She stood back as he drove in a circle, pausing beside her again with his elbow resting on the open windowsill.

'By the way. The job was advertised today, and I've already completed my application.'

Claire clapped her hands before clasping them together. 'Oh, that's fabulous. Now we wait?'

'Yep. I sent it to Dad to check it over and when he gets it back to me, I'll do any alterations required and submit it.' He moved the vehicle slowly forward, calling back, 'Keep your fingers crossed and say prayers for us both!'

'Don't worry,' she whispered as the car drove away. 'I will.'

23

That evening, with the hay neatly stacked in the shed and Rhys's double-checked job application submitted, the four of them shared a barbeque and several thirst-quenching drinks.

'What are the chances of you getting the permanent position, Rhys?' Ginny asked.

He blew out a despondent breath and shook his head. 'I really don't know. The inspector seems happy, but I've got no idea how many competitors I have—or what their qualifications are. I'm also pretty young for the role ... but you never know,' he finished with a hopeful shrug.

He met Claire's gaze, a little surprised at the fervour in her over-bright eyes. His chest tightened, and he swallowed a gulp of beer to dampen his dry throat.

'If you don't get it, where will you go?' Claire's voice was soft, almost inaudible.

'I don't know. Back to district office, I guess.' He shrugged again. 'I'm trying not to think about it.'

'Fair enough,' Kirk said. 'Now you've lodged the application, you might as well forget about it until they contact you—and think about when we can get together to go back to the mine. This time, we could spend a bit of time investigating the old hut. You never know, it might be worth rebuilding, so we've got somewhere to stay when we go up there.'

Claire shook her head. 'I don't think so. Remember, a mother and child were both killed there and the thought of sleeping right where it happened is too disturbing to contemplate, no matter how long ago it was.'

Rhys grimaced. 'I agree with Claire. I'm not a great believer in ghosts ... but I wouldn't want to put too much to the test.'

Kirk was sitting, and Ginny leaned over his back, wrapping her arms across his chest. 'I'm with Claire and Rhys. Visit the area if you like, but if you're going to build anything, why not make it a tribute of some sort to those who lost their lives there. If you want a more stable place to stay when you go on your fossicking breaks, why not build a natural-looking shelter out of the timber and brush that's around the mine area? It would make a good hide then for bird-watching as well.'

Kirk tilted his head back, his white teeth bright in the thicket of black beard. 'That's a great idea. No wonder I love you so much.'

Claire rolled her eyes at Rhys before attacking her steak with a ferocity more akin to sawing wood. Rhys lifted an eyebrow, a little surprised at Claire's reaction. Obviously, despite her approval of Ginny and Kirk's relationship, Claire still struggled with the demonstrative side of their mutual love—and Rhys suspected it triggered happy memories of her father.

'I agree with Ginny,' Rhys said. 'Perhaps next time I get more than one day off in a row, we could make a start on it?'

'Before you go racing into the bush with Kirk, I was hoping we could go for a ride together,' Claire said. 'You haven't seen much of the farm yet. Only the falls and the track to the mines, really—oh, and the hay shed.'

Rhys swallowed his mouthful of salad. 'Tell you what. My next day off is this coming Sunday. How about we go riding then—and in a fortnight's time when I get my next long break, we'll head for the hills?'

Claire beamed, pointing her fork at him as she spoke. 'It's a deal. Put that in your phone diary right now so you don't forget.'

A deep laugh burst from his throat, and he shook

his head. 'As if I would forget something as important as that.'

RHYS HAD SETTLED into the police quarters quickly, even picking a bunch of wildflowers on his morning run to put in a jar on the coffee table. It looked—and felt—homely, enhanced by the lingering drift of Claire's perfume for a day or more after each of her visits.

Following the barbeque, he filled the rest of his week with routine paperwork, assignments, and another road accident, this time involving a rusty farm ute and a cow wandering on the road.

The days were drawing in and Rhys glanced at the office calendar with surprise. He had been in Featherwood Falls for more than three months. It wouldn't be long before he would need to wear thermals for his early morning run. And, if they were returning to the mines for a camping break, it might be best to go soon, before the heavy frosts and cold southerly winds blew in.

Despite having not seen Claire for days, Sunday arrived more quickly than Rhys expected. He drove into Featherwood Station before seven-thirty, ready for whatever Claire had planned for them. A tiny smile touched his mouth as he walked through the gate, sure the day would involve more than just a ride on the new horse.

He was right.

Claire welcomed him with a hug before dragging him to the kitchen. 'We're having a big breakfast and Mum's made a quiche for lunch.'

'I hope you're feeling energetic,' Ginny said as she poured tea into mugs. 'Kirk is doing a building job over at Kallala at the moment, so it's just the three of us today.'

'Okay,' Rhys said, plonking himself in a chair. 'What's the plan?'

Ginny put a plate of eggs on toast in front of him while Claire stood behind her, head tilted slightly as she mouthed, "sorry".

'I want to drench the merino wethers and I thought seeing as you two are going for a ride anyway, perhaps you could bring them down to the shed. We'll run them through the race and check them, administer their medication, and then you could go for a second ride this afternoon and put them in a new paddock.' Ginny's voice rose, filled with hope and expectation.

Rhys nodded. 'Of course, Ginny. Whatever needs to be done will be. By the way—remind me what a wether is again? Remember, I have horse and cattle experience but know nothing about sheep.'

'Don't cross your legs when I tell you this.' Ginny

smiled. 'They're the desexed male sheep—our wool growers.'

'Ah.' Rhys squirmed, swallowing any further questions. No doubt the how and why of castrating sheep would be another experience he would take part in—if he was still here, that was.

Pushing the thought to the back of his mind, Rhys demolished his breakfast while Ginny and Claire discussed the finer details of bringing the sheep to the woolshed and which paddock they would be taken to afterwards.

Half an hour later, Claire called the horses to her. Akela arrived first with the two old ponies shuffling as fast as their legs could carry them. Splash walked alongside, as though on standby should they need help.

'He looks like a nice temperament.' Rhys nodded toward the Appaloosa.

'I can't believe how nice he is. He's really kind to the others—almost like you would expect a favourite uncle to be.'

Rhys nodded his approval, the anxiety that had been gnawing his insides easing. 'What happened to his tail?' He pointed to the short, ratty strands of brown hair that hung from his tailbone.

Claire raised her eyebrows. 'I don't know. He came like that, so I assume he must have been in a paddock somewhere with calves or other animals that chewed his tail. He's so placid, he probably hardly knew what they were doing.'

Rhys's confidence increased at the comment, and he grabbed the halter Claire handed him and slipped it over the gelding's head.

After grooming and saddling, Rhys cautiously mounted Splash in the round yard, conscious of Claire's critical eye.

'Let your reins out a bit. He doesn't enjoy having pressure on his mouth,' she called. 'Now squeeze with your legs and walk around twice to get the feel of each other.'

Rhys followed her instructions, slowly relaxing into the gelding's stride. It had been almost ten years since he'd been on a horse but, like riding a bike, he was relieved that he hadn't forgotten how—although, he conceded unused muscles would probably protest by the end of the day.

Having ridden Splash almost daily since his arrival, Claire assured him she was confident that he and the horse were compatible. She opened the gate and rode alongside him on Akela, three of the kelpies trotting behind.

'We'll walk for the first bit if you like,' she said. 'Just until you get used to each other.'

Rhys nodded, allowing his long legs to stretch a little lower, remembering his sister's constant instruction of "weight in your heels and drop them down so only the ball of your foot rests on the stirrups".

Claire led the way up the track past the cattle yards and through the gate onto a ridge that stretched three quarters of the way across the farm. Running along the wide, gentle land to the west, a network of paddocks provided grazing for the cattle and sheep. While on the steeper country beyond them, native bush filled every hill and crevice. Before they reached the turnoff they'd taken when hiking to the mines, they picked their way around an outcrop of granite boulders. As they emerged from the shelter of the rocks, Claire reined Akela to a halt and Rhys rode up beside her.

Drawing a whistling breath, he sat mesmerised. 'Wow. Just wow!' he said.

'I know. It kinda takes your breath away, doesn't it?'

'Sure does. It's amazing that you can't really see all this from the other side of the valley. It's so ... private and absolutely stunning.'

'Yep. When our great-grandfather signed up for this block, I reckon most of the locals would have thought he was mad. From the bottom of the valley, all you can see is scrub, so you would never know all this lovely grazing land is even here—and the best part is that it's sheltered from the westerly winds. There's always been a bit of a dingo and wild-dog problem, but that boundary fencing you saw when we came back from our mining trek has stopped most of that issue.' She turned to him and smiled. 'It's great country for raising sheep and cattle—and a gorgeous part of Australia to live.'

Energised by Claire's enthusiasm, Rhys pointed to the paddock in front of them, dotted with grazing sheep. 'Are those the fellows we're looking after today?'

'Sure are. We'll go down and open the gate into the paddock next door, then the dogs can bring them through. It joins a fenced race that goes all the way back to the yards. Makes shifting stock much safer and easier on us all.'

'There's a hell of a lot of fencing to take care of, isn't there?'

Claire huffed. 'I know—it's a never-ending job checking and repairing it. Most of the paddocks have an electric wire around them now, which helps keep the cattle away from them—and predators. Actually, I have to admit, I'm not sure how Mum and I would have coped if it wasn't for Kirk. After he settled here, he and Mum spent weeks replacing sections that hadn't been looked at since Dad died.'

Rhys stared at her for a moment. 'So, you're comfortable with Kirk potentially being a member of your family?'

She sighed. 'Yes, I am. Dad would have liked him—and I do, too. It's just ... since I've been home, I can feel Dad around the place, and it's taking a while for me to get used to seeing Kirk where it should have been my father.'

Rhys didn't know how to answer that, so he said nothing, hoping she could feel the sympathetic vibes he was sending.

She straightened and reached over to him, touching his hand gently. "Thanks for ... just being here.' Then she shot him a grin and whistled the dogs. 'Come on. We've got a job to do.'

24

*I*t was late morning by the time the flock of almost five hundred sheep filled the yards. Rhys slid off Splash with a grateful groan. His thighs ached, and it took a few seconds of standing on two feet before the circulation in his legs and backside returned to normal.

'We'll unsaddle the horses and leave them over there.' Claire pointed to a pen at the end of the woolshed where an ancient pepperina tree shaded most of the area from the midday sun.

Hobbling behind her, Rhys led Splash to the allocated yard and began unsaddling him. With both horses seen to, Claire grasped his hand, and they strolled to the personal door at the side of the shed.

'You made it.' Ginny looked up as they entered, peeling the lid off a container as she spoke.

Laden with food and flasks of both tea and coffee, the table near the wool press was almost full. Ginny now placed the sandwiches in the middle.

Inside, the shed was tidy, its darkened interior highlighted with dust motes floating in the sunlight that shone through the open windows. Rhys inhaled the scent of lanolin and sheep manure and smiled at Ginny.

'We did. I might be stiff tomorrow, but by the look of that spread, I certainly won't be hungry!'

'Here, have a drink of cold water first.' Ginny handed both him and Claire a large tumbler, and Rhys took it gratefully, swallowing the cool liquid without a pause.

With lunch over, Ginny fastened a container of drench on Claire's back and adjusted the dispenser gun. 'Come with me, Rhys. You and I will fill the race, then Claire will administer the medicine orally to each sheep. Once she has dosed all those in the race, I'll release them and close the gates again, then will give you a wave to push the next lot up. Are you okay with that?'

'Yeah. Sure.' Rhys waved back, convincing himself there was nothing to it. If Ginny and Claire could do this on their own, then any help he could provide would be a bonus—right?

Things didn't quite work out as simply as he'd expected. Standing amidst a cream swirl of woolly bodies, he soon realised that sheep thought differently to people—or maybe they didn't? He threw up his hands in a helpless gesture as Ginny gave the command to push up the next lot.

Claire walked toward him, chortling. 'I'll show you.'

She pointed to the two dogs lying quietly outside the yards, waiting for a command. Immediately focusing on her, they leapt the fence at the flick of her finger, despite the lack of verbal instruction. Then, creeping slowly, their bodies close to the ground and their eyes glued to the flock, they patrolled back and forth, holding the sheep in a tight group while Claire grabbed the first animal and turned it to face the open gate into the race. It leapt forward, and she released it, standing back as the rest followed it in a rush.

'See, they like playing follow the leader. I'm sure you've heard the term "follow like sheep" ... well, there it is. You just have to think like they do.'

Rhys grinned and gave her a mock salute. 'Got it.'

For the next three hours, they progressively worked their way through the process with no further trouble. Rhys's admiration for both women rose as he witnessed the efficient and methodical inspection each animal was given. While Claire walked backwards amongst the tightly packed animals, gently squeezing a measured dose of drench into each mouth, Ginny did a rapid inspection of the wool around each tail and cast her eyes over their hooves. Now and then, the women would single out a wether that needed his toenails trimmed or had signs of fly-strike. They marked it on the top of the head with a thick chalk stick and then, as Ginny released the majority into the large side yard, those requiring extra attention found the gate swiftly closed in their faces, forced to run straight ahead and up into the woolshed instead.

When the process was completed and the final sheep released, Rhys helped hold those animals inside while Ginny and Claire trimmed their feet or cleaned around their backsides by shearing the wool off and spraying a medicated liquid on them.

'Geez, I didn't know you had to do so much with sheep.' Rhys rubbed a greasy hand through his mop of hair, his admiration escalating.

Ginny raised her eyebrows. 'It's all part of good animal husbandry, and I've never thought about it, really. I guess both Claire and I love the sheep, so we don't see the work involved as a chore—more a way of ensuring the stock are happy and comfortable. After all, their wool is our pay packet.'

Rhys nodded. His limited experiences growing up had given him a healthy respect and understanding of cattle and horse management, but now he looked at the sheep in a new light. They were smaller and easier to handle—and he rather liked the smell of lanolin and the sponginess of their beautiful, soft wool.

'Okay. So ... now we take them back to their paddock?' He glanced over to where the horses were dozing, swishing flies as they stood nose to tail under the pepperina tree. His thighs twinged at the thought of having to ride for another two hours and he bit back a grimace.

'Yes.' Claire lay a hand on his arm and looked at the sky. 'It'll be dark in another hour though, so I think we'll take the ute instead. They don't have to go as far as they did this morning. Remember that gate I hooked back while we were bringing them here? It's the paddock they'll be going into, so we should make it before dark.'

Ginny followed Claire's gaze and nodded, chewing her lip. 'Good idea. I'll take the horses back to the stables and brush them down while you two do that—and dinner will be ready by the time you return.'

Relief flooded through Rhys. Somehow a pleasant horse ride with the woman he admired so fervently hadn't been quite what he had expected—but then, he didn't mind surprises, especially when they involved Claire.

KIRK HAD STILL NOT APPEARED by the time they sat down to eat, and Rhys fidgeted as the subject he'd been trying to suppress for so long rose to the forefront of his mind.

'Umm ... I've been meaning to talk to you about something Mr Ward's solicitor said.'

Both women looked at him as if he had suddenly grown two heads.

'What do you mean?' Claire said, her forehead wrinkling.

'The thing about Mr Ward and Donald—and your father—being cousins.'

Ginny shook her head. 'That's rubbish. If it were true, Lyndon would have known and perhaps the relationship between him and Nigel may have been different.' She shrugged. 'I don't know where this is coming from—or why it's suddenly been mentioned.'

Rhys's heart jackhammered. 'Perhaps you could ask Donald next time you see him—just to confirm whether he's got proof. You know, DNA results or something.'

Claire gazed at him with an open mouth, her eyes wide. 'You know something, don't you?'

Ginny's face paled, and she held a hand over her mouth. 'What!'

The seconds ticked in the ensuing silence. Rhys took a deep breath before he spoke.

'The solicitor sent me a copy of the letter of authority for Donald to act on Nigel's behalf—and in that, it confirmed a match in Nigel and Donald's DNA.

All I'm suggesting is that it might be a good idea to clarify the situation with him.' He faced Ginny. 'I've been told most of what happened after your husband's death and leading up to Nigel's arrest, and I'm pleased due diligence has prevailed and they have locked him up. However, the reasons for Nigel doing what he did puzzled me.'

'But he was greedy—he told James he wanted the farm because of the mine.' Ginny's face had morphed from shock to disbelief, pink spots appearing on her cheeks.

'Think about it, though. If he is Donald and Lyndon's cousin, do you think he could have been driven by a desire to be part of this family? He must have been jealous of the respect Lyndon garnered in the community—not to mention the beautiful property he had inherited.'

Ginny exploded, her eyes flashing. 'It might have been in the family for generations, but Lyndon and I worked our butts off to pay his parents every cent this place was worth. We even had to give up a block of land we owned to finance Donald into the farm he chose—all because he was such a selfish and obnoxious prick, neither Lyndon nor his father could work with him. If Nigel knew he was Lyndon's cousin, why the hell couldn't he have approached the subject civilly and talked things over with Lyndon? We're very reasonable people—but he had to kill my husband

and terrify the living daylights out of me!' she finished with a sob, and Claire jumped up and wrapped an arm around her shoulders.

'I think you'd better go,' she muttered, but with a firmness Rhys had not heard before.

His heart ached as he drove back to the station. He'd blown it. Sagging into his seat, he stared blindly down the main road, oblivious to the beauty of his environment, and turned into his driveway.

Hidden secrets caused so much pain and angst? If unravelling them brought nothing but hatred for him, why did he want to stay in Featherwood Falls so desperately?

He trudged inside, locking the door behind him, and slumped on the couch. He stared at the painting on the wall—two fortunate children playing with their beloved father.

Because I want my children to have the same sort of life that I had, that's why.

25

*I*t was the following Friday afternoon before his phone buzzed and Claire's name lit up the screen. He snatched it up, his belly churning.

'Hi,' she said.

'Hi.'

'Are you okay?'

'Yeah. You?' Rhys answered hesitantly.

'Yes. I'm really sorry about last Sunday.'

'So am I.'

'Mum and I are over the shock—and you were right. We rang Uncle Donald, and he confirmed the DNA match.'

Rhys's stomach settled as she continued.

'Apparently Nigel only found out after his mother died and he got a copy of the death certificate and other documents from the solicitor. But regardless of that, Mum and I had no right to "shoot the messenger" so to speak, and I'm really sorry. Umm—would you like to come for dinner tonight? Kirk's home and we thought we could plan our next trip up to the burned-out hut. Have another look at things and see if we could help Kirk build himself a little shack or something.'

Rhys sucked in a breath. Was becoming involved with Claire's family the right thing to do? If he intended to live in this town, it was important to be unbiased—but how could he be? He stiffened with a jolt. *My feelings for Claire have gone way beyond the friend stage.*

'That would be lovely. Thanks.'

An audible huff of relief sounded down the phone. 'Great. See you around six?'

'Okay. I'll be there.'

He tapped the red icon before turning back to the box of records and diaries dated 1960-1965. Following his revelation the previous Sunday, he had re-read the 1937 logbook before continuing through the rest of the decades stored in the back room. Although interesting, nothing had revealed itself as being more than routine life in a country police station. He wasn't quite ready to relinquish them to the state archives until he understood every minor event that had made this place the community it was.

At five minutes to six, he drove toward Featherwood Station, his insides tumbling with pleasure, familiarity, and a good dose of trepidation.

'Hello.' Claire was waiting at the gate as he approached her, the regular six-pack of beer and bottle of wine tucked under his arm.

'You look beautiful.' His breath caught as he gazed into sparking grey eyes. Her hair hung over her shoulders, a cloud of gold against her clear, glowing complexion.

She ducked her head. 'You look pretty spiffy yourself.'

He grinned, remembering how dirty and dishevelled they all were the last time they'd been together. Tonight he had taken extra care, shampooing his hair and spraying a liberal dose of the new Hugo Boss aftershave his sister had given him for Christmas. To recover from disappointment and fill in the time, he'd spent two evenings during the week doing random breath testing out on the main highway and the less trafficked roads—and caught up with an overflowing washing basket. Now he wore freshly ironed moleskin trousers and a plain green shirt with the zip-neck merino wool jersey he saved for special occasions.

A chill wind had sprung up earlier in the day—a reminder that winter was not far away. At the door, he toed off his polished RM's and stepped into the living room, immediately absorbing not only the warmth from the fire but also the atmosphere.

Ginny rushed over and hugged him. 'I'm sorry about my outburst. It wasn't your fault, and I was very rude.'

'It's okay. You weren't rude. Just shocked—and I totally understand that. I admit, I was a little, too, when I first read the letter.'

'Come in. Have a beer.' Kirk clapped Rhys on the back, almost jolting the six-pack from his grip.

It was as though the discussion about cousins had never taken place as the evening progressed. Ginny and Kirk exchanged banter, skylarking like a pair of teenagers, and Claire rolled her eyes.

'Kirk's been really busy this week over at Kallala, so it's been just Mum and me all week. Can't you tell?'

'So, when are we heading for the bush again, Rhys?' Kirk sliced the roast meat, glancing at Rhys over a pair of half-glasses that made him look like an absent-minded professor.

'It's the long May weekend coming up, so I'll be on traffic duties throughout that, but I've got three days off afterwards. Will that suit?'

'Sounds great. How about you, Claire?'

'I can work around it. I'll get the project I'm working on finished this week and then, if I have to, I can work over the long weekend as well—and have the same days off as you guys. Will you be okay, Mum?'

Ginny nodded. 'Of course. It's time to put the rams with the ewes, but the dogs can help me—and I'll do it before you all head off, just in case I have any problems.'

Light-hearted conversation continued over dinner and, after clearing up the dishes, Ginny handed Rhys a pile of DVDs. 'Your choice tonight. The pickings are slim, but there's some good movies there, even if they are old.'

He flicked through them, choosing one labelled *Everest*. 'This okay?' He turned it over and read the blurb. 'True story. I like that.'

Claire leaned on his shoulder. 'Ooh, I haven't seen that for years. It's great—but I'm glad we've got the fire on.'

Rhys gave her a quizzical look, uncertain about her meaning. An hour into the story, he understood completely and pulled her more tightly against him on the squashy couch as they stared at the horrendous blizzard on the television. Ginny sat at the other end, knitting as she watched, while Kirk lay in the recliner chair with one socked leg propped on the footrest and the other stretched out in front.

When the movie finished, Kirk thumped the footrest into place and pointed the remote at the television. 'Lucky we're not dealing with that kind of weather here.' He grew solemn for a moment. 'Mind you, I saw plenty of it in the Snowies. Not as high as Mt. Everest, of course, but still pretty easy to lose your life if you're not careful and the weather turns nasty.'

'What was living down there like?' Rhys asked Kirk while Ginny lay down her knitting and put the kettle on.

'I didn't know any different, so for me it was great. Caring family, plenty of friends, and lots of great places to hike and ski. Suppose it's why I like it here. Not as cold, but still four defined seasons and lots of bush to escape to.'

It was on the tip of his tongue to ask what had brought him to Featherwood Falls, but something stopped him as he vaguely recalled Claire mentioning his wife had died and things had gone wrong for him. With last Sunday's conversation still burning in his mind, he was wary of bringing up any more subjects that could cause overflowing emotions.

As he and Claire shared a kiss beside his ute an hour later, Rhys held her tight. 'I thought you might like to know I got an interview for the permanent position.'

She drew back and stared at him. 'Fantastic. When?'

'Next Wednesday. I have to go to district office in Warwick for it.' He shrugged. 'I wish I knew what competition I'm up against, but I don't. So I'll just have to do the best I can and try not to stuff anything up.'

She squeezed his hand between hers and smiled. 'You won't. I've got a good feeling about this. You just need to believe in yourself and give it everything you've got.'

They hugged again, and he blew out a slow breath. 'Oh, I will. There's no problem there.'

He slid into his ute, and she bent her head through the open window to plant a last kiss on his lips. 'Talk tomorrow?'

He smiled. 'I hope so.' And he drove away.

A life here for as long as I want—and Claire at my side. What more could I wish for?

26

*A*lthough waiting at the roadworks had been stressful, glancing down at his watch every thirty seconds, Rhys was almost glad he was held up. It had left no time to sit in the station waiting room, mulling over whether he had done enough preparation. He walked into the district office with three minutes to spare before being called in to the interview room.

He glanced around, absorbing the atmosphere as he stepped inside. The room was the largest in a row of offices facing the corridor, all fronted in half-glass walls. They had covered some windows with charts and hanging cork boards that blanked out most potential onlookers. Thin carpet covered the floors, ensuring any noise was deadened slightly, and behind the desk, a smaller window looked out on a paved area between the main building and the watch house.

'Please sit down.'

He didn't recognise the woman who spoke, assuming she must be the delegate from the human resources area of Brisbane or Toowoomba mentioned in his letter confirming the interview.

Inspector Jones shot him a brief smile before introducing the other two in the room, Sergeant Ryan from Regional Office and Mrs Leanne Ackerman.

He shook hands and sat in the chair opposite, pushing his feet hard against the ground to prevent his legs from shaking.

Beginning with some niceties regarding his time in Featherwood Falls, Leanne then continued with an overview of the position, expectations, and duties—all of which Rhys was acutely aware, having been there for almost four months.

Sending a silent thanks to his father, he glanced at the matrix he had drafted. The spreadsheet was in large, bold type—enough to catch his eye and jog his memory should he forget what he was going to say. Along the top row, key selection criteria words were highlighted, and underneath, in larger cells, was the abbreviated list of examples showing his ability and experience in each of the required standards.

His practice of reading it aloud to himself each evening for the previous week, together with writing and re-writing examples on paper, meant he didn't need to refer to his matrix at all. At the end of the interview, he stood and thanked the panel for their time, filling his lungs to their fullest with deep, satisfied breaths.

'We'll let you know some time in the next week or two,' Leanne said.

Rhys smiled, tucked his folder under his arm, and dutifully followed the sergeant back to the main office. Several staff members were leaning in their chairs or standing, obviously discussing something either too interesting or too unimportant for outside ears as their murmurs faded when Rhys walked in. In recognition, two called out a hello and Rhys replied with a nod before the sergeant opened the front door and Rhys passed through it taking a deep gulp of fresh air.

It's one thing to say gidday to comrades when it's a casual visit, but job interviews have a unique set of rules.

Before he drove home, he called into a café, bought himself a steak burger and soft drink, then walked across the road to the park—the opposite end from the spot where he and Evie had met on the day that seemed forever ago.

He ate the burger with gusto, gratification, and a touch of exhilaration filling his chest. Then he pulled out his phone and rang Claire.

She answered on the first ring, her voice calm but tinged with a discernible tremor. 'How did it go?'

'Okay, I think. I was happy with both the questions and the answers I could give, anyway. Don't think I can do any better than that.'

'Well done. Of course not. You gave it your best and now it's over to them,' she repeated, her tone brighter now, her relief and enthusiasm akin to his.

'Yeah. I'm going to ring Dad to let him know how I got on, then I'll head home.'

'Great. Will I see you tonight?'

'You bet. I'll pop in to see Lola and Frank first. They know I'm here, and why, so I'd like to spend a bit of time with them since they've kind of become my pseudo grandparents.'

'Oh, I've invited them for dinner tonight so you can catch up with them then. If you don't make it before we eat, I'll keep some for you.'

'Thanks heaps. That'd be great. See you tonight.'

'Drive safe. Bye.'

His smile widened as he swiped the end icon and scrolled down to his father's number.

After talking at length with his parents, he ambled back to his ute, buoyed by hope and happiness.

By the time he reached Featherwood Falls, he had relived the interview and put it to the back of his mind. Regardless of the outcome, his next goal would be to enjoy the camping trip in the hills and come clean to the Shepherd family over what he had read in the 1937 police log—although there was one thing he needed to do first.

IT WAS AFTER FOUR, the western sun hitting him right at eye level as he drove down Dingo Gully Road.

He parked well away from Taylor's cowshed and walked cautiously toward the rhythmic thrum of the milking plant and the sound of cows mooing.

Standing well back from the concrete bay, Rhys waited to be noticed. The radio blared while Bruce and a younger man dashed up and down the pit, washing cows' udders before attaching or removing cups from their teats. He wasn't sure how long he stood there, finding the process fascinating and developing a new respect for the humble dairy cow. Methodically, each one trekked into position, waited for the mouthful of grain to drop into the feeder in front of them, and patiently stood still until the process was complete and the row of cows released.

Eventually, the younger man looked up and nudged Bruce. Beckoning Rhys, the older man climbed out of the pit and tramped through the vat room to the outside air.

'What's the problem?' His leathery face wore a grumpy expression, his mouth drooping at the corners.

'Nothing, Mr Taylor. I thought I'd pay a visit to see if you're still having trouble with the motorcyclists.'

Bruce grunted. 'Not as bad. They still come past every day, but at least they slow down now and ... I suppose the cows are getting used to the noise.'

'That's good to hear. If there's any more trouble, please let me know.'

Bruce nodded curtly. 'I will.' He turned away but stopped. 'There's a truck that comes past every week now, though. It doesn't bother us none, but I've never seen it until a few weeks ago and doesn't belong to any of my neighbours.'

'Did you get the registration—or notice any business name or any other form of identification on the side of it?'

'Nuh. Just a little Pantech, like a food delivery company might use.'

'What about the driver? Is it the same person each time?'

'I think so. A little fellow—Asian. Barely see over the steering wheel.' Bruce snorted. 'Anyway, I've gotta get back to me cows,' he finished and stomped to the shed.

Hmm. Rhys frowned as he returned to the car. He hadn't expected a "thanks for checking on us" but was surprised Bruce hadn't rung him to report the strange vehicle—especially after making such an issue about the motorbikes.

27

There was an air of jubilancy around the Featherwood Station dining table that night. Frank and Lola arrived before Rhys, and after their meal, Claire topped up everyone's glasses while they bombarded Rhys with questions about his interview and the probability of him staying permanently in Featherwood Falls.

They were almost finished their after-dinner coffee when the conversation turned to the revelation of Lyndon and Donald being Nigel Ward's cousins.

'I'm not sure how or what the connection is?' Ginny's round, hazel eyes met Rhys's gaze. 'Lola, you know more about the town's history than I do. Can you help?'

Her earrings clinked as they swung below the mop of grey curls. 'I've only heard gossip—you know what these places are like. One person says their grand-mother told them about such-and-such, then it goes around the neighbourhood like wildfire and what someone doesn't know, they make up. Before long, it's all out of proportion and no-one knows what the actual truth was.' Her round face creased, and her head tilted to the ceiling, as though delving into long-forgotten memories.

Rhys's gaze roved around his companions as he weighed up the options. He couldn't show them private police documents, but they already knew about the fire and the deaths—so, he reasoned, all he was doing was clearing up decades of misconceptions and gossip.

Clearing his throat, he said, 'I found something of interest in the station's storeroom.'

All eyes turned to him.

'Go on.'

He met Ginny's wide-eyed gaze and rubbed a hand through his hair. 'There's been a bit of a ... delay in archiving documents here, so I've been going through them to see what needs to be thrown away and what needs to be kept.'

Frank threw his head back and laughed. 'I can just imagine the problem you're talking about. It's called neglecting your duty.'

Rhys ignored the intimation, knowing it probably referred to his predecessor, and continued, 'I found police record books backdating to the 1930s—and I've been reading them.'

'Do you mean diaries kept by the station?' Claire asked.

'Yes. All police carry notepads in their pocket and used them to jot notes of every incident or event attended, including anything that may be needed for a court procedure or reference at a later date. In previous decades, the station diary, or log, was left in the office and they transferred any information noted by individual cops into it at the end of the day. Now we enter it into the computer.'

'Okay, so what have you found?' There was a sense of urgency mixed with trepidation in Ginny's voice, as though she wanted to know but was afraid of what might be revealed.

'It's the 1937 diary I've found interesting—particularly after hearing about Turtle Ridge having a name change to Camel Hump and the bushfire that killed a family.' He glanced at the others, perceiving their undivided attention.

'W-what did you find out?' Lola asked quietly, her hooded eyes drilling into him as though desperate to get to the core of the story without delay.

'The writing was hard to read in some places, but it's clearly documented that although a fire went through the hills and general district, it didn't begin with a weather event ... It was deliberately lit by the man who first shot his wife and daughter—the man you refer to as Wild Willy.'

'Really?' Kirk dragged his chair closer and leaned his elbows on the table.

'Apparently, when the bodies of the wife and daughter were found, it was obvious they had both been shot.' Rhys glanced at his companions. There was not a sound in the room as he continued, 'William Gerard McMahon, or Wild Willy as he was known, has never been found ... But—and this is a big but—a few days after the fire, a teenaged girl arrived here, at this very house.'

'What!' Ginny held a hand over her mouth.

'Her name was Jo-Lee McMahon, and she said she was the elder daughter of Wild Willy. According to the records, he was a drunkard and inclined to go into wild rages—hence the name, I suppose. Anyway, according to Jo-Lee, he shot her mother and young sister in a drunken rage. Somehow, she missed being killed and hid in the bush—but not before she watched her father set fire to the cabin. I don't know how she escaped the blaze because it seems to have taken off easily and burned for days.'

He paused, and before he could continue, Ginny jumped in.

'What happened to her?' Then she leaned back in her seat, her eyes meeting his. 'Oh. Let me guess.

Angus invited her in and put her to work—under the guise of "caring for an orphan".'

He nodded slowly. 'It seems he offered her refuge for housework and caring for his ill wife. Minor details weren't recorded, but, reading between the lines, it appears she lived on Featherwood Station for about a year after old Mrs Shepherd passed away, by which time their only son—Lyndon's father—was at boarding school. Except for the occasional mention in the next few months that Wild Willy was still missing, there was nothing more about the incident—or Jo-Lee.'

'I still don't understand?' Claire said. She turned to her mother. 'Did Grandad ever talk about all this?'

Ginny shook her head. 'Never. He probably knew nothing about it. I mean, that was just before the war, and in those days, every property employed quite a few staff. In this district, there were a lot of Chinese who worked in the mines and grew vegetables. They were great workers and were quickly snapped up on any property. Anyway, Grandad was just a child and, even in the years I knew him, he never talked about his parents.' She screwed up her forehead. 'Hang on a second. There's an old bible in the study. You know how people used to write birthdates and stuff in the front of them? I'll get it and see if it sheds any light for us.'

She hurried away, returning while Rhys and the

others were still mulling over the information revealed so far.

Placing the fragile volume on the table, Ginny opened it, beaming as she ran her finger down the inside cover. 'It's a bit faded, but it looks like Angus Shepherd married Maisie McKenzie in 1919. Then, in 1931, there is one birth listed, Douglas Roy.' She looked up. 'That was Lyndon and Donald's father. There's nothing else mentioned here, but I'm sure he married Jeanette in 1965 and then Lyndon was born in 1967. Donald was born five years later, in 1972.'

'Crikey,' Claire chirped. 'They were not a very fertile family, were they? I thought people had about ten babies before they turned thirty-five back in those days.'

'Not everyone was that fortunate.' Lola's voice was soft, tinged with sadness.

Rhys's chest squeezed with compassion. Frank had only ever mentioned their son, Ryan, once—and although Lola smiled when she spoke of their only child having worked "away" since he was sixteen, Rhys was yet to meet him and hadn't delved into what seemed to be a private subject.

'Okay, Rhys.' Claire narrowed her gaze as she fixed her eyes on his. 'I feel this is leading somewhere important. Can you tell us more?'

He took a deep breath. 'Since hearing about Nigel's

declaration that he and Donald are cousins, I've been over the logbooks again and taken a bit more care.'

'And ...' Claire's eyes sparkled with feverish excitement while the others waited in silent anticipation.

'There's a notation in 1938 about the officer in charge here having to witness a document transferring a portion of land from Featherwood Station to Jo-Lee McMahon. Angus Shepherd named it Glenrowan, and it seems she must have lived there until her death— and then it was bequeathed to her only daughter, Flora, who by then was married to Jim Ward.'

Ginny spluttered. 'Flora! That was Nigel's mother, and she was such a sweet lady. So, who was Flora's father?' The room froze in total silence for a few seconds as the truth encompassed its occupants. 'Ooh! Lyndon's grandfather—Angus bloody Shepherd.'

'There's nothing in the logs to confirm that. But I reckon that's your answer—given that Donald and Nigel's DNA matches.' Rhys lay his hands quietly on the table in front of him as his eyes roved around the group.

Lola drew a long, noisy breath. 'Well, that puts one puzzle to rest. Now we know Flora and Nigel have Chinese ancestors, which is where their got their small stature and straight, black hair from. And ... although the rumour has always insinuated Angus Shepherd was a bit of a "ladies' man", in this case he obviously did something right—not only acknowledging Jo-Lee's child was his but also giving her an excellent farm!'

Claire nodded, her eyebrows knitting in wrinkles above her nose. 'I get all that now, but I can't understand why no-one has ever mentioned this before. Or why after all these years, Nigel told Donald they're cousins—when he goes to jail?'

'I suspect, like dozens of other families around the world, people keep secrets they don't want their children to know—for a whole raft of reasons,' Kirk said, his voice low and serious. 'Maybe Nigel found out something after his mother's death and his tendency to think irrationally fed a jealous streak. It must have been to do with his belief the mines on Featherwood Station contained wealth—and he truly believed he deserved a share of it all.'

Ginny got to her feet and began gathering the empty coffee cups. 'We'll never know the reasons for Nigel doing what he did—but I for one am pleased he's now getting the care and mental health help he obviously needs—and, although we've lost Lyndon, we'll never forget him and can now put the whole matter behind us.'

A murmur of agreement filled the air, and they dropped the subject as they discussed the upcoming camping trip to the mine.

Hours later, long after Rhys had returned to his apartment behind the police station, he lay on his back, staring at the ceiling, hands clamped behind his head. He was solely responsible for revealing a history that might destroy the community's respect for the Shepherd family—a respect they had held forever.

He groaned and rolled over.

Why do secrets come with so many complications—especially when they involve people I really, really like?

28

*M*orning mist hung in the valley, shrouding the village as the three hikers sat on a rocky outcrop, munching their morning snacks. A flock of corellas circled, screeching above them.

The breeze had a chill to it—a reminder that winter was approaching, while a string of thin, white clouds floated high above.

Rhys met Claire's gaze as she twirled her ponytail. It had been more than a week since the dinner at Featherwood Station and, except for a couple of texts confirming the final arrangements for today's trek, he hadn't seen her. Not that it surprised him after the cooler than usual dismissal her family had given him. Despite gossip over the years insinuating there were a lot more blood ties in the district than the community realised, both Ginny and Claire must have been surprised to receive confirmation that the Wards had not only been neighbours, but also part of the Shepherd family—sort of, anyway.

'We couldn't have chosen a more perfect day,' Claire breathed.

'Sure is. Not too hot either, so hopefully we'll make faster progress,' Rhys answered, shooting her a warm smile that released any remaining threads of worry.

'Let's push on, aye?' Kirk swung his backpack in the air, slipping his shoulders through the straps.

'Need a hand?' Rhys didn't wait for Claire to answer, hoisting her pack off the rock and holding it to her back.

'Thanks.' She smiled, turned away, and began striding on up the track.

Rhys hurried to fall in behind her. Walking was easier, due to a combination of Kirk's vigilant slashing each time he returned to the mine and the slowing of growth with the change in the weather.

'I reckon leaving that couple of hours earlier than we did last time will give us a chance to dig out a bit more of the tunnel and see where that seam of quartz leads us,' Kirk called to the others.

Rhys glanced behind him, giving Kirk a wry grin. 'Yeah. You hope.'

The midday sun had slid to the west by the time

they reached the clearing where the hut had once stood.

Kirk looked at his watch. 'I suggest we set up camp here for a change.'

'I'm not sure, Kirk.' Claire's voice had a worried quaver. 'It feels spooky—like someone or something is telling us we shouldn't be here.'

Kirk dropped his pack on the ground. 'Let's have a more thorough look around first then—after we've eaten lunch.'

Rhys stemmed the hot breath of relief as his stomach rumbled. 'Sounds good to me.'

They ate quietly in what Rhys determined was unified peace and respect for their surroundings. A wallaby hopped close by and, ignoring its human companions, dropped its head to the short grass and began eating. Another arrived, then another, and within a few minutes, a mob of the cute macropods were spread across the clearing.

Kirk stretched and reached for his pack to stow the empty lunch container, and with that movement, the wallabies fled with frenzied bounds. 'Whoops. Sorry about that.' Kirk shrugged. 'I'm going to have a poke around.'

'You do that. I'm staying here for a rest.' Claire turned to Rhys. 'What do you want to do?'

'I'll stay here with you,' he said with a slow smile. 'You could get lost out here.'

She laughed and slapped him on the arm.

'I reckon I could find my way home without a problem ... but you? Hmm.' She trailed off, her cheeks pink as Rhys moved closer to her.

NEITHER TOOK notice which way Kirk had gone until the crack of timber sounded, followed by a muffled roar.

'What was that!' Claire leapt to her feet, ready for flight as she imagined a wild boar charging out of the scrub at any minute.

Rhys grabbed her by the wrist while putting a finger to his lips. 'Shh.'

Poised as though frozen in time, they both faced the area from which faint sounds of moaning emanated. Seconds passed before the sound faded to nothing.

Claire grasped Rhy's arm and their eyes met, wide and filled with fear.

'Kirk!' Claire yelled as she ran toward the edge of the clearing, stopping short where the land dropped away to a rocky ledge.

'Where are you, Kirk?' she called again, pausing for a moment and closing her eyes to hear better.

The low moan came, and she scrambled down the rocks, ignoring the scratches from sharp edges and random scrub that stuck out. Grateful for Rhys's presence immediately behind her, she swung an arm back and clung to him as she called again. 'I can hear you, Kirk. Please ... make another sound so we can find you.'

'I'm here,' the faint voice echoed, a high-pitched whine sounding more like a woman than the deep tones of the Kirk they knew.

'We're coming!' Rhys pulled her with him, cautiously stepping toward the sound. 'He sounds like he's fallen in a hole somewhere—and we don't want to follow.'

Claire's wide gaze met his before swinging to the ground. They crept toward a patch of boulders, intertwined with rough grass and shrubs, yelling repeatedly and halting between each call to hear Kirk's reply. They were close now, his responses infrequent and strained.

A small plank of rotting timber stood at an odd angle at the foot of one of the smaller boulders, and Rhys dropped to his hands and knees and crawled closer, dragging the foliage to the side as he went. 'Kirk! Can you give us another call, please?'

'Ooooh.'

The groan rose from the ground immediately in front of Rhys. He leaned forward, and peered through the undergrowth at the black hole.

'Is it a well? Or another mine shaft?' Claire whispered.

'I'm down here.' The thin voice echoed and a splinter of relief ran through Claire.

'Are you hurt?'

'Ankle. I think I've broken my ankle.'

Rhys swung his gaze to meet Claire's. 'It's okay, mate. We're here, and we'll get you out,' he spoke calmly, beckoning Claire to join him. 'Claire's with me, but she'll nip back to where we left our packs and bring torches and the climbing tape.'

He nodded at Claire, and she leapt to her feet and scurried away.

'Is THERE a ladder or anything down there resembling footholds?' Rhys called into the darkness.

'Don't think so.' Kirk's voice was short now, intermingled with noisy breaths. 'Too dark to see.'

'It's alright, Kirk. Claire won't be long. We'll lower a torch down to you so you can have a look around while we work out what we can do to get you up here again.'

The time seemed to drag, but it was barely three minutes before Claire returned with a water bottle in a drawstring bag, two head torches, a handheld flashlight, and a bag stuffed full with climbing tape. She knelt beside Rhys and spoke firmly. 'It's Claire here now, Kirk. I'm going to lower some water down to you and the torch will be in the bag with it.'

Sending a silent prayer of thanks to her father for insisting the girls used bowlines and other correct knots to secure anything on the farm, Claire glanced at Rhys.

He nodded, and together they released the bag into the shaft. Rustling sounds rose to meet them, and Rhys looked at Claire, pointing to the mark on the tape. Leaning toward Claire, he murmured, 'That's the ten-metre marker. Thank God he didn't fall any farther.'

A faint beam of light shone, catching Claire in the eyes as she bent over the hole. Blinking, she pulled back, and Rhys took her place. 'Have a good look around you, Kirk. And at your ankle. Tell me what you can see.'

'Ankle's on a funny angle. Reckon it's busted.' The information came in short bursts, interspersed with the throaty sounds of someone in pain. 'Looks like an old mine shaft. Wider here ...' His voice trailed off.

Rhys drew a deep breath and ran a hand through his hair. 'Righto. Hang on, Kirk. We're working out a way to get you back on solid ground.'

Claire gazed at Rhys. Her head tilted to one side. *How?* She mouthed.

Running a hand down her cheek, he whispered, 'We'll use the climbing tape.'

She swept her gaze around the area, frowning. 'But

there's no tree close enough or strong enough to tie it to … and I don't think I could support your weight if you abseil down.'

Her pleading eyes met his and he rubbed his chin.

'Right, this is what we'll do. You're strong and are lighter than me. If we loop the tape around that narrow boulder and my waist, I reckon I could support you going down—and pull you back up afterwards.'

'So, I won't stay down there with him?'

'No. With only the two of us here, one of us needs to go for help while the other remains with Kirk—and the gear and food. If we can make him comfortable, we can work together then. We need to call emergency services—and Kirk will need the CareFlight helicopter to get him to hospital.'

She nodded. 'Okay. How should we do this?'

Before he had a chance to speak, she answered her own question.

'I'll bring our backpacks here, so we can access anything we require, then you can drop me down with everything he needs for the moment … and then I'll go for help. I'll take water, my phone, and a head torch.' She held up her hand as he opened his mouth to protest. 'I know the tracks better than you do—and anyway, I'm faster.'

Rhys didn't dispute her statement, instead nodding his approval.

Within a few minutes, their gear surrounded them,

and Rhys gathered two of the straightest and smoothest branches he could find to use as splints. Then, while he ran the climbing tape around the base of the nearby boulder, Claire sorted through the first-aid and snakebite kits, laying out two crepe bandages and a packet of painkillers.

'I hope this rock doesn't decide that this is the time to move.' Rhys raised an eyebrow at Claire as he tested the knot.

'Don't say that.' Her words were sharper than she intended as her face paled.

'Sorry. I promise you'll be fine.'

Feeding the tape out, he stood a metre back from the shaft and looped it around his hips, tying it again before strapping the opposite end around Claire and weaving it securely under her arms and through the leather belt she wore around her waist.

Around her neck, Claire hung the drawstring bag that had held her sleeping bag, now filled with water, snacks, and the medical supplies. She drew a deep breath and nodded to Rhys.

'I'm ready.'

29

Claire dropped into the darkness below as Rhys let the tape out gradually, her feet walking backwards against the shaft wall as she went.

Although thin, she was tall and well-muscled and, conscious of the amount of energy Rhys would expend in controlling the speed of her drop, urgency replaced her fear. After what felt like minutes rather than seconds, her feet touched firm ground and she called to him.

'I'm down! It looks like there's a few remnants of a rotten ladder still in the walls. That might help me get back up?'

Without waiting for his reply, she crouched in front of Kirk, her head torch blinding him for a moment.

'Sorry.' She turned the beam to red and ran her

eyes over his face. It was pale, and he groaned as he attempted to move his legs to allow her more room.

She focused on his left ankle, rolling the leg of his jeans up. Even in the dim light, she could see the swollen limb lay at an unnatural angle and she bit back her shock.

'I'm really sorry, Kirk, but we need to get that boot off. Here, take a couple of painkillers.' She handed him a drink bottle and pressed two tablets out of their foil. Then, while he gulped them down and swallowed a few mouthfuls of water, she extracted the crepe bandages and splints.

As gently as she could, she unlaced his boot and eased it off his foot. Despite her care, he groaned, and a sharp pain shot through her, as though it was her own leg and not his she was trying not to hurt.

He leaned forward, holding his knee while his breath came in noisy pants. They sat for a few moments in an attempt to let the pain ease a little.

'Are you okay with me bandaging it now?' She struggled to keep the anxiety out of her voice, desperate to make him as comfortable as possible and run for help.

'Do what you have to do. I'll hold the splints still while you bandage.'

In awe of his strength, Claire strapped the injured ankle to the best of her ability, then squeezed his hand.

'I'm going for help now. Rhys will be up the top, so yell if you need anything.'

His mouth softened into a semblance of a smile, and she jerked the tape.

'Pull me up, Rhys.'

Her pulse thumped so hard she was sure both men would hear it as Rhys hauled her up the shaft a few centimetres at a time. At irregular intervals, her toe touched a spike driven into the wall, possibly the anchors for a ladder, and she used them to assist in the assent. With a relieved grunt and Rhys's powerful grasp, she flopped onto the grass at the top, puffing and her muscles twitching.

They both lay for a few moments, recovering.

Claire was the first to regain her energy, and she hauled herself to her feet, tied her jacket around her waist, and slipped her phone and head torch into her pockets. She picked up her stainless-steel water bottle and reached up to hug Rhys once again.

'Take care,' he whispered in her ear. He shoved a piece of paper into her hand. 'Here are the coordinates we took last time we were here. The emergency team will need them.'

'Okay. I'll just tell Kirk what we're doing.'

She squatted next to the gaping hole in the ground.

'Kirk, I'm going for help while the sun is still high in the sky. Rhys is here with you, and I'll be back as soon as I can. Are you okay?'

A strained grunt replied, and Claire's chest squeezed with compassion.

'See you as soon as possible.'

She met Rhys's worried gaze and touched his arm for a moment before setting off at a jog.

STUMBLING over a tree root covered in leaves, Claire slowed to a walk and checked her phone again, searching for a signal. She had covered the three-kilometre distance in her usual swinging stride, alternating with periodic jogging when the track was clear. One bar appeared briefly. Narrowing her eyes, she focused on an open stretch of bald rock just off the track, around five hundred metres away. Making her way toward it, she trod warily. The last thing she needed was a fall and a smashed phone screen. It was the one item that would bring help for Kirk—and if something happened to it, she would have to hike all the way back home.

Shaking her head, she clamped her lips together and strode on, wishing they had invested in an EPIRB or a satellite phone. At the base of the granite mound, she slid the mobile back into her pocket and buttoned the flap, freeing both hands to climb the steep slope to the plateau above.

'Yes!' Her heart thumped as she stared at the three-bar signal and, before it disappeared, she tapped the "Home" number.

It rang for what felt like ages before her mother answered. 'Claire. Is everything alright?'

Breathing a rapid sigh of relief, Claire spoke slowly and clearly. 'Mum, I don't know how long I'll have reception. Please call emergency services. Kirk's fallen into an old mine, and we think he's broken his ankle.'

'Oh no!' Ginny's strangled cry hit Claire like a slap in the face. 'What happened?'

'I'll explain later. Calm down so we can work out what needs to be done before the bloody signal drops out.' Her stern tone sounded harsh, but she continued, hoping that Ginny was registering what she was saying.

'Can you direct them to the following coordinates.' She glanced down at the note Rhys had given her and read them out. 'Have you got that, Mum?'

'Of course.' Ginny appeared to have recovered quickly, and Claire relaxed a little at her familiar, efficient tone. 'I'll call them now and will wait at the end of our road. I'll get them to follow me to where the bush track begins—and we'll see you at the top.'

'But you don't know where to go?' Confused panic filled Claire for a fleeting moment.

'It's okay, darling. Remember, I've lived here for more than thirty years—and I know the way, even if it has been a while. Now get back to Rhys and Kirk and leave the rest to me.'

'I'll wait here for a few minutes while I've got service. Ring me once you've spoken to someone so I can report to the guys.'

'Will do. Stay calm, Claire. The men need you.' And Ginny hung up.

Claire paced up and down the granite, waiting for her mother's call. She glanced at her mobile again. The signal had disappeared. Muttering an oath, she sighed, pleased she had decided not to place the emergency call herself.

Within a few minutes, soft music floated from the device in her hand, and she swiped the screen before pressing it against her ear.

'The SES are rounding up their troops and will get here as soon as possible. CareFlight is on call.' Ginny offloaded more details before taking a deep breath and continuing. 'It's okay, Claire. Help is on its way and while I wait for them, I'll get Lola to come and stay at the house in case of phone calls or anything. Frank will no doubt want to be part of the rescue, too, but someone will need to mind the shop. Anyway, they can sort that out.'

Ginny sniffed before speaking again.

'How is he?'

'I'm not really sure, Mum. Rhys is doing what he can—and I just hope help will arrive before dark.'

The phone went dead.

'Damn!'

Desperate to waste no more time, Claire tucked the device into her pocket and began the trek back, her relief at knowing help was coming now overshadowed with concern for Kirk.

As she trudged along the track, ignoring the branches catching her clothes and whipping at her face, she whispered 'Please, please hurry.'

'KIRK! CAN YOU HEAR ME?' Rhys leaned over the edge of the shaft, the beam from his torch scanning the depths below.

A breathless, 'Yep,' answered.

'Good. Is the pain easing?'

'Maybe. I might take a couple more?'

Rhys huffed. 'No, mate. Two painkillers every four hours. Sorry, it's for your own good. As soon as the paramedics get here, they'll sort you out. You hungry?'

'Nah. Bit cold though.'

'Righto. I'll tie your jacket to the rope and send it down. Reckon you can put it on?'

'I'll manage.'

Rhys had continued talking to Kirk at regular intervals to distract him, as well as ensuring he remained conscious.

'Can you use the handheld torch to have a look around?' Rhys called. 'Tell me if you see any minerals in those walls,' he finished with a grin.

'Okay.' Kirk responded to Rhys's question in a stronger voice.

Rhys lay on his belly, his head and shoulders hovering above the shaft, while Kirk flicked the powerful LED beam around the base of the mine.

'Shit!'

The exclamation startled Rhys, its tone thick with disbelief. 'What? Have you found gold?'

'Definitely not.' Kirk's voice was quiet now, the words an incredulous quaver. 'Looks like ... a skull?'

'Like a kangaroo that's fallen in? Have another look —there's probably more than one if they were unlucky, like you.'

The seconds ticked by, the only sounds the chitter of birds in the scrub. Rhys shone his torch down the shaft, about to call out again, when Kirk's deep voice resonated,.

'It's human.'

Rhys's veins turned to ice.

Sitting back on his heels, Rhys frowned. Human bones? It was certainly possible, given the terrain and the history of the area. His heart skipped a beat as his eyes swept the surroundings. Wild Willy? 'You're sure?'

'I reckon I am.' Kirk's answer came slowly, each word stilted and clear. 'I think it's a complete skeleton

—fully dressed. Looks like there's something lying next to it, but I can't see from here—and my ankle doesn't want me to move.'

'Don't worry, mate. Once help arrives and we've got you on your way to the hospital, we'll have a closer look.' Rhys ran a hand through his hair while his mind went wild.

'I'm back!'

At Claire's call, Rhys stumbled backwards, dizzy with relief. He scrambled to his feet and crushed her against him. 'Thank God. Did you get through?'

'Yes. Emergency services are on their way. They'll have a helicopter standing by. I guess once the foot team gets here, they'll send someone down to get him into a harness, then winch him clear of the mine shaft. Not sure how long we have to wait, but Mum said she'll lead—so hopefully there won't be a problem with anyone getting lost.' She glanced up at the sky. 'I reckon we've only got two to three hours of daylight left, though.' Grimacing, her flushed face filled with concern. 'How is he?'

'Doing okay. He asked for more painkillers, but I didn't give him any. Umm, there's something else. He reckons there's a human skeleton down there with him.'

Claire clapped her hand on her mouth, her eyes huge. 'Wild Willy.'

Rhys shook his head. 'That's what I thought.' He

waved an arm toward the remains of the timber shack. 'Could be, though. If he lit the place up and did a runner, who knows, he might have fallen down his own mine shaft? As soon as we get Kirk sorted out and have phone service, I'll let CIB know and they'll organise a team to retrieve the remains.'

'Cripes. I didn't expect our camping break to be this eventful?'

'You're not wrong.' He drew her away from the shaft and lowered his voice. 'I reckon we need to do a bit of preparation for the retrieval team.'

Claire nodded. 'I've got to sit down for a few minutes, Rhys. I'm pooped.'

Taking her by the arm, he led her to a log near the edge of the clearing. 'Of course. Sorry. I'm a thought-less bugger.'

She slumped on the rough bark seat and pulled a chocolate bar out of her pocket. 'I'll be fine in a few minutes. Just need an energy boost.'

'Have a rest and then perhaps you could move to the top of the shaft and talk to Kirk while I gather a bit of wood and light a fire over here in the clearing. It'll make us easier to find—and give a bit of warmth once the sun's gone down.'

Their eyes met.

∽

CLAIRE READ the expression in Rhys's gaze and her stomach did a flip.

You don't think they'll get here before dark.

She had only been involved in one search and rescue years earlier—a child who had wandered away and got lost in the bush. It had been twenty-four hours before they found the little one and it had taken the whole town days to recover from the ordeal.

She swallowed hard, reassuring herself that at least this time there was no search. They knew where they were. But a rescue in the dark, especially in this area strewn with rocky outcrops and thick bush, would not be easy for any of them.

30

Shadows grew long as the last of the sun sank in the west. With its departure, the temperatures also dropped, and Claire unrolled their sleeping bags.

Rhys lowered Kirk's down to him while Claire boiled water on the fire. She had just poured them all a mug of tea when the sound of a helicopter cut through the stillness.

'Coo-ee!'

At her mother's familiar call, Claire grabbed her torch and ran. 'We're here! Over here!'

Lights bobbed through the bush while they called to one another.

The joyous reunion was short-lived as Rhys led two of the four rescuers, donned in fluorescent yellow vests, to the edge of the shaft. 'He's down there.' He squatted and called to Kirk, 'Help's arrived, mate. Won't be long now.'

Within minutes, the leader of the team had relayed information via a satellite phone to the helicopter and a massive spotlight was switched on, turning night to day.

Ginny collapsed on the ground next to the shaft, her breath hitching in faint sobs of relief while equipment was being prepared by the others to extract Kirk.

'Kirk, darling. How are you feeling?' Her voice strengthened as Claire knelt beside her mother.

'I'm fine. Not sure I'll be much help mustering those cattle later in the week, though.'

Ginny flung a smile toward Claire when he answered, his deep-throated growl resonating up the shaft.

The chopper hovered overhead, their words deafened as the wind from the blades thrashed the surrounding foliage, flattening shrubs and whipping twigs and leaves from the trees.

A paramedic shinnied down the ladder hanging from the chopper's open door, a rucksack on his back. He was pursued by a second responder, this time lowering a stretcher to the ground.

Everything seemed to happen in a hurry, and Claire pulled her mother back from the shaft before sitting her on the log she had rested on earlier in the day. Handing her a bottle of water, she perched beside her and watched in awed silence as first one, then a second paramedic disappeared down the now well-lit shaft. Minutes later, they returned to the surface with Kirk swaddled in harness and with what vaguely resembled a cricket pad wrapped around his left lower leg.

They lay him on the stretcher, securing him in place while he sucked on a green pain whistle.

'Okay, Mum. Let's find out what the plan is.' Claire took her mother by the arm, and they scurried to the prostrate patient.

Ginny reached for Kirk's hand while Claire caught the attention of one paramedic.

'Where will you take him?'

'It looks like he's got quite a nasty fracture there, so we'll be whipping him straight to Brisbane. I reckon they'll want to keep him for a couple of days while they get him sorted out.' He smiled kindly at Claire. 'Don't worry, love. He's in expert hands.'

She nodded, returning a brief smile. 'Thank you.' She waved toward her mother. 'If she hasn't already, Mum will give you his details. I know she'll be following the helicopter as soon as she can.'

A few minutes later, they winched Kirk into the chopper. Then the door shut, and it swung away to the east.

As the flashing lights disappeared, the bush settled back into a semblance of calm.

Rhys glanced around the group and cleared his throat. 'What's the plan for everyone now? Head back to Featherwood Falls?'

The leader of the rescue party held out his hand. 'Kevin Truman. Sorry I didn't introduce myself properly before. Bit busy and all that.' A smile spread on his weather-beaten round face, and Rhys grinned, shaking the extended paw.

'We'll head back now.' He turned to the three other members of the team. 'What do you reckon, fellas? It's that or camp here for the night and get out in the morning.'

Rhys, Claire, and Ginny joined the discussion before arriving at the decision to have a quick bite to eat, pack up the gear and ensure the fire was out, then make their way back to base by the use of headlamps. Ginny stepped from one foot to the other, unable to sit still.

Claire moved close to her mother, regularly resting a hand on her shoulder or arm as they repacked Kirk's rucksack.

She'll be desperate to get to Brisbane to be with Kirk— and I don't blame her. Claire glanced at Rhys, meeting his kind eyes, and her breath hitched. *I guess that's what love really is.*

THEY SETTLED into a natural formation with Claire and Ginny leading, and Kevin, the team commander, following closely. The two youngest members of the crew, both athletic men in their twenties, tramped a few metres behind Kevin, and last, Rhys and Rob, the fourth member, bringing up the rear.

Conversation was erratic as they negotiated their way through the thick bush before the track opened up and glimpses of twinkling lights in the valley below filtered through the shrubbery. The wind had increased, blowing against them and bringing the occasional sound of a vehicle travelling on the main road through town.

Tramping cautiously in the dark, Rhys tipped his head back as a vaguely recognisable smell assaulted his nostrils. He sniffed the air, but the wind dropped, and the scent was gone. As they continued down the hill, a small clearing provided a brief glimpse of a light shining from a shed near the back boundary of Glenrowan.

Rhys narrowed his gaze, slowing to focus on the area. The outline of a building was just visible through the trees and would have gone unnoticed if it wasn't for the uncurtained light.

He excused himself as he pushed past the young

men to reach Ginny and Claire. 'Is that part of Glenrowan?' He pointed to the light, and the group paused, following the direction of his index finger.

Ginny frowned. 'It's certainly Glenrowan—that fence is their back boundary. But the shed must be new because the Wards had no buildings on their land except the packing shed near the main road and what's around the house.'

'Maybe they've had to build another facility for the tomatoes?'

At Claire's question, Rhys raised his eyebrows.

Ginny gave a small shake of her head. 'If that's the case, why wouldn't they build it near the front road where transport trucks could easily access it?'

'Good point.' Rhys pondered over Ginny's comment as they continued walking. They crossed a bare granite ridge before descending onto the last stretch of track a little before midnight. The wind was stronger now, blowing from the southeast, and Rhys zipped his jacket to his chin.

He took a deep breath, relief driving him on as they neared the end of what had turned out to be an extraordinary day. The smell hit him again.

'Eeew. What's that horrible stink?' Claire exclaimed.

'Yuk. I can smell it, too. Some sort of chemical? Perhaps Lars has sprayed all the weeds,' Ginny added.

Rhys shrugged as realisation dawned. A flashback to a nasty job from his early days of policing—in the depths of a sleezy, junk-filled farm at the back of the Gold Coast.

Keeping the thoughts to himself, his mind raced as they loaded the gear onto the assortment of vehicles parked in the paddock. Another fifteen minutes and they would be back to Featherwood Station, and he had only one focus—to get through the rest of the night as quickly as possible and ring James Avery at first light in the morning.

Light streamed from every crevice of the homestead, the veranda illuminated as though in daylight when the weary hikers eventually tumbled out of vehicles and trod their way up the path.

Lola greeted them effusively with a touch of her hand, a hug, and a sympathetic word while Frank stood at the stove in Ginny's kitchen, stirring the contents of a large saucepan.

'Come and sit down, everyone. Have a bowl of hot soup and some fresh bread before you go shooting off home.'

With wild earrings swinging, she bustled everyone inside, including Ginny, who appeared to accept this takeover of her home with relief, plonking herself at the head of the table and resting her head on her hands, elbows propped on the polished timber.

As they ate the tasty food, the group visibly perked up, agreeing that the next step was to get home to their own families and beds as soon as possible.

And a little over half an hour later, Rhys's vehicle was the only one left in the yard.

'I'm sorry it was such a traumatic day for you.' Stroking Claire's hair, he held her in his arms while she leaned against him, exhaustion once again taking over her body.

She pulled back, her arms still loose around his waist, and gave him a smile.

'Thank you for everything. You've been fantastic today. I don't know what I would have done if it had just been Kirk and me up there.'

'Don't think about it. We're all safe now—and you need sleep.'

He squeezed her again, then reluctantly released her and stepped toward his ute.

'I'll ring you in the morning.'

She nodded. 'Sleep well.'

Doubting sleep would come easily after the events of the day, he grinned as he slid into the vehicle and started the engine.

With the knowledge the Stanthorpe office was taking care of his calls, and being disturbed during the night would be unlikely, Rhys stood under a hot shower for much longer than usual. He tumbled into bed relaxed and warm while the wind howled outside, thrashing a tree branch against Rhys's little home. He drew the doona up around his neck and was asleep within seconds.

31

The sun filtered through the bedroom blind when Rhys woke the following morning. He glanced at the bedside clock, one eye closed. Could it be right? He blinked and rubbed a hand over his face. Almost eight-thirty?

Slinging his legs over the side of the bed, he stretched before pulling the cord on the blind, allowing the autumn sunshine to flood the room.

Astounded he had slept so heavily and for much longer than usual, he took a few minutes to splash his face with cold water and do some stretches. An ache in his lower back reminded him of the previous day's activities—at least twenty kilometres of walking, plus the physical exertions of getting Claire in and out of the mine shaft and dragging fallen branches to form a fire. Add the heightened adrenaline that came hand in hand with emergencies—no wonder he'd slept well.

Half an hour later, he sat in front of the desk phone in the station office, his long legs stretched out under the desk.

'Detective Senior Constable James Avery.'

'Hi, James. It's Rhys, from Featherwood Falls.'

The sound of a chair scraping on a timber floor filtered through the airwaves. 'Rhys. How're you getting on, mate? Sorry, I still haven't got down to collect that money,' he blurted as though feeling guilty about neglecting his earlier promise.

'That's okay. I know you're busy—and it's not going anywhere.'

'Have you received any more? Only you mentioned the packages had been arriving every three months, according to your postman.'

'No. Three months have been and gone and there's been nothing. Umm. Something else has cropped up, though, and I'm looking for some advice.'

'Sure. Fire away.'

Rhys downloaded the events of the previous day, highlighting the discovery of the skeleton at the bottom of the mine shaft and his suspicions of who it might be following his unearthing of Wild Willie's story in the police logbook.

'Geez, Rhys. You really have dived in the deep end

there. It seems it's a busier place than district office at the moment.'

Rhys gave a small laugh before switching to the subject of the shed at the back of Glenrowan.

'Call me suspicious minded, but something is going on there. I'm sure of it. The problem is, I've got no evidence and no reason to do an inspection—unless someone else knows more than I do or has powers I don't.'

'So, you thinking what I'm thinking? Do some surveillance, then if it shows anything worth investigating, get a warrant and pay a surprise visit at daybreak?'

'That sounds like a good place to start.'

'Okay. I know you're supposedly on days off, but I think we need to get onto it straight away. If you don't mind, I'll bring a couple of my team with me and come down. We'll have a chat about things and get the ball rolling—not only to explore this mine shaft you mentioned, but to see if we can arrange an inspection of Glenrowan.'

'Sounds good.'

'Righto. Leave it with me. I'll get the guys organised here and call you on your mobile before we leave, so you've got an idea of when to expect us.'

They disconnected the call, and Rhys returned to his tiny living room to unpack his rucksack. He put a load of washing on, startled to receive another call from James within minutes.

'We're leaving now. See you in an hour.'

Rhys glanced at his watch. That made the meeting at eleven. 'Okay. See you then.'

He threw off his jeans and shirt and dressed in uniform while the washing machine gurgled and hummed in the laundry beside the back porch.

Returning to the office, Rhys gathered his notebook and rang Claire.

'Hi,' she answered immediately, and his face softened.

'Hi. How are you feeling this morning? Tired?'

'A bit. And sore—but I'm sure poor Kirk is worse.'

'He will be. Any news?'

'Yeah. Mum rang the hospital after everyone left here last night. They said he was stable and has to wait until sometime today for the orthopaedic surgeon to see him.'

'Poor bugger. Is your mum going to Brisbane?'

'She's already there. Left at six o'clock this morning and rang half an hour ago to say she arrived safely and was parking the car. I think, depending on how long they reckon Kirk will be there, she'll get a motel close by somewhere and walk to and from the hospital.'

'Okay. Is there anything I can do to help while she's gone?'

'No. We talked before she left and we'll leave the cattle for a few days—at least until we know what's going on with Kirk. I'm here to feed the animals and run the dogs. Oh, and exercise the horses ... If you get any time off while she's away, you might like to come for a ride with me? I think Splash is quite happy with you on board,' she finished with a small giggle.

'Okay. I've got the CIB fellas coming shortly. We'll be organising for the skeleton to be extracted, so, with yours and your mother's permission, of course, a forensic officer will take care of that. I guess they'll need me to take them there, too. Is that okay?'

'Of course. I want to find out who it is as much as you do.'

'Umm ...' He dithered for a moment before continuing, 'We might also request access to inspect the shed at the back of Glenrowan from Featherwood Station. I'll let you know what's going on as soon as I can.'

'Oh. Sounds intriguing.'

He breathed a long sigh. 'Yeah. I have a few suspicions and could be proven wrong—but something tells me I won't be this time.'

'Would you like me to nip over and do another night time inspection?' she joked.

'Don't you dare.' His voice was soft, but his words came out more harshly than he meant. 'Don't go anywhere near that place.'

'Don't worry. I won't. I'll be lying low while Mum's away. The last thing I want is for that revolting Lars to realise I'm here on my own.'

'You don't have to be,' he said firmly. 'If you need a bodyguard, I'd be delighted to oblige.'

She laughed—the same rich sound he loved so much.

'Okay, Romeo. You do your work, and I'll do mine, and we'll talk again later. '

'Sounds good to me.'

They said goodbye, and he slipped his phone into his pocket, the smile on his face widening.

FOR THE FIRST hour of their meeting, the discussion focused on the events surrounding Kirk's fall, the discovery of the skeleton, and the possibilities of a cold case being solved after more than eighty years.

'I know you're hopeful, Rhys, especially after hearing about what you found in those old logbooks ... But remember, nothing is in the bag until the tests are done. If these bones are a match for Nigel Ward's DNA, then I reckon we'll be able to close the case. But ... you know, it could be anyone. Only time will tell.'

Rhys gave a curt nod while Paul, one of the younger officers, tapped his pen on the desk.

'Okay. You mentioned something about suspicious activity in a shed on Glenrowan?' Paul asked.

'Yeah. There was a distinct aroma on the wind last

night—one I've smelled before. I'd like to see if we could arrange surveillance of the place and gather evidence in the hope we can understand it. Even if I'm wrong—and I hope I am—those Shepherd women next door have already gone through enough and I want to ensure they're safe.' Rhys slumped in his chair while the other men digested his comments.

'You're right, Rhys. This is what I suggest we do.' James placed his notes in front of the others, and Rhys's hopes leapt. 'We'll meet here at six in the morning equipped with everything we need to get in and out of the mine shaft, declare the site as a crime scene if that appears to be what it is, and prepare it accordingly. Rhys can show us where he spotted the shed, and we'll work out the best place for a camera. Then I guess it will be a waiting game for a couple of days. Forensics will take care of the bones and provide us with results in due course, and Rhys can check the camera after, say, three days and report on what it reveals.' He nodded at Rhys. 'Okay by you?'

'Yep.' *Now we're making progress.*

IT TOOK LESS than an hour to arrange a forensic officer who was prepared to hike the twenty-kilometre round trip to retrieve the bones. Rhys would lead, and James,

Paul, and Oliver, the two uniformed associates from district office, would accompany him together with the forensic officer whose name was Stephen Muller. With that sorted, they turned their attention to arranging which surveillance camera to use and discussing further subtle inspections of the area, including Dingo Gully Road.

'You believe whatever's going on in this shed has something to do with those two bikies who laid the complaint against you?' Oliver asked.

'Yes. And I don't trust that fellow Donald Shepherd hired to run the farm. My suspicion might only be a gut feeling—but it hasn't let me down in the past.'

'Right then. We need to gather evidence in order to prove you're right—and we need to begin now.' James got to his feet and held his empty mug out. 'After another coffee.'

They laughed. While Rhys got up to make another round of drinks, he took stock of his companions. Smile wrinkles around his eyes and mouth highlighted James' kind face. From the detective's experience and the few comments Rhys had heard when at district office, he guessed him to be around early fifties, but with his slight, athletic build, he looked younger. Paul and Oliver were of a similar age to himself, and both looked fit and strong. Rhys exhaled quietly while enthusiasm bubbled. He was desperate to understand both issues—leaving only one unsolved secret that he doubted would be unravelled: that of the money sitting in the safe.

He filled the kettle and stared through the kitchen window, his eyes narrowing.

If this raid on Glenrowan reveals what I reckon it will, I'd lay my bets on those money packages being connected.

32

*A*s soon as Rhys finished the day's duties, he changed out of his uniform and drove to Featherwood Station as the shadows lengthened. Rain threatened, and he frowned at the thought. Hiking up to the mines in bad weather was not what they needed, and he hoped that this time, any precipitation would bypass them.

Claire was at the kennels when he arrived, and the kelpies ran toward him, their tails wagging and tongues lolling with excitement.

'Hello, you lot.' He ruffled their ears and made a fuss of each before strolling toward Claire. The dogs bounded alongside him as he walked then leapt into their respective kennels to gobble their kibble.

Claire smiled, latching the cage doors before turning toward him. 'Perfect timing. I've just finished.'

She linked her arm in his. 'Come and join me for dinner. I've made shepherd's pie.'

'Yum.' The skin around his eyes creased as he smiled.

'I can't wait to hear what the plan is,' she said.

She opened a bottle of cabernet merlot and poured them both a glass.

'So ... tell me.'

He downloaded the details of their meeting, adding the bit about needing her permission to set up a camera somewhere close enough to Glenrowan to capture any activity but far enough away to not be detectable.

'You know you have our permission. Mum would want to know what's going on there as much as I do—even though, deep down, I hope it's nothing to worry about and the shed is full of boxed tomatoes waiting to be collected.' She raised her eyebrows hopefully and poured a second glass of wine. 'Can I come with you?'

He angled his head slightly. 'You can—but what about the jobs around here? Won't you have to feed up? Anyway, what if your mother rings? If you're in the bush with us, you won't be able to talk to her. And, besides that, I want you to be safe—especially if there is something going on next door.'

She slumped. 'Yeah. You're right. I suppose if someone like Uncle Donald turns up and finds no-one here, they might just come looking and find the vehicles parked at the edge of the bush. We don't want to blow your cover.'

He laughed and took her hand. 'You've been watching too many cop movies.'

'Okay then. I'll drive you to our usual parking spot so you can leave whatever vehicles you don't need back at the station. That way, it won't appear as though we've got something really juicy happening here on the off chance that someone flies a drone or a plane over our place.'

'How about we work that out when the guys arrive in the morning? For now, I'm happy to hear how Kirk's getting on—and eat that delicious food that's driving my stomach crazy.'

'Kirk's fine, but it'll be another four or five days before they'll let him come home. Mum's staying down there with him, so I'm in charge here. And I say we eat first—and then decide what comes next.'

She kissed his cheek and, with a chortle, picked up a pair of pot mitts and moved toward the oven.

RELIEVED THE RAIN had not arrived, Rhys waited for James and his team in the main office as the night moved to daylight. For the second time in as many days, he rechecked his rucksack, ensuring he had all the equipment, food, and water.

His nerves jangled. He'd only been to the remains of the hut twice and, although sure he wouldn't get lost, was acutely aware that they would test his leadership skills today more than ever before.

Right on six o'clock, a police four-wheel drive, exactly the same as the Featherwood Station vehicle, pulled up outside.

Locking the door behind him, he swept up his rucksack and strode to the vehicle. 'Gidday, all.'

Windows rolled down and without stepping outside, Paul introduced Stephen Muller, the forensic officer sitting in the front passenger seat. James got out of the driver's seat and walked around the back to open the rear door, and Rhys laid his pack on top of the others, filling the storage area.

Three of them in the back seat was a squeeze, but they all agreed the fewer vehicles required, the better.

Claire was waiting and invited them in to use the bathroom or have a hot drink before they headed off.

James shook his head, his impatience to get going obvious to all.

Four hours after leaving Claire at the gate into the bush, Rhys was delighted to wave his arm around the clearing in front of them. 'This is it, fellas. The shaft is over there where those logs are.'

After a few minutes to recharge energy and have a drink, Paul and Oliver set up a rope ladder that dangled into the shaft while Stephen unpacked his equipment.

Knowing it would not be a quick procedure, Rhys gathered firewood and lit a fire before unpacking the food Claire had put together for them.

Taking turns, the men joined Stephen at the bottom of the mine, assisting with sample collection and photography.

An excited call from Oliver echoed up the shaft. 'There's an old rifle here!'

Over lunch, they studied the weapon and skeleton, and Rhys produced the photocopy he had made of the logbook notes from 1937.

'Yep. That rifle definitely appears to be an old military .303—the same as the one reported missing in the log.' James squinted at the rotting timber stock and the rusted barrel.

'I think you're right. Looks like this is the missing man. Guess we'll soon know, anyway,' Rhys replied.

'Okay, one last trip into the depths and we'll bag the items and then get going. If we muck around much longer, we'll be in the dark.'

With the skeleton, gun, and remnants of clothing securely bagged and labelled, the men packed up and began the return trek. The wind had strengthened again and late in the afternoon, as they approached the spot where Rhys had sighted the shed only two days earlier, they halted.

'This is where I first smelt the chemicals,' Rhys said. 'And there's the shed.' He pointed, and they crowded around.

Sniffing the air like a bloodhound, James grimaced. 'You're right. I'd know that stink anywhere. A meth lab.'

The energy seemed to increase between them, and a five-minute discussion ensued, working out where the best place to put the camera would be and running through the potential risks.

Using the binoculars, James remained silent for a few moments. 'Rhys. Has that road always been there?'

'What road?'

James handed the binoculars to Rhys and pointed while Rhys focused the glasses against his eyes. He removed them for a moment, squinted toward the shed, and lifted the field glasses again, confirming James's discovery. A thin brown line ran between two rows of fencing.

'Shit. You're right. That's new. You can see the fence lines have been there a while. There's even a broken post halfway along—but the actual road looks as though it's new. There are hunks of soil along the edges with grass growing out of them.' He turned slowly, the binoculars glued to his eyes as he followed the road to the south. He gasped as it disappeared into a block of pine forest—the same forest that began on Dingo Gully Road farther up from Taylor's dairy farm.

Swinging his gaze back to the shed, he held his breath as he focused on it. There was no sign of life, but he waited for another couple of minutes before facing his companions. 'I knew those bikies were up to no good.'

'What are you talking about?' Oliver asked.

As patiently as he could, Rhys summarised the interaction with Bruce Taylor, the two bikies, and the subsequent complaints laid against him soon after arriving. He added the conversation he had had with Lars and the details Claire had shared after seeing Lars and the bikies outside the Stanthorpe pub.

All four men stared at him in silence before Paul moved. 'I'm with you, Rhys. There's something going on here. I'd bet my life on it. Let's get that camera up asap.'

It took a while to find the exact spot suitable for the camera. With everyone satisfied it was well concealed yet in the right position to pick up any movement, they continued their hike to where they had parked the police vehicle that morning.

Stephen was quiet, and Rhys shot a glance at his exhausted face.

Once again, Claire must have heard the vehicle approaching, as she was waiting at the gate when they pulled up.

The sun had just set, the skies a mix of vibrant orange and pink. As the men tumbled out of the Land-Cruiser, the horizon faded quickly, leaving the valley filled with muted colours that darkened with every minute.

'I've got a pot of pumpkin soup on cooking. Thought you might all like some before you head home again?' Claire offered.

Oliver nudged Rhys. 'Don't get that sort of invitation very often.'

'Thanks, Claire. That would be very welcome,' James said.

33

*T*hree days later, Rhys and Claire rode toward the site where the camera was installed. Mounted on Splash, Rhys felt comfortable and was enjoying the ride more than he had on the previous occasion. *Probably because I'm fitter.*

It was to be their last night together as Kirk and Ginny would return to Featherwood Station the following day—complete with crutches, a plastered leg, and a list of instructions from the orthopaedic surgeon.

The cattle Rhys and Claire had moved bellowed in the distance, the newly weaned calves indignantly calling their mothers as though their separation had been their fault.

Rhys grinned. 'Those babies are not happy.'

Claire snorted. 'Babies! Not anymore. They're

nearly as big as their poor mothers, and if the cows don't get a break from them over winter, they won't do an outstanding job of rearing their new calves come spring.'

'I know. We used to do the same on Mum and Dad's place—although our little herd wasn't exactly big. We fed the calves extra hay and a bit of grain to get them through winter and no-one seemed to suffer.'

'That's really why I wanted to get them weaned before it gets any colder.' She looked toward the southern sky. 'The weather report says we're in for a cold snap next week.'

Rhys nodded. 'Let's hope we can get this issue sorted out before then. I don't fancy the early mornings once the temperature drops below freezing.'

They drew to a halt at the gate leading into the bush and dismounted.

'Shall I come with you? The horses will be fine tied up here,' Claire said.

'Sure. We'll be back within the hour. Will they stand here that long?'

'Yeah. They've done a bit of work this morning, so they'll be glad of a rest.'

Within minutes, they were traversing the ridge inside the bush, heading off the main track toward the boundary between Featherwood Station and Glenrowan.

Rhys paused and Claire pressed against him,

following his gaze as they remained in the shadow of a large leptospermum shrub, bent over to avoid its small, prickly leaves.

'What are you waiting for?' she asked.

'Just checking there's no movement here. I doubt they'd see us, but we need to be careful. If I'm right, we're dealing with dangerous people, and must take every precaution.'

'O-kaay,' Claire said slowly, her eyes widening.

'You stay here. I'll nip over to the camera, switch the cards, and be back in a couple of minutes.'

He darted away, sticking to the cover of the bush. Minutes later, he was back and, clutching hands, they hurried back to the horses.

Once home, they unsaddled and brushed the horses before releasing them.

Rhys kissed Claire. 'I've got to download whatever's on this card and get it to James as soon as possible. I'll be back as soon as I can.'

'Okay.' Her gaze followed him to the vehicle with an ache in her heart as that now familiar face remained etched in her mind.

When are they going to decide if you are staying here or being moved on? I can't bear it much longer.

RHYS COULDN'T BELIEVE what he was seeing. He recorded the times, noting that the black ute arrived around daybreak each morning, followed by two motorcyclists an hour later. The vehicles drove along the new road, however, at ten o'clock each evening, a farm utility turned up, emerging from the trees near the Featherwood Station boundary. The previous afternoon, a white Pantech truck had also driven along the dirt road, and less than an hour later, the recording showed it leaving again.

Rhys replayed the footage, peering closely at the screen to identify the drivers. Although he couldn't see their faces, he was certain the driver of both the black and the farm vehicles was Lars. His white hair stood out while his build showed a tall, well-muscled man. Of the bikies, Rhys couldn't be sure. Both wore beards but under their helmets and leathers, at that distance they could have been any motorcyclist. As for the van, it was impossible to see the driver's face, but, when he zoomed in, he could make out both the registration number and confirm the driver was small and dark-haired.

A surge of adrenaline pumped through his veins. He had been right.

He saved the footage to the computer and attached it to an email and forwarded it to James. Picking up the phone, he dialled.

'Rhys. What's happening?'

'I've just sent you the recordings from the last three days. I was right. Have a look at it and tell me what you think. I'm certain the driver of both the black and farm utes is Lars, but it's hard to see who the others are. Seems all but the white truck is there every morning for about an hour. Lars gets there real early, and the bikies turn up about an hour later.'

'Righto. Give me a second and I'll pull it up.'

Rhys waited, staring impatiently at the clock as the seconds ticked by.

Eventually, James spoke again. 'Yep. I don't think we should wait any longer. I'll get a warrant this afternoon and organise the boys to do a raid at seven in the morning. Okay with you?'

'Absolutely. I've had the afternoon off today to make up for the other day, but I'll be back to normal tomorrow.'

'Good.' They worked out the finer details, including who would be where, how they would converge together and where they would meet for the early morning briefing.

'I'll take a run out to Dingo Gully Road in my ute shortly—have a look at that road and make sure there are no padlocks or electric fences we've got to get through. I'll call you back afterwards and let you know.'

'Perfect. Thanks, Rhys. I should have the warrant by then. I'll nip next door to the courthouse now.'

Without wasting another minute, Rhys clapped his battered Akubra on his head and glanced down at his filthy jeans and shirt. 'Perfect,' he muttered.

No-one will even know it's me.

He snatched up his keys, locked the doors, and strode to his ute.

Passing Taylor's farm while milking was in session, he slowed, eager to avoid attention, and continued along the gravel before slowing again as the road ran into dirt. As with the new track that had appeared at the back of Glenrowan, it was smoother here than it had been earlier in the year.

He turned onto the forestry road and followed the track in a northerly direction. At the end of the thick swathe of pines, a stretch of horizontal wires held together at intervals with fibreglass posts ran across the track, and Rhys's heart sank. He got out and walked to the end where it connected to the main wire fence and touched it carefully with a finger. Reassured it wasn't electric, he unhooked it and pulled it back, his heart thumping in his chest.

The last thing he needed was to be caught on a private road without permission—*if it is one?* He drove through the temporary gateway before stopping again and re-erecting it. As quickly as he dared, he covered another two kilometres before the familiar row of trees that surrounded the shed came into view. Content with his discovery, he did a U-turn and parked so that he could reinstate any grass his wheels had disturbed. With a small, leafy switch from a nearby shrub, he covered the signs of a vehicle, and hurried back to the station, taking care to ensure the gate was exactly as he had found it.

After another conversation with James, his evening passed in a state of feverish anticipation.

He phoned Claire and told her what would be happening. 'So don't leave the house yard if you can avoid it,' he finished. 'The animals can wait an hour or two. We really need to get this lot cleaned up first.'

'Okay. I get it. A couple of vehicles will be driving past our house really early in the morning—before daybreak—and will head to the back corner boundary where officers will be dropped off. Then the cars will leave and park out of sight until called. I'll make sure the first couple of gates are open for you, and after that, you will ensure you leave every gate as you find it.'

'Correct. The dog squad will wait here at the station until they get the word to come. James will be with me and a few other guys. You probably won't hear anything more until it's all over.

'Okay.' Her voice shook. 'Take care, Rhys.'

'I will. I promise.'

34

*T*apping his fingers on the steering wheel, Rhys's heart thumped as he waited for Xavier, the young constable, to open the gate.

'We've struck it lucky with the fog. Should muffle the sound of our engines.'

Rhys met James's gaze as the detective spoke, catching the repetitive twisting of his wedding ring out of the corner of his eye. *You're as keyed up as me.*

A heavy mist hung over the valley, stretching along the creek until it reached the bush on the hills. It was cold and Rhys leaned over and turned the heater up before driving through the open gateway. He stopped well clear to allow the following vehicle room to pull up behind him and waited for Xavier.

The door slammed and James swung around,

frowning. 'Quiet, mate. And make sure your phones are on silent.'

'Sorry.'

'Remember, stealth is the key. It's a raid, not a bloody party.'

Rhys raised an eyebrow. James had previously shown an elevated level of calm in the dealings they'd had. It seemed that this time he had a lot riding on his shoulders, and efficiency was paramount if execution of the warrant was to be successful.

Rhys glanced in the rear-view mirror at the three in the back seat. While Duncan had more than twenty years' experience, Xavier and Mark, the constables, were on their first big assignment. Another five officers occupied the vehicle behind them.

Not a word was spoken as they traversed the farm, sticking to the tracks that wove around the hills and avoiding the higher areas where sound could travel. The fog thickened as they neared Glenrowan and the vehicles crawled, increasing speed only when met with random patches of clear visibility.

'This is it.' Rhys braked in a dip at the foot of a fog-shrouded hill and waved toward it. 'That runs down to the back boundary of Glenrowan.'

The second vehicle pulled up beside him and five men got out.

'Right.' James spoke quietly, his voice low. 'Chris, you and Selwyn take the vehicles back to the station.

You know the plan from there. The rest of us will cover the last five hundred metres on foot.' He pointed into the fog. 'Stay close to Rhys as we climb the hill and descend to the boundary. He knows the way and, although this fog is helpful, we don't want anyone getting lost. Rhys, Xavier, Mark, and I will each station ourselves near the four corners of the building. Malik, Chad, Colin, and Duncan, as discussed, you will wait in hiding until signalled. Once we're in position, we lie low until the bikies have arrived and are inside with Lars.' He glanced around the men as they murmured and nodded in acknowledgement.

'Chris and Selwyn will bring reinforcements.' The two-way crackled softly on the front of his vest and he squatted, pulling it to his mouth. 'Go ahead.'

'Dog squad are in position.'

'Got that.'

He stood again and nodded. 'They're in the southern plantation, so we've got all exits covered.' He turned to the two youngest officers. 'We're dealing with tough men here. Be on your guard.'

With a final equipment check conducted, Chris and Selwyn got into the vehicles and slowly drove away. The others flanked Rhys and James as they climbed the hill in the eerie grey light.

Weak morning sunbeams filtered through the mist as they hunkered down in their respective positions. Rhys pressed his back against the melaleuca trunk, rearranging the prickly leaves so he could peer through them.

The sound of a vehicle approaching drifted toward him and he froze, his pulse pounding in his ears. Blanketed by the fog, he was unable to determine which direction it was coming from but there was no denying the rattle of a Toyota utility. The engine died and a door slammed before quiet descended once again. Not even a bird call broke the silence.

Rhys lowered himself to a squat, stretching his back and rolling his stiff shoulders. Time seemed to tick slowly, and his mind drifted to a vision of Claire, curled in a warm, cosy bed.

The distinctive rumble of Harley Davidsons approached. Rhys shot to a standing position again. He glanced at his watch. Five minutes to seven.

Hairs on the back of his neck rose as the muffled sound of voices carried through the bush. A door clanged, the ring of metal on steel, while a whiff of chemicals assaulted Rhys's nostrils.

From his post, he could make out Duncan's bulk on his right—nothing more than a dark mound tucked behind a pile of dirt in the ditch alongside the track. A sense of reassurance touched him. Duncan was built like a front row forward and, although not a fast runner, he was strong and determined—the perfect partner for the job. The others were out of sight, but

Rhys was sure they would be tensed, ready to pounce the second they received the command.

It came suddenly—James's voice firm over the two-way radio. 'Bring the cars and dog squad up now. We're going in.' There was a moment's pause. Then he said, 'Go, go, go!'

As he ran, Rhys glanced to his right. Duncan was only metres away and though the mist impeded his line of sight, footsteps sounded behind him.

He hammered on the door. 'Armed police. We have a warrant to search the premises. Open up immediately!'

Scuffling noises came from inside and a second later, the sound of glass smashing echoed in the fog.

'Stand back!' James's command filled Rhys's left ear and he leapt back as without hesitation, Duncan and Malik rammed the door with a metal battering ram.

Rhys and Duncan charged through the door at the same time as Lars rushed at them brandishing a length of steel. Duncan bent over and launched himself at the man's legs, bringing him crashing to the concrete floor. Tramping on the wrist that held the weapon, Rhys snatched Lars's spare arm and twisted it behind his back. Lars emitted a strangled yell, and the bar flew across the ground as he lay face down amongst an array of broken glass and liquids.

It happened so quickly, Rhys barely had time to think. One minute he was facing the evil-looking

Viking, and the next he was snapping the handcuffs around the man's wrists. He shot a glance toward Duncan. 'You alright, mate?'

'Yeah.' A wide grin spread across the big man's face as a trickle of blood ran down his forehead. 'Still got it.'

Rhys returned the grin as they marched Lars outside, turning him to face the wall.

'Piss off!' Lars growled.

Within minutes, two more bikies emerged from the shed, cuffed and escorted by Chad, Colin, and Xavier.

'We're missing one,' James yelled. He bent his head and spoke into the two-way. 'Dog squad, there's a suspect on the loose.'

A panting voice surged over the radio. 'He dived out the window and headed for the bush. I lost him. He's gone to ground but he's here somewhere.'

'Righto, Mark. The dog's on its way,' James replied.

Another voice responded by radio. 'Dog squad here. ETA three minutes.'

'Great. Mark, keep watch but don't contaminate the area.'

'Roger, received.'

While they waited, James directed two officers to search the handcuffed suspects and handed them a wad of evidence bags and a black marker pen. 'Record all possessions found. Rhys and I will conduct a quick search of the shed.'

A row of vats lined one wall and a table sat near the

door, laden with clip-seal bags of white powder. It took no time to verify the contents of the shed indicated a sophisticated drug lab operation. 'We'd better get out of here,' James said. 'It's not safe. Best left to the experts to dismantle it.'

Rhys followed him outside as the dog squad arrived and screeched to a halt. A handler leapt from the vehicle, a lead in hand, and within seconds had the dog harnessed.

'Where are you, Mark? Which way did he go?' the handler said into his radio.

'Mark here. On the western side. He can't have got far.'

The dog handler disappeared around the side of the shed as the paddy wagon and support vehicles arrived.

Fifteen minutes later, Mark and the dog handler returned at a steady pace, a bloodied and battered bikie between them.

Mark inclined his head toward the suspect. 'We'll need an ambulance. This fella's got some nasty cuts from diving through the window.'

James nodded and pulled a mobile phone out of his pocket. He punched in a few numbers before speaking. 'Ambulance please.' It took a few moments to organise the assistance before James ended the call and faced the officers. 'We'll take them to Warwick to begin the process and leave this mess to the drug squad.' James glanced around the growing crowd of officers as the fog thinned and the sun warmed their backs.

'Good work, fellas.'

It felt like the middle of the night when Claire woke to the sound of vehicles driving slowly past the house. She glanced at her bedside table. Five o'clock. Outside a boobook owl hooted, and her heart leapt. It had begun.

For the next five hours, she heard nothing. She tried to go back to sleep but couldn't. Her mouth was dry and her pulse pounding. Giving up, she dressed and made herself a pot of tea.

By eight o'clock, she had completed a book cover she'd been struggling with. The author had given her little guidance, telling her to do what she liked but then voicing her unhappiness with whatever she'd come up with. This time, though, Claire was sure she had nailed it and she smiled. Maybe all she'd needed was a solid dose of nervous excitement and an early start.

The sun was high in the sky, the chooks squawking in protest at their lack of breakfast before the sound of a vehicle approached the homestead.

She glanced through the window, confirming it was the police before she ran into the yard.

Rhys pulled up and rolled down the window. His face glowed with a mixture of happiness and relief.

'Did everything go according to plan?' Claire asked.

'Sure did. Like clockwork. We got Lars and three bikies—including the two I questioned after Bruce Taylor's complaint.'

'And the shed? What was in it?'

'A methamphetamine laboratory. It was the chemicals they use in the production that we smelt when we were coming back from the hut.'

'Wow! So, no dope?'

Rhys laughed, turning to the officer beside him. 'That was a bonus we hadn't expected. You know the poly-tunnels you had a look at?'

She nodded. 'Yeah. Full of hydroponic tomatoes.'

'Well, they didn't contain just tomatoes. Tucked in the middle of several rows of the fruit was a plantation of marijuana—in every poly-tunnel.'

'Cripes. Worth a bit, then?'

The other officer leaned forward, a smile across his face. 'You could say that. Millions, I would reckon. It was no small setup, that's for sure.' He paused. 'I'm Duncan.'

Claire's jaw dropped in astonishment. 'Hi Duncan. So, what happens now?'

'We'll be busy for a couple of days. The drug squad

will take over the removal of everything necessary. The culprits will go before the court, and we'll be tracking down your uncle for questioning, not to mention the white Pantech.' Rhys reached for her hand. 'Sorry, it's all so close to home for you.'

Claire shook her head. 'I can't believe it. Right here in our quiet little town. A drug cartel, a historical death that hopefully will answer a lot of questions that have been asked for decades—and a newfound relative that I'm not sure is welcome given the last couple of years' events.'

Rhys touched her face. 'I know, love. I've gotta go now and get all this stuff sorted out, but I'll ring you later.'

She nodded and managed a small smile. 'Okay. Mum and Kirk should be home by then.'

'Good. I look forward to hearing how everyone is. See you later,' he said softly.

'See ya.' She remained glued to the spot as the vehicle drove away.

Despite her head spinning, a warm glow filled Claire. He had called her love. Did that mean he really felt more than he let on? Suddenly, the importance of him being assigned the permanent position seemed irrelevant. No matter what happened, she was certain their lives together were only just beginning.

35

*S*oon after lunch, Rhys looked up as the door opened for the umpteenth time. 'Frank. How are you?'

The snowy-haired man beamed, his eyes almost disappearing in the surrounding folds of skin. 'I'm good. More to the point—how are you?'

Rhys tilted his head a little. Why would Frank be asking ... unless he had already heard whisper of the early morning events. 'Fine.'

'So, it is true? That lot on Glenrowan have been growing drugs?'

He flashed Frank a wry grin. 'Yeah. There's been a bit going on there—but they've been busted now, so hopefully once everything's wound up, life around here can return to normal.'

Frank snorted. 'What's normal? Lola's always said

these little towns have secrets as big as the big cities do —it just takes a time to uncover them.' He frowned, his tone lighter as he continued, 'She's been talking to Ginny and apparently, Ginny's bringing Kirk home today. Another incident on the mend, aye?'

'Yes. That was all unfortunate.' Rhys glanced around him as if to confirm he was alone again. 'Did Ginny say anything more?'

'You mean about the skeleton in the mine?'

Rhys met the old man's knowing expression.

'Yeah,' he said casually. 'Good to have that sorted out, too—at least we know what happened to the old scoundrel.'

Rhys raised an eyebrow. 'We haven't received confirmation yet that it was Wild Willy.'

'Yeah—but I bet you my last cent it is him.'

Rhys wasn't so sure, but he certainly hoped so. Although he hadn't read every station log yet, he had found no other reports of people missing in the area— other than a couple of children who had been found safe and well.

'Righto. I can see you're busy, so I'll head off.' Frank inclined his head toward the scattered papers on Rhys's desk. 'Catch you tonight at Ginny's. We're all heading there for dinner.'

'Okay. See you then.'

The door closed again, and Rhys returned his attention to the computer.

As the afternoon drifted on, Rhys's energy waned, and by three o'clock, he yawned and stretched, fighting to stay awake. The adrenaline had long since worn off, leaving him a ragged zombie, and he gave up and closed the computer.

'Coffee, I think—and a quick nap,' he said aloud.

He locked the door and was on his way to the kitchen when the phone rang. Groaning, he resisted answering for a few seconds. Then he snatched it up, chiding himself for even considering the thought.

'Rhys.' The deep tones of Inspector Jones emphasised his name with a pleasant lilt.

'Hello, Inspector.'

'I wanted to congratulate you. Not just on your diligence, but your leadership, too. Great results.'

'Thank you, sir. It's been a busy time, but I'm happy we got to the bottom of the Glenrowan issue, anyway. Just have to see what forensics come back with the skeleton from the mine, I guess. Hopefully that may be another mystery solved.'

'Yes, I'll be following that up—we should have received a result by now.'

'How did the interview go with Donald Shepherd? Is he the ringleader?'

'He denies all knowledge of the drug business. Is adamant he employed Lars to supervise the growing of corn and tomatoes and nothing else—but time will tell. He might be telling the truth. We'll see what the investigation reveals.'

'Okay. I'd be interested to hear how Donald and Lars met?'

'Well, Mr Shepherd claims Lars approached him at his property one day looking for work.'

There was a pause, and Rhys frowned. 'Really?'

'That's what he said. We have to accept his version in the absence of any other evidence to the contrary.' The older man cleared his throat. 'There's another thing.'

Rhys's interest piqued. Hadn't they covered everything?

'You have been chosen as the number one applicant and are offered the position of officer in charge of Featherwood Station. Are you prepared to accept it?'

Rhys's jaw dropped. Barely able to contain his excitement, he forgot his weariness. 'Yes, sir.'

'Congratulations, Senior Constable Rhys Morton.'

'Thank you, sir.'

'I'll have someone bring the paperwork out for you to sign. I'm proud of you, and I know your dad will be too.'

Rhys could barely speak. 'Thank you,' he said again.

'Oh, by the way. James Avery has briefed me on the money that turned up at the station. When the officer brings out the paperwork, would you please give the package to him?'

'Okay. Will there be any further action taken regarding Stan?'

'Well—this is the situation. Stan is not talking to us. The only thing we have at the moment is the package of money. We don't know where it came from and there is no offence in sending money to a police station. Therefore, there are no elements to substantiate an offence against Stan.'

'But what about the suggestion made by the bikies indicating I shouldn't be here—and them mistaking me for being Stan initially? To me, that indicated some sort of bribe had been made to turn a blind eye on their activities.'

'Did they actually mention Stan's name?'

'No. They only asked where the old fella was.'

'I understand. But at the moment, that's a suspicion and certainly not sufficient evidence to substantiate a charge beyond reasonable doubt of any magistrate or jury. The cost of extradition would be substantial, and with the risk of a failed prosecution, it has been decided not to pursue the matter further. The money will be lodged as unclaimed and after three months, will go into consolidated revenue.'

'I see. Frustrating, sir—but I understand.' Rhys sighed. Frustration seemed to be part and parcel of this job.

'I'll leave you to it—and look forward to catching up with you soon,' the inspector said and then ended the call.

Delight gradually took over from disbelief, and Rhys fizzed with excitement. With the permanent position came security, respect from his peers, and the realisation that his dream was coming true. He couldn't wait to tell Claire—and his parents.

'That's fabulous! Congratulations,' Claire shrieked down the phone.

They talked for several minutes, their voices high-pitched with glee like those of excited teenagers.

'I can't wait to see you tonight,' Claire said. 'I won't say anything to Mum or Kirk. You can tell everyone over dinner.'

'Thanks. Frank said he and Lola are coming, too.'

'Yes. Lola's bringing dessert and Mum's already rung to say she'll be home in time to cook a roast dinner. It's my job to thaw the meat and prepare the vegetables.' She chuckled. 'I admit it will be good to have them home again.'

Rhys silently agreed. While it had been wonderful spending time with Claire , the days had been fraught with action, and he'd been too distracted to enjoy their growing relationship as much as he wanted to.

HE WAS WALKING out the door that evening when his mobile rang.

There was no caller ID—just the words "Private Number" on the screen. He hesitated and was about to put the phone back in his pocket, unanswered, when he changed his mind and swiped the green icon. 'Hello?'

'Rhys. It's Stephen Muller. I've got your results.'

Rhys waited while Stephen paused. 'And?'

'The samples are a positive DNA match with those of Mr Nigel Ward. It looks like you were right. The bones we retrieved from the bottom of the mine shaft are those of William Gerard McMahon.'

Rhys's legs shook, and he slumped into a chair in the reception area. 'That's fantastic to hear. Could you confirm how he died?'

'It appears to be suicide. Bullet to the head. The scenario as discussed with the CIB suggests he must have climbed into the mine shaft, covering the entrance with boards after him, possibly to escape the fire. He may have sobered up while down there, realised what he had done, and subsequently taken his own life. I was suspicious from the minute I saw the angle the gun was lying. Looks like he must have sat with his back against the wall and set the gun up in front of him. Over the years, both he and the gun had fallen and disintegrated to a degree. My team has studied the photos and samples at length and our findings support my report. There'll be a few loose ends to tie up, but I reckon the coroner's office will sign that one off now as a non-suspicious closed case.'

'Thanks, Stephen. Appreciate your call.'

'No worries, mate. I thought you'd be interested to know.'

'Yeah. I was ... am. Thanks again.' He ended the call and got to his feet again, this time with an unexpected spring in his step and a wide smile on his face.

I reckon tonight's the night for celebrating. Old Ned won't believe his luck when I buy a whole carton of beer— and a few bottles of wine.

36

*C*laire hovered by the French doors, fingering the lacy frill around her neck. Her skirt flowed around her ankles, and she tucked the strand of loose, silky hair behind her ear. Tonight she had gone to extraordinary lengths to look good—surprising herself even more than her mother.

Her insides tumbled with anticipation, her eyes twinkling. It had taken everything she had to keep her joy from bubbling over at Rhys's news and, before Ginny and Kirk arrived home, she had danced around the living room like a five-year-old.

The dining table looked beautiful, and while Ginny and Lola fussed in the kitchen, Frank had taken control of serving drinks. Kirk sat in the recliner, his plastered leg resting on the footstool and a contented grin on his face.

Flames leapt in the fireplace, and Claire cast her eyes around the room as the sound of Rhys's vehicle reached her. She was sorry about only one thing—that Briony and Alex, her beloved sister and Scotsman, weren't here with them.

She rushed outside to greet Rhys, throwing her arms around him as he attempted to get out of the vehicle.

He hugged her to him for a long minute before their arms softened, and she drew back.

Claire's smile faded.

'Are you alright?' Rhys frowned.

'Yes. But I am so sorry.'

'About what?'

'For being so erratic. I'm not usually the sort of person who runs hot and cold—but I was so worried you wouldn't get to stay here ... I didn't want to let my feelings go and both of us get hurt.'

Rhys appeared to almost crumple with relief, and he laughed.

'You funny girl.' He nuzzled into her neck and hugged her again. 'We would have found a way. I might have even given up the force and become your jackaroo if it had come to that.'

'Really? You'd do that for me? Give up the job you love?'

He chuckled again, softly this time. 'Well, I would have considered it, anyway.'

It was her turn, and she let out one of her rich laughs. 'I'm glad neither of us has to give up anything —especially each other.'

'Me too.' His smile stretched, and he pressed a kiss on her forehead.

She dropped her hand and squeezed his, clasping it tightly. 'Come on then. Everyone's waiting to hear about what's been going on while Mum and Kirk have been away—and I can't wait to celebrate ... Senior Constable Rhys Morton, Permanent Officer in Charge of Featherwood Falls Police Station. Good grief, what a mouthful.'

They turned toward the house and she opened the gate ahead of him. Light spilled onto the veranda, illuminating the garden while a boobook owl hooted from the shadowy cover of a tree nearby. Laughter and muffled conversation floated through the air.

Rhys's fingers wrapped around Claire's again, his strong, roughened skin gentle as he pulled her closer. She leaned into him and met his smile.

'New beginnings?' she murmured.

He dropped her hand and wrapped his arm around her. 'Yes, new beginnings.'

ACKNOWLEDGMENTS

I loved writing Rhys and Claire's story, however, I could not have done it without my wonderful family, assistants, and support crew.

To Anna and Lauren at CREATINGink, thank you both for your editing support and suggestions. I truly value your expert assistance and ongoing friendship.

Frank Honsa, book cover extraordinaire—thank you so much for stepping in and taking over after my lovely cover designer became ill. I love your work and appreciate all you do.

Getting the information and procedures correct in any story involving crime and the law is fraught with challenges due to differences between the Australian states and territories, even if only slight. My struggles were eliminated by the help and guidance of my husband, Roger, whose forty years in the Queensland Police Service has served us well—not only in the community, but for my stories, too. Thank you from the bottom of my heart.

To Dianne, Jennifer, Kathie, Patricia, Deb, Carly,

Deborah, Fiona, and Alice—my sisters, advanced readers, and much-valued proofreaders—thank you all so much for your patience, constructive critique, and professionalism.

I love you all.

ALSO BY HEATHER REYBURN

Tullagulla Series

The Cedar Tree

The English Oak

The Pepperina Grove

A Tullagulla Christmas

Fantail Ridge Series

Peninsula Promises

The Lupin Fields

The Scent of Promise

Featherwood Falls Series

A Stranger in Featherwood Falls

Secrets in Featherwood Falls

Sparks Fly in Featherwood Falls

Clouds over Featherwood Falls

A STRANGER IN FEATHERWOOD FALLS

To lose a loved one is tragic, but to lose a lifetime of dreams? Unthinkable.

Alone on a two thousand hectare sheep and cattle property, Ginny Shepherd questions her husband's sudden death, convinced it was no accident. As a series of farm related incidents unravel, heightening her suspicions, her livelihood is put under threat. Featherwood Station is Ginny's lifeblood—her passion, her home, and her haven and she is determined it will stay that way. But it seems someone else wants the property as much as she does and will stop at nothing to get it.

When a stranger finds a forgotten token gifted to him as a child, distant memories set him on a path to pursue his grandfather's dream. But, greeted with more questions than answers, he finds life in the heart of

Queensland's Granite Belt more difficult than expected.

A smouldering attraction forms between he and Ginny, alarm bells sound and frightening events escalate. Ginny's life is in danger.

Is the stranger who he says he is? Or could it be that someone has a grudge to settle?

SPARKS FLY IN FEATHERWOOD FALLS

Fed up with life under scrutiny, Ashleigh Paton considers her grandmother's favourite saying— *"Escape to the Country! A Change is as good as a holiday."*

The advice ignites a yearning in Ashleigh to leave city life and all it involves. A teaching position in Featherwood Falls could provide the answer, one she hopes will offer the new life she craves. After all—what could go wrong? It's better than being unemployed and the reward could be the peace she desires.

Damian Cartwright has a secret. Like his eccentric great-aunt, a reclusive life in the bush suits him. Except now his son, Charlie, is old enough to start school, and old enough to be subjected to ridicule. It's time for action, even if that involves calling a truce with Charlie's feisty new teacher.

When unexplained events occur in the area, young

Charlie forces Ashleigh into seeking answers. But uncovering the truth proves more shocking than imagined and sparks fly in more ways than one.

Can Ashleigh extinguish the inferno without destroying all she has gained? Or will her dreams be over before they begin?

CLOUDS OVER FEATHERWOOD FALLS

In a town teaming with secrets, three women find themselves inexplicably entwined.

At the edge of her future, sixteen-year-old **Zoe** teeters, uncertain. The vibrant city with its dazzling lights, familiar sounds and scents, exudes adventure and a dream career. But when unexpected tragedy strikes, she is left to navigate the world on her own, gripped by loneliness and fear.

Lola is feeling the weight of her years. Despite a loving husband, a flourishing business and a circle of faithful friends, something is missing. While she pours her soul into a menagerie of sick and abandoned animals, her heart aches for the return of her only child.

At forty-two and lonely, **Emma** is free at last. Lost love and an unwavering commitment to her late mother have confined her to the quiet charm of Featherwood Falls. And while her role as teacher's aide at the local school fills her days, she longs for something to happen—something that will transform her existence and redefine her life.

Can Featherwood Falls offer the key to uniting these women? Or will a dangerous voice from the past destroy family bonds, challenging the discovery of love and hope.

ABOUT THE AUTHOR

Heather Reyburn enjoyed an idyllic childhood in beautiful New Zealand, before settling on the Darling Downs in Queensland. With a passion for nature, animals, reading and all things farm related, it wasn't long before her rural lifestyle inspired dreams of writing stories of her own. She loves happy endings, history, suspense, and characters who remain with the reader long after "The End". When not writing, Heather is often found in the garden or spending time with her husband and family.